the moons

fire rooster to earth dog

Yuxin Zhao

The Moons: Fire Rooster to Earth Dog

Yuxin Zhao

ISBN 978-1-940853-19-2

Cover adapted from a photograph by Jiayi Chen.

Published by Calamari Archive, Ink.

https://www.calamaripress.com

the MOONS in FIRE ROOSTER

the MOONS in EARTH DOG

the moons

fire rooster

火羅

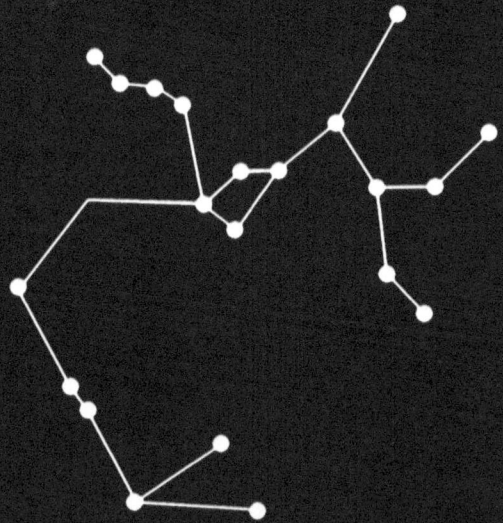

SAGITTARIUS

11/8

1. last night the fire alarm went off 2.5 times in 4 hrs. i covered my head with the comforter. after a while i started to wonder if i was the only one hearing it? no doors opened, no footsteps … was the alarm only sounding in my room? was i hallucinating? i fell asleep after the last 0.5 time and was woken up 0.5 hours later by the noise of the blender. someone making a breakfast smoothie. corned beef, swiss cheese, sauerkraut on bagel. medium chai (hot)

2. 1 orange. this time the oranges are sweeter, but harder. don't know whether it means i'm bad or good at picking out oranges. the other day C and i both changed the background image of our chat. now mine is a pic of her standing in front of a mirror in her dorm, face half-hidden behind her phone, dressed in a dark-grey knit skirt, a light-grey knit coat, and a sky-blue sweater with a koala on it. it's a kids' sweater. we like to imagine us living together as a family. we'll mix up all the kids' clothes and wear them ourselves at random. yesterday had a revelation, i realized the phone in her pic is exactly vertical. scrolling through the chat window, the right edges of her dialogue boxes pass the long edge of her phone, 1 by 1, they make perfect parallel lines.

3. 1 slice of bbq chicken pizza. medium watermelon lemonade. thought it'd be strange, but it was good.

11/9

1. a nurse tries to draw my blood and fails. she thought it would be easy. she found my vein, but i wouldn't bleed into the syringe. she tries twice on my left arm, once on my right. she says, i'm

going to be mad at you. if you're not a bleeder, you should have told me so i wouldn't poke you like this. you'll walk out like a pin cushion. after 3 failed attempts, she says let the doctor try, she's good at getting people to bleed. the doctor tries on my right arm and fails in this way: she inserts the needle—no blood comes out; pulls out the needle and reinserts it—no blood comes out; pushes the needle deeper inside the vein—no blood; shifts the needle under my skin so it pierces the vein from a different angle—no blood; nudges the needle around so it pierces a different vein— no blood comes out and it starts to hurt really bad. that other doctor 6 years ago had failed to draw my blood in the same way. and remember being carried to a hospital at the age of 5 and someone sticking a needle in my arm, and that someone failing too? i've always been a person from whom it was hard to draw blood. 6 years ago that doctor felt she could try as many times as she pleased. it didn't hurt, but caused a bruise the size of a fist. now, this doctor apologizes and leaves the room. i hear her and all the nurses discussing who is going to try and draw my blood next. i hear someone say they work in the er. this er nurse had a different uniform because they worked at henry mayo. such a strange name for a hospital. the other day i told C about how when i was 5 a doctor said i had a shorter trachea than most other people and C said she would like to see me hiccup. while i was waiting for nurse no.3 i carefully studied the poster on the wall behind me, the one that teaches people how to examine themselves for breast cancer. it starts with what is breast cancer and goes into the 4 stages of breast cancer and ends with detailed instructions of how one should feel one's breasts with the pad of 3 fingers. begin on the outer circle and close in. press the nipple to check if there's any discharge. such a graphic reminder that part of your body could go wrong just like that and even if it doesn't, you'll die anyway. it was a long wait, but satisfying to finally see my blood quietly float into a glass tube. the nurse and i laugh at how hard it was and she asks, would you like to hold it? she hands me my blood. it is not as warm as i expected. lukewarm at best. scrambled eggs with hash browns. last night the alarm went off again. wonder if it will go off every night from now on. C says someone must have been smoking.

2. slept for 1.5 hours. intentionally sleep past lunch. considered sleeping longer so i didn't need to have dinner. chicken quesadilla

3. 1 bite size brownie. 4 chips with guacamole. C watches *rick and morty* during lunch and is disgusted by the jelly bean episode. she says the jelly bean wants to rape one of the kids and is smashed to death with a toilet seat. can't imagine how this could be disgusting. sometimes i feel closed in and don't know how to react. i am experiencing the typical fantasy of marrying one's 1st love. when i told mom about C in the summer, she said, i hope it works out for you in the 1st try; otherwise you will be so hurt. i decided not to tell her how hurt i had been. no matter what happens with C i don't believe i'll ever be hurt as much again. she has canceled my capability of wanting to die and brought back my childhood fear of death to a degree. that day mom also asked me why i liked C. i told her C was cute and she wanted examples. i said, there was a time when i was especially frightened by death. i would be sitting in bed reading and all of a sudden the thought of death occurred to me and i was too afraid to do anything. that was when i'd just started talking to C. i said i was afraid and she said she was too. she said she didn't know how to face that dark eternity either. i told mom i'd never thought of death in that way before, as a dark force for us to face, and she didn't find it particularly cute. once when C was upset with me she brought it up. she said, what kind of person uses this as an example of cuteness? i said i couldn't think of anything else at the moment. she was worried this would make my mother not like her. she said, make sure to tell your parents you fell in love with me 1st and chased me for a long time so i'd be your girlfriend. i said, then they would dislike you because our daughter is so nice how could you not fall in love with her 1st?

11/10

1. dream: i take the bus to see C. sitting on the bus, i realize it is driving backwards at a high speed. i tell everyone it's going backwards. they look out the window and say, yes it is. C lives in a university. when i get off the bus i can't remember where she is. i call her so she can come pick me up and take me to eat drumsticks in the cafeteria. yesterday before sleep i asked C if she liked the

smell of apartment heating. she said heating had no smell, except maybe a faint smell of sunlight. i said i liked the smell, but i couldn't describe it. 2 pepperidge farm shortbread cookies.

2. sesame fried chicken with rice and coleslaw. maybe they think sesame dressing plus ginger equals asian food.

3. fries with ketchup. 1 bottle of naked juice. been watching *twin peaks* the whole day. this morning after i wake up C asks if i'm still sleepy. i'm so sleepy i have a headache. i talk to her for a while and we do the good-night routine so we can go to bed at the same time. i've almost fallen back asleep when G texts me. i can't sleep afterwards. when C wakes up she says she had a terrible nightmare and then gets angry at me because i didn't tell her i wasn't sleeping. she says she didn't want to sleep but i forced her to because i was sleepy. she says, why didn't you talk to me? i stayed up late and you were not there. i start to remember all the times we'd had these half-fights because of my sleep or lack thereof. it's such an intricate thing: how long should we talk before i sleep? how much sleep should i get? when should i wake up? how many messages should i send her while she's sleeping? how many messages should i send in response to what she's sent me? and then there is that feeling of sadness again. i don't think i can ever completely figure out what irritates her. but can you figure everything out with anyone? when you are 16 hours apart from someone it becomes especially hard to find a mutually satisfying slot for sleep. and i always think back on the 1st time she cried after we got together. she said her heart ached. she said when she cried she experienced physical pain. now i understand how she felt.

11/11

1. cheeseburger with mushrooms. small cup of coke.

2. crackers with guacamole. grapes. apple cider with whisky.

11/12

1. last night in the old house of H's parents, i had my play performed by 3 people, one as the salesman, one as homeowner-to-be, one as the rug. it felt like i had given it out, that it no longer

belonged to me. afterwards, H drove me and A back to campus. it was around 12:30 when we got back. i could tell C was worried and maybe angry but i didn't know to what extent. she waited till this morning to tell me not to stay in someone else's place till that late. but it's safe, i say. we were just talking. she says, if you are in other people's houses writing code i won't be worried at all. but if you are all reading your work to each other and talking i can't bear the thought of it. i don't know why, but i don't like it. you are having deeper communication. i tell her there was no deeper communication because it was packed. we were taking turns talking in small circles and we were saying the most meaningless stuff like "don't touch the white dog," "everyone loves the cat there are so many hands touching the cat," "this place is 20 minutes away from everywhere; if you hear people say a place is 20 minutes away from another place this is where they are talking about." but C doesn't care. she says, would you be worried if i went to my male classmate's house and stayed till past midnight? i wanted to say not if there were 20 other people at the same time, but instead i tell her i would be. this time it takes too long for me to admit i've been wrong so that when i finally say it she says she doesn't want me anymore. she says, if you have a girlfriend you won't have any nightlife. she says, you are not behaving. you won't go out at night again before the semester ends. at this point i am crying but also wonder if it's meant to be funny, especially when she says if i do it again she will tell my mother. she will tell my mother i stay out late, way past bedtime, and how can i still have a girlfriend? i don't love her and don't care about my family, which i assume means her and me. my 1st relationship might be failing because of my ignorance. partially due to all the exclamation marks she puts after every sentence, i find it a little difficult to take what she says seriously, and i almost laugh, imagining how mom would react to this. i have the feeling that she has some inaccurate estimations about my mother. but still, i keep crying because once again i believe her words fully when she says she doesn't want me anymore. once again i feel that i am a newly adopted dog and maybe should i say it to her face? maybe she only wants a dog. i tell her i feel like a dog and she gets really into it because we say it all the time, how we are each other's puppy and puppy owner at the same time. she tries to bring everything back into the puppy routine and puppy talk me and bring me to her lap by saying i'm her silly puppy and i'm so small she needs to teach me everything. i tell her i'm not a real dog. she says, i love you more than you can imagine; starting a long-time relationship is very difficult. there are things about me that you may think you can tolerate but actually can't in the long term. i decide not to tell her i've never felt like a puppy owner. i decide not to tell her, if you love me that much how can you always talk about breaking up? she says she is the kind of person who pushes the other away when she's angry or sad. she says she would rather push me away 1st than have me push her away because i get too annoyed. every time i stay. if i did this to her she would be gone. at some point i wonder if this is the person i made love with only 2 days ago. she seems restrained, far away, though she is indeed ½ the world away. she says she will try to change. i promise not to worry her again. she says, let's get married and live together. i won't stop you from going out at night. yesterday i meant to tell her about the performance but i didn't know what to say so went to sleep. we'd been together for 170 days and i fell asleep thinking how close it was to ½ a year. she apologizes and apologizes and apologizes and i see my eyes swollen in the reflection on my phone. her eyes must be swollen too. she goes to sleep at almost 5 in the morning. had i said i was still sleepy when she asked me after i woke up, maybe none of this would have happened. 1 blueberry bagel with ½ an avocado.

2. medium matcha (iced). at dusk the eastern sky is pink. yesterday while driving to the house, E asked me what my plan was for winter. i told her i was going home. she said, where is home for you? i told her it was the 2nd time i got this question and both times it had been phrased in the exact same way. the more i consider it, the more i feel it has been posed to me 3 or 5 or 10 times, but i know it hasn't. only twice so far.

3. 3 eggs scrambled with honey-roast turkey breast and guacamole. C wakes up and says i'm not being nice enough to her, and let's raise a child together. she says her whole face is swollen because she's been crying all night. i say, yes, let's raise a child together.

11/13

1. 2 pepperidge farm shortbread cookies (finished the pack from the other day).

2. half a southwestern chicken wrap. 1 bite of brownie (baked by P).

3. medium mocha (hot)

4. C brings up the topic of children again. she believes getting married (living together) will solve all our problems and actually i think so too. she says she wants a baby like me. i tell her i need some mental preparation for getting pregnant. i say, what if the baby is not like me? she says, it has to be. your genes are strong. i say, but a baby like me will be hard to raise. she says, we'll do it together. we can also ask your mother. i say, ok. in fact i was not hard to raise at all. i didn't cry much except when i couldn't see my mother. the only thing i didn't like to eat was any kind of baby food. i started to demand an adult diet when i was barely 1. since C and i make 2 mothers, i don't think a baby like me would cry very often. ½ a southwestern chicken wrap.

11/14

1. 3 bites of brownie.

2. 1 tuna melt sandwich: sourdough, tuna salad with celery, pepper jack cheese.

3. small cold brew with half and half

4. 1 drumstick with barley, beets, diced carrots. C's friend asks her what my birthday gift for her was. she shows the friend a picture of the stuffed otter. for my birthday she gave me a stuffed duck. we are still in the stage of giving each other stuffed animals, like 2 high-schoolers. now that daylight saving time has begun, we both say see you tomorrow when i'm about to sleep because even if i wake up at 8am, it will already be midnight on her side. i remember saying it for the 1st time. it was a sentence inserted by me at the beginning of our relationship, so that we both felt there was some promise for the future. guess she liked it too. a large part of our daily conversation is devoted to this sort of promise and i feel that, had i shied away from it even only once, we would not still be together. the prospect is so significant that

to a certain extent what is happening now no longer matters, so long as the likelihood of our shared future is preserved. we are always imagining it, talking about it, gravitating towards it, while also avoiding describing it with too much detail. or maybe we still lack the capability to describe it in that way. we are living the now and the *now* is a path into the future. already we are not entirely here. already we are married and have a real dog, a real cat, a stuffed dog, a stuffed otter, a stuffed duck, and a stuffed rabbit.

11/15

1. 1 bite of brownie. last night i downloaded a selfie app that enables users to take selfies with a variety of animal ears. C was excited and told me to send her short videos of me tilting my head, flapping my extra pair of ears. a lot of the ears looked either strange or ugly on me. how can C appear so natural? natural facial expressions have never been something i'm good at. users can also adjust the size of their face and eyes, so that in the final picture the former appears smaller and the latter larger. this function has produced many selfies with distorted skull structures. why are we humans so interested in wearing animal ears? i decide to try out all the ears and send C a picture/video every day. what i have realized so far: mouse ears seem to suit me better than anything else, since they are round and won't make my face seem too narrow or pointy, even though i used to believe i had a round face; the fact that my upper incisors have pushed themselves out through the gums above their designated place gives my upper lip a slight bulge that hinders full closure of my mouth. for the 2nd time in 10 years i consider getting braces. the 1st time happened before last summer, when C told me she was going to see a dentist. i asked her if she thought i should wear braces. she said, you don't have to if it doesn't affect your health. i said, it doesn't, but i wanted to ask if she thought it would make me look better. but that would have sounded strange, too daring, thrown out by a mere friend. dad has been trying to persuade me to get braces. he always says, you are too young, you don't understand the long-term significance of it. maybe after you find a boyfriend you will wish you did. and i would say, if he likes me he has to like my teeth, otherwise i won't like him. i've

been compared to rabbits and squirrels and am happy with both comparisons, but to a certain extent dad is right too. if i tell him this, would he be more willing to accept C as my girlfriend?

2. scrambled eggs with hash browns

3. medium cold brew with half and half. i realize i don't know what's in half and half but keep using it because the cold brew is good that way. if i switch to 2% milk my feelings might change.

4. small cup of chicken pot pie soup. 1 cake with cookie chips. to my left some strangers are talking about church, sin, and how to be a cat owner. one of them says, "i didn't know that in order to be a cat owner you have to finger your cat." then he drops something. the person next to him says, "this is what you get for saying the p word out loud." the 4 of them leave together through the glass door. because of all the reflections, they seem to have disappeared into the world behind them.

11/16

1. scrambled eggs with hash browns and 7 broccoli. today a hum follows me and sticks on my left foot. i move from my bed to the cafe to the lounge and it won't go away. it seems to be inside my foot, which is cold and twitches a little when i tuck it under my thighs. maybe it's because it's now sock season and i haven't been wearing socks. but in summer i had the same numbness too.

2. medium matcha (hot). G calls and says she doesn't think boys find her attractive. she tells me there is a boy she's interested in making into her boyfriend, to whom she's sent some signal, but he only ignores her. i ask her what the signal is. she says, i invited him to go to target with me. i say, that's not a signal. he could have thought you wanted him to carry groceries for you. she says, but i didn't let him carry anything. i say, how could he know? supermarkets are not that kind of signal, in general. she says, maybe. i keep thinking of her words, *i sent him a signal*. i wonder if she is a firefly. then i think of the moment when i have just stepped out from the train platform and caught sight of C, out in the midst of a crowd, looking around, waiting. i like to run towards her, especially when there is no need to. and then

we are embracing, kissing, wanting all the strangers to see while already forgetting their presence. once in august she came to see me with her ikea stuffed dog, and i held the 2 of them in my arms. we took it to the mall and pretended to feed it grilled beef. we took pictures of it with all the pelicans on my shirt. after the train platform kiss we hold hands, and at this moment, together again after our separation, heading to the subway, my fingers woven into hers, i find myself at the highest of completion. it surprises and even scares me, how hand-holding alone can feel so intimate and sensual. once C said, when we got back to our hotel room, that every time we hold hands she imagines how the same hand had touched and would again touch her body later at night. she said it felt like foreplay, the part of foreplay that was always happening, never dropped, as long as we were close enough to each other. we would sleep with our hands clasped together, to feel safe. we need these moments of safety and getting married is the ultimate safety reservoir, the one we drink from day and night, vast, boundless, inexhaustible.

3. spicy shrimp avocado roll (8 pieces). we have developed a new habit. what was once virtual sex is now often practiced in the form of phone sex, which makes it harder for me to think of something to say. most times we don't say much. we just keep saying each other's name. i'm always worried one of her roommates will barge in, since she doesn't have her own bedroom.

11/17

1. my body temperature is higher than hers. she told me that after the 2nd time we slept together. she said the 1st time she thought it was my bed, that my bed is small for 2 people and we had to squeeze tight. she thought the bed was too small, that was why my breath was so hot against the back of her neck. after the 2nd time she realized my whole body was warmer, and she has been looking forward to spending winter with me ever since. sleeping alone, she often feels cold. i'd make a nice blanket she says, long as i don't flip over. once she woke up halfway through the night and found me so far from her that she got angry. she felt as if i had left her. she also said i flinch in my sleep like a dog. after she realized i had a higher body temperature, she was happy.

she said, it's something only your girlfriend can find out. even yourself wouldn't know. 1 blueberry bagel with cream cheese. medium watermelon lemonade.

2. on my way to vons i see a dead leaf that looks like a tiny dead mouse. on closer inspection i see it's a dead leaf, not a dead mouse. B is going to the desert for a week with her boyfriend, and i saw her packing a huge grey canvas bag. set on top of everything else was a whole head of broccoli. C still wants to cut her hair but hasn't yet. long hair takes too much time to wash. she told me she'd like to start wearing nail polish again, now that we are so far apart. but she hasn't done that either. she is always in the lab. yesterday i took 2 pics using the selfie app with my breasts exposed and i thought my nipples were beautiful in the sun. i haven't sent them to C. maybe she'll find them funny because i have 2 rabbit ears on top of my head and gold stars and hearts around my face. a selfie app is surprisingly close to having a sexual application. remember 5 years ago i went to the seaside with mom and dad and got sunburned? mom insisted i apply plain yogurt to my shoulders. i was lying in bed, stripped to my underwear, yogurt spread on both shoulders. that was the 1st time i felt the impulse to take pictures of myself. 5 years later i sent the picture to C.

3. self-made sandwich: 2 pieces of wheat bread, 2 slices of bologna, lettuce, salad dressing. C calls me and we make love. then she says she wants to give me her water. she says, if i give you my water will you bear my child? i say, it doesn't work that way. she says, no? and i start to cry. she tries to comfort me. she says, if you don't want to, we won't have children. but it's not that. i am still figuring out why i cry. i tell her if i say yes then i will do it; i will let myself be pregnant and give birth to a baby. it is such a significant decision, one that comes with a series of changes in my body and our life, and i can accept it only if there is no 3rd person involved. she says she wants a child like me and my child is also her child. i feel powerless. even if i agree to get pregnant it will feel like i am losing myself to something over which i have no control, nor can i put my finger on this terrifying something. so i cry and cry and we never finish making love this time.

11/18

1. C's been having a ringing sound in one ear. she says she will go to bed earlier. after C goes to sleep i always want to sleep in, as if i now have a reason to be lazy. 2 eggs scrambled with lettuce and honey-roast turkey breast.

2. small brown sugar bubble milk tea

3. rosemary potatoes with coleslaw

4. 1 slice of pepperoni pizza. i'm reading a book called *treasure from heaven*. from the blood stain left on his shroud, we know jesus christ's blood type is ab, a universal donor. i tell C about this and she is not happy. she says she doesn't like christianity because she did not grow up with it. when i talk to her about it, i suddenly become foreign. i tell her i think the historical events are intriguing. she says the stories of zodiac signs are more interesting. i've been considering this all day, whether we should have a child. but even if we decide to, it would still depend on the policy at that time, so pointless to talk about. C shows me her knitted gloves and tells me to guess which animal they are. i say monkeys. C says, yes! you're smart. everyone else thinks they are sheep. G calls me and says a schoolmate of hers from panama told her she was pretty. then they kissed. a man i've never heard of. i ask G if they are close friends and she says, no, i met him yesterday. could he be one of those people with asian fever? could he be looking for easy sex? am i being paranoid? i'm relieved to know G is not interested in him.

11/19

1. scrambled eggs with hash browns. 1 small cup of chocolate milk.

2. medium hazelnut latte. today i feel especially in love and am paralyzed. C has made a list of everything she will take me to eat when i go back. she likes meat. the list makes me eat less. i am so paralyzed, i can't bring myself to do anything. i say to her, we should have a dog. i tell her now every time i see a kid i am thinking about whether we should have one, but does she want to start with a dog? and she says yes. she says we can walk the dog every day after work. we can go get groceries and cook and eat

and wash dishes together. i say i won't let her because she hates washing anything. she says, let's get a dish-washing machine. why haven't we thought of it before? though i've always found dishwashers a bit hard to trust. she says we will machine-wash our underwear too. the only 2 things your hands will ever wash are yourself and me.

3. 2 pieces of wheat bread with chocolate spread.

11/20

1. this morning before work we make love. written like this, the distance has disappeared, is left out of the description, whereas what really has happened is i masturbate and reach orgasm twice while exchanging messages with C and she feels satisfied and goes to sleep. 2 mini croissants. 1 small cup of nonfat milk. the card system is not working again and one of the cafeteria staff gives me free breakfast. today at work my nose bleeds, through my left nostril.

2. 1 slice of dutch apple cheesecake pie. dutch apple? 1 small cup of soup: chicken, barley, mushrooms.

3. medium coffee with half and half and brown sugar. still haven't checked what half and half is. an actress is recording herself reading a passage and the 2 phrases i remember are *curse my fate* and *at heaven's gate*. i'm reading *a lover's discourse* and i wonder if i am reading it in the wrong way, since mostly i just reflect on my relationship with C and pick and choose, *yes this happens too*, or, *that's not the case in our relationship*. whenever i'm thinking of her, my ultimate fantasy is for us to lie in bed, me holding her from behind, browsing delivery menus together. it can be any season, preferably at dusk, when the sun is setting and darkness is soon to prevail. i know she won't agree with me on that, but the shared life in our imagination is oftentimes a life of suspension. we're suspended from social duties such as working or interacting with other people and in this isolated idealized space together. the only times we've talked about working, we transform it into a pathway we take so that we can reinforce and reaffirm our togetherness: in the morning we struggle in bed together because we don't want to go out into a world that is

not *ours*, we kiss each other goodbye before we have to exit *our* space, after work *we* reunite and go back home hand in hand, the reward for another day of adventure in the *not-us* world. there is an omission of what this work actually is or is going to be, both because neither of us knows for sure yet and it is not (as) important to the relationship. to work is a means to ensure a shared life, and the actual content of work, though it matters to the individual, ceases to weigh as much when 2 individuals form a space outside of it with even more intensity.

11/21

1. 1 blueberry bagel with cream cheese. 1 tiny cup of tea with half and half. today is free bagel day.

2. sandwich: 5 grain bread, tuna salad, lettuce, cheese

3. 13 fruit candies. 43 corn chips. from the care bag given out by student affairs. the bag also has a toothbrush and toothpaste in it, both of which i happen to need. besides these: some more snacks, a word search book, and a bottle of hand sanitizer. today P gives her dog a bath and the dog shows up at school still damp, then rolled around in a discarded plastic bag drenched in alcohol. C is in a meeting. i'm reading *never let me go*, so i can wait for her without falling asleep. then there comes the fleeting feeling that i am sitting in our living room, waiting for her to physically come back and sleep in the same bed with me. small matcha (hot).

11/23

1. dream 1: mom found out about C and argued with me. woke up and forgot all about what she said, but i know i didn't win the argument and feel my chest bursting with anger and sadness. the one thing i remember is her calling me a pervert, which she has done before. dream 2: i was sitting near a pond. it was so deep i couldn't see the bottom, and there were fishes the size of cars swimming by, swallowing shiny white bits of flesh. watching them, i got scared. a man sitting next to me put his feet into the pond and said, "this is a pond designed by me. see, the water is just over the ankle." i looked again and found the pond shallow as

he'd described. just as my fear started to subside, a woman told me we had to come back tomorrow and see the pond. we had to do it every day. i grew even more scared. then i realized we were trapped on the roof, behind a clear glass window. roast turkey, vegetable stuffing, cranberry sauce, mixed greens, mashed potatoes with mushroom gravy.

2. tall white chocolate mocha. is today my toast day? i wonder if i will still drink iced coffee when i get old. it doesn't seem too good for little kids either, so what is a reasonable age range of iced coffee drinking?

3. key lime pie ice cream. C tells me her mother used to own a kindergarten, between the time when she was in 4th and 5th grade. the kindergarten had a tiny slide. her mother took some pictures of her playing on the slide, though by that time she had grown to be very unlike a kindergartener. i told C how i had to do an elementary school interview. i was 5, sound asleep when the teacher appeared in our living room. i don't remember anything about the teacher or what i was asked during the interview, or why i had to go through an interview to enroll in an elementary school (i was later told it was popular). all i remember is being carried out from bed, in my mother's arms, into my 1st failed interview and the 1st little piece of world that found me unqualified.

4. 2 pieces of wheat bread with lite spam

11/24

1. 1 small bowl of beef pho (4 slices of beef looking significantly different from those in the picture). when i'm in the shower 3 hairs of mine get stuck to the wall and create the shape of an elephant. have almost finished *a lover's discourse*. G went to new york with her friend from high school and she complains to me, "she doesn't know anything. she doesn't know how to call an uber. she doesn't even know how to cross the street! she'll walk when the signal says stop and there are cars coming towards us. i have to keep an eye on her, it's like traveling with a little daughter. i only recently got rid of my ex-boyfriend but now i'm on a trip with someone just like him." this mother-daughter metaphor and the comparison with her ex-boyfriend make it seem like an

example taken from *a lover's discourse*, except their relationship is of a completely different nature. C wakes to a nightmare: i was back, she brought me home with several other friends. at night the 2 of us slept on the same bed. she had fallen asleep, but i started to lick her. she sat up and found all her stuff gone. she realized i didn't actually love her, that i had been scheming with the others to steal her belongings. she tells me never ever do this. she says she wants to come out next summer so she can bring me home and not care too much about how intimate we are. i tell her if she gets thrown out i will take her in. she's afraid of my dad. we can outnumber him, though i'm not sure which side mom will take.

11/25

1. yesterday C was telling me how much she loved my body, and i got worried and sad. i told her, what if you grow tired of my body over time? what if you are fed up with the same reaction from me every time we have sex? what if you start to find me boring, at 1st only a little, but quickly ½ of me turns boring in your eyes, then over ½, then almost every part of me, then all of me? she said, but i won't. will you get tired of me? if you won't then i won't either. at that point, out of nowhere, i suddenly realize what i'd like for lunch tomorrow (today). then i don't feel worried or sad anymore. so cal sandwich. as i sit here eating, a little girl throws her napkin into her elder sister's plate. the elder sister picks it out, but the little girl throws it in again. i wonder if the elder girl will remember this afternoon, when they have both grown up, and accounts for it like this: that abnormally warm afternoon in november, my little sister was being annoying, etc. etc.

2. C had another nightmare: she came to see me at my place, but my parents found out. i had to see her off at the bus station near the apartment. as we were saying our goodbyes, she looked up and saw my dad standing on the balcony, watching us. my initial reaction to her dream is we don't have a balcony, but i refrain from saying that. now i think i shouldn't have told her about my nightmare yesterday. maybe she has her own nightmare because i have said so much about my parents, my dad in particular. 2 pieces of wheat bread with lite spam.

11/26

1. woke up at 5 in the morning. no message from C. got worried. was she unhappy? was she anxious about her lab tasks? i messaged her and waited. couldn't sleep without seeing her, but once i'd seen her it had been too long and i wasn't sleepy anymore. when we are in the middle of virtual sex, i have a habit of exiting our chat and scrolling down the screen, occasionally even opening a new app. sex creates such a division between us and the others that the chat as a space also gets transformed, turning into an isolated, heated room. through frequent exiting and reentering, the difference is repeatedly examined and reaffirmed, and it feels both unreal and strangely soothing. scrambled eggs with 2 sausages. self-serve parfait: 11 pineapple 6 cantaloupe 18 honeydew with blueberry yogurt and strawberry yogurt. saw what looks like a tiny bug in my eggs. i bring it to the cashier and say, "i'm not sure what this is," half wishing she'd say it's a fried green onion. she says, "it looks like mosquito part."

2. large jasmine milk tea with boba. a man says, "give me a large thai smoothie with no balls."

3. 2 pieces of wheat bread with lite spam. today while we are having sex, C starts to picture something i don't want to do. i tell her i don't want to, but she ignores me and goes on. i tell her again and again but can't make her take my words seriously. i begin to feel powerless like i'm losing control and it might have been the 1st time i ever really get angry at her. she says we should decide on a phrase that means "i seriously don't want to." i say i said i seriously don't want to. what phrase could stand in the place of the actual words it's supposed to function as? she says, then let's pick a sticker we don't use very often and have it mean "i seriously don't want to." we pick a squirrel with its back to us, cheeks puffed, getting angry. to its right are the words, "i am angry," in a child's handwriting.

11/27

1. 1 slice of buffalo chicken pizza. 1 small cup of lemon iced tea. should try harder to remember i don't like buffalo chicken. today C and i decide on which kind of dog we want and come up with

a name for it. in beijing people with a lower income are being forced out of their homes because of a fire that took place in an apartment building a week ago and killed 19 residents. those who have been ordered out are not locals. now they must either go back to where they are from or find a new job in another city.

11/28

1. wake up feeling dizzy and get scared. C says maybe i haven't slept well and tells me to sleep some more. dream: we travel to a small city in japan and look for places to get ramen. we take the elevator up a building and sit down in a restaurant, leafing through the menu. then we realize the food here is not good and leave without eating anything. i have the feeling that recently i have been demanding too much from C emotionally. how could she tell me the best way of dealing with my family, of coping with the fact that people are being removed from their homes, of accepting the impossibility of knowing whether children have been molested in a particular kindergarten and if it's the case, who has done that? there is an article about the effort of making french gender neutral or at least more gender inclusive and some people are scared that french as a language is in danger. i don't understand this. what kind of threat could be posed by inventing feminine versions of masculine nouns? how could a gender-neutral pronoun diminish the uniqueness of a language? hot pastrami french dip with giardiniera. i don't know what these words are, i'm copying what's on the cafeteria website. mom texts me at 4 in the morning (in their time zone). she says she fell asleep but was startled awake because she heard me calling her name. it gives me shivers. i say, you were dreaming, go back to sleep. she sends me a rabbit sticker saying ok. she downloads every set of stickers i send her and uses them whenever she gets the chance, as if through the act of sticker-sending we'd be better connected.

2. medium ginger peach tea. the kind of dog C and i decided on was the great pyrenees and the breed has a spanish/french origin. my biggest concern is it would eat too much and grow too large, especially since C is so small. she is not really that small, but somehow in my mind she appears small. she is not much shorter

than me, but i imagine her as someone i can easily carry around with one arm. in reality i can't.

3. 1 small bowl of salad: lettuce, grilled tofu, macaroni with mushrooms and onions. french fries. make love with C while sitting in the cafeteria. surprisingly no desire to move and sit on the sofa in a corner, where no sight can penetrate. having it all happening in the phone feels private enough. afterwards i go to the choir concert, J sang at 8pm. it's the 2nd time i've heard a funeral mass, the 1st time being 4 years ago at a stranger's funeral. after intermission J sits down next to me. at some point, a phone starts to ring and won't stop. the sound seems to be coming from inside a backpack behind us. J grabs the bag and presses her ear to it and zips it open to search for the phone. the ringtone continues. she takes the bag and runs to the back, as if it will explode and she was determined to dismantle the bomb. C keeps asking me where i am. she says she is going out for lunch with her schoolmates because 2 of them have just received their scholarships. they go to a hot pot place that also has karaoke. it's noisy. she doesn't like it (she doesn't like karaoke in general). she says it's not very respectful to the food.

11/29

1. 1 piece of wheat bread with chocolate spread

2. bbq steak salad: tri tip, romaine, corn, black beans, grape tomato, red onion, cilantro, tortilla strips, ranch dressing. there is a fancy trout salad being served. gold beets, brie cheese, prosciutto, salami, laid in rows next to smoked trouts and whole pears and baguettes. many stop to watch. small matcha (hot). search online for tarot cards. decide to go with the classic deck because i already have a strong connection with it. before long i might start looking at all the zodiac stuff, which i've never believed.

3. 1 slice of pork and jalapeño pizza. 1 slice of chocolate mousse pie. get rid of all the jalapeño before eating. L remarks, "you are only eating triangular food." we start to talk about something called soyland, a powder drink that's designed to replace everyday meals in a healthy and efficient way. i wonder what

would happen to one's teeth if they only drink soyland for 10 years. L says he's fine with his teeth falling out. someone says "no teeth diet."

11/30

1. 1 blueberry bagel with cream cheese. C sends me 28 voice messages when i'm in a reading, saying things from "i love you" to "do you love me?" to "i'm a little cat" to "i'm a small motor" to "what are you then?" but when i'm finished and leave the room she disappears. recently i've been feeling that she disappears to touch herself more often and it starts to step into the realm of an act of small betrayal. but maybe she has just gone to get dressed (as it turns out, she has fallen back asleep). when i took the train to la to see *lady bird*, sitting to my left were a mother and her daughter. before the movie was a trailer for *call me by your name*. the mother crossed her arms and huffed, and kept her arms there until the trailer ended.

12/1

1. 1 small cup of butternut squash with ancho chili and apple soup. why do i decide on this? it tastes so strange. medium hot apple cider. 1 chocolate cookie sandwich. 1 cherry stollen.

2. medium mocha (hot). 1 almond sea salt cracker. today i receive my deck of tarot cards. i shuffle the deck and draw. when i don't know what to ask, i always think in my mind, *should i stay here or go home?* the card i get is the high priestess. yesterday i dreamed i was walking to a building to meet C, but there was a strong wind and heavy rain and it was nearly impossible for me to move forward. woke up after i reached the building, without seeing C. then another dream: C was licking me but i didn't feel much pleasure and felt the need to feign. she wouldn't let me lick her. this morning C says when we make love she wants me to be brutal—in language that is, not physically. she says when we make love she feels masochistic, and is afraid i'd find that abnormal and abominable. she says if i could say something harsh or call her lustful she'd feel taken into possession and therefore safe. i don't find it disgusting at all. she keeps telling me to say no, if that's not what i want. i tell her i want everything she wants.

12/2

1. had trouble sleeping last night. by the time i wake up, C has gone to sleep. i missed her by a mere 3 minutes. i am left facing all the messages she has sent me, alone, with no response. now, looking back at this morning, i realize i have been sad the whole day since getting up. scrambled eggs with hash browns. 4 chunks of pineapple, 9 chunks of honeydew. 1 small cup of fat free milk.

2. today i am thinking of all the things i can't do and feel depressed. cheese fries with ground turkey and chili with lettuce. yesterday i did a celtic cross spread for myself and another one for C. it took me hours, looking up the meaning of each card. i told her the cards suggested she was being manipulative in our relationship. today i do a 3-card spread for myself. i sit there considering the result while eating cheese fries. a lot of the cards i've drawn for myself have to do with making decisions, but about what? we have entered another period of frequent lovemaking. C has a fantasy of me being touched by the paws of stuffed animals, but it is a skill i can't master. tonight she tells me to hold the leg of my huge easter bunny between my legs. she says, do you like it? is it big enough? it strikes me as something you'd ask about a penis, and for a second i am frozen. tonight we're on the phone for 3 hours. later G calls me. she is so afraid she'll be scolded by her mother when she goes back home that she can't sleep. she asks when i'll be back and says, by that time i would have slept with my friend. she is deciding between sleeping with her best male friend and a certain ex-boyfriend who claims to have had sex with 10 girls. i tell her to choose her friend. she says, but he's a virgin. i've always been amazed by G's ability to 1st disagree with what i say, then reiterate my words a while later as her own thoughts. she doesn't even bother to rephrase anything.

12/3

1. C says she wants to bury her face in my neck and smell me. says we will gradually smell the same. i say we will look more and more alike too. our friends already think we look the same, though if one is to look at our features individually none of them has the same shape. cheese fries with ground turkey and chili

with lettuce, left over from yesterday. G asks if she should get back together with her ex-boyfriend. i draw a 7 of wands. then i draw the reversed star on whether she should sleep with him. i didn't get my period last month and thus failed to practice using a tampon. maybe i'll redirect that energy into learning tarot reading. dream: someone sets up a bomb in my bedroom. 3 policemen and their dogs come to inspect the cleanliness of the living room, so i tell them to search for the bomb on their way out. they find it and defuse it by letting it explode in a jar. i tell them the suspect is coming over later and if they wait for a while they can surely arrest him. but they are not interested and refuse to linger. last night i asked C how much she loved me and she said, as much as you love me. i said, you told me you loved me more than i could imagine. i've been trying to figure out the part i can't imagine. she said, that was a long time ago. i said, last month. i almost opened this document to look for the actual date when she got upset and said that. but i would prefer her saying, as much as you love me, than feeling accused and lost, caught up in this unimaginable part of love. sometime last week mom asked when i was going to see C. after i told her, she said, you have to pay attention to what you say and do. it's not a very open environment after all, and you 2 are still students. i said ok, but i wasn't sure what she meant. then i recalled once C told me we were being stared at because someone saw us kissing on the escalator, a quick kiss, she turning back, me grabbing her sleeve. she was really excited. she said, did you see that man staring at us? did you see his face?

2. venti peach passion tea lemonade. 1 cheese danish.

3. 3 eggs scrambled with lite spam. spam: the best thing to scramble with eggs. no need for extra oil or salt. this morning after eating the leftovers, i hiccuped for 10 minutes. then i hiccup again after drinking lemonade. then i hiccup again while talking to C. C said in the beginning we were 2 dogs who had never met each other. she liked me and followed me around. i was soft in heart enough to be her friend. slowly we could hold paws, then knot our tails together, then go home and shower and sleep on the same bed.

12/5

1. scrambled eggs with vegan patty, squash, green and red peppers, onions. we were promised free bagels for today 2 weeks ago, but the people fail to show up. maybe they too get stuck in the traffic jam caused by the wildfires, cream cheese melting in the back of their car.

2. medium matcha (hot). many can't make it to the school. we are talking about the apocalypse. L says it's a boring apocalypse because there's no power shortage or tornados, even though he's the one with the most trouble driving home. P says she was driving under a beautiful blue sky but when she looked in the rearview mirror, smoke was gathering and everything was yellow and grey. J was on the phone with a friend and didn't know there was a fire until she drove into the fire zone. she told her friend, looks like there's a fire. her friend said, oh, do you need to leave? she said, i can't right now. and she just drove on and drove through the wall of dust and smoke. wish i had seen it. i guess we are all looking forward to something unusual, something that takes us out of our routine, which by now has been going on for 15 weeks and getting old. maybe not quite as dramatic as a tornado, though a power outage would have been nice, for a few hours, like that time back in philadelphia. the light that comes right after a period of darkness can be nothing short of exhausting. P buys me coffee for looking after her dog. small coffee with sugar and 2% milk (hot).

3. plain bagel with cream cheese. 6 almond sea salt crackers. i'm calculating how much i've spent since september and i run the calculation 5 times. today is windy and sunny in the way that makes me feel as if i were back in beijing, but right away i start to debate whether i should be allowed to use the word back. today is the 4th time i have been asked, where is home for you? i need to do the calculation again and again so that i feel safe enough to come out to my father if he demands a reason for me going to see C again. i suppose i won't get beaten; i doubt he knows how to do that, since neither him nor mom has ever hit me (considering how common a practice it is for chinese parents to beat unruly children). in my case it won't be this bad anyway. even if he wants to chase me out, i can always talk to mom in secret.

12/6

1. woke up to a nightmare at 3am, mouth wide open. ever since finding out my left jaw had a chewing disorder 6 years ago, i had never opened my mouth this wide. i closed it. did i swallow a giant bug? there was a sound above my head, coming from outside the window. was it the wind? a knock? could someone be at my window, maybe with a screwdriver, trying to break in? the sound was low-pitched and continuous. when i was lying there looking around the room, comforter tucked tight around my body, the darkness seemed lighter and lighter over time. surely it is how one's eyes work, but i wondered, is someone holding a flashlight to see if the room is empty? should i sneak out of bed and go to the living room, where i can easily run out through the front door? if i move, should i bring my comforter with me so that i won't freeze? or maybe the bathroom can also be an option. i half sat up and looked at the window. no one was there. texted C and told her i was scared. it was all too clear to me, at that moment, that we were so far apart, and i regretted telling her about my worries. i said i was going to just lie in bed for a while, trying to sleep. i realized the sound must be coming from upstairs. as soon as the thought occurred to me, i heard heavy footsteps. someone in the room above me was stomping around, opening and closing doors. now i could recognize the sound as not aggressive, not hurried, calmly taking its time. a burglar or thief wouldn't spend the whole night working on a locked window. it took me 2 hours to fall back asleep. caesar salad with chicken. P and i watch *coco* this afternoon. she asks me how long i've been with C and where C is right now. when i tell her C's in china she says, hardcore. reminded me of the way she sings along to the music in her car. i never expected to be associated with this word.

2. medium chai (iced)

3. 1 small cup of indian corn soup

4. the fire carries on. sometime past 9pm we all receive an emergency alert on the phone, saying, strong winds overnight creating extreme fire danger. stay alert. listen to authorities. i mention it to C. she is in the middle of menstrual cramps. 2 almond sea salt crackers. key lime pie ice cream. i think of the steam iron,

an object of adulthood, one that i've never considered buying but now seems indispensable if we want to build a successful family life. i ask C if we will buy an iron. she says it's too heavy, she prefers a garment steamer.

12/7

1. chicken, tabbouleh, hummus, baba ghanoush, tomato, and cucumber salad

2. small caramel macchiato (hot). i see someone peeling an orange, and he struggles to get all the white stuff clean. watching him, i feel happy. said to myself, this is exactly how anyone should peel an orange.

3. 4 almond sea salt crackers. i draw a card for our relationship and get the hierophant. the 1st day i received my deck, C said she wanted to see if we were going to get married but quickly backed out, too scared to see what would come up. if the act of me drawing a card indicates i'm less scared, then why am i? on the other hand, the hierophant stands for marriage alliance, captivity, servitude, mercy, and goodness, inspiration. it seems like quite a nice card. should i tell C about it? will she be worried that the result is only temporary and the evidence already gone as soon as i insert the card back into the deck? will she frown at the card because it shows a religious figure, a priest? maybe she'll feel relieved, even just a little bit. the wildfires strike on. today we have 7,000 acres with 15% controlled, and yesterday it was 5,000 with 5%. statistically, the situation seems to have improved. mother asks if the fire is close to where i am. i tell her no. really it depends on how she defines *close*. later in the shower i find a long cut on my back. don't know how it happened, but it's already healing. this evening is the 1st time one of C's roommates comes back when we are in the middle of sex. had C not been on her period, it could have been more awkward. her voice cools down quickly. though it's only a bit, i can sense it anyway. in that voice she says she'll wait for me. i say, wait for me to what? she says, i'll wait till you come. i can hear what her roommate is saying. i'm afraid she'll start to answer what's being said to her. for a while i lie on my stomach, trying to find the situation stimulating, to

recall all the fanfictions that have this kind of phone sex. what are the sexual scene setups that excite me when i read them? i hope one day i can make a list in 2 seconds. i realize i know very little about my body. my shoe size, my pant size, what color suits me, how much bleeding to expect, the amount and look of normal vaginal discharge, my favorite sex position and sensitive areas— all of them lay beyond my self-knowledge. 16 years have passed since i had that sudden itch that almost led to the loss of my right nipple, and understanding the word nipple could be the biggest discovery i've made so far. i admire C for her ability of knowing what she wants physically. she says we'll find out together.

12/8

1. dream 1: C and i have a large dog that looks like a small white bear. it bites me on my left hand while playing. i laugh as i try to shake loose its bite. i sense the dog is happy too, but i'm worried my hand will get hurt. dream 2: i climb up a ladder and find my friend's license plate in a hole. i plan to return it to financial services, which i recall, correctly, as located down the hallway past the library. dream 3: i am watching a tv show of young actors re-staging old movies. a young woman escapes from a wealthy family for whom she has been a servant for many years. as she gets cornered by them in a tiny hotel room, she jumps out the window and crushes her skull. i eat a purple grape and watch her die. 5 almond sea salt crackers. spaghetti with 2 meatballs and cauliflowers. 1 small cup of coke.

2. medium mocha (hot). i ask mom if i should bring something for everyone in my family when i go back. she says, toothpaste? C wakes up and we talk about which model of vibrator we should buy. there are so many different models. she says, i need to study this carefully.

12/9

1. last night C got upset at me because when we were on the phone, the signal was really bad and she couldn't hear what i was saying. i started using eye cream several days ago so it would be a waste if i cried. was up till almost 2 and had trouble sleeping

even after her apologies. she kept apologizing and saying i love you, and lying there, imagining our life together, i started to cry. the heat was on. the night before i had trouble sleeping, lying next to my comforter in shorts and t-shirt, thinking, it's so hot; what am i supposed to do with it? i was too tired to stand up and open the window. fell asleep at some time past 3. maybe i'd been waiting for C to post something. did my sleep really depend on her online post? i could infer 90% of the content before seeing it. but this was how bad i wanted reassurance, reassurance of any kind, as long as it could happen right then, right in front of my eyes, on the screen i was holding. i wake and find she has bought the vibrator we agreed on yesterday. pork sandwich with french fries and coleslaw. feeling guilty for not counting the fries.

2. medium raspberry iced black tea (iced). 1 tempera green bean. doesn't taste like green beans. 3 french fries. i keep crying on the wrong day. i realized that when C wants me to touch her but has to do it herself because i'm still sleeping, she feels i have abandoned her by not playing with her, and the situation causes discontent on her part. my eyes have been swollen the whole day and tomorrow they will surely get worse. it takes us more than 3 hours to get it straightened out. then we make love. she brings up the vibrator but when i try to incorporate it into the imaginary setting, she laughs under her breath. the remark on the insatiability of one's partner (can't be satisfied with fingers alone and therefore requires a vibrator/dildo) is a line we have encountered countless times in fanfictions; so frequent, so vulgar and unaware of itself as an unrefined sentence, it has turned into something laughable. we let it slip. nevertheless, it is now so much easier to hear every word she says as coated in irony.

12/10

1. again had trouble sleeping last night. in the past 2 days the small frictions between C and me bring me back to reality: the dorm after S comes home, usually sometime after 2 in the morning. she always holds an electronic device that plays what sounds like the news or tv show. then she will fix something to eat in the kitchen, with the tv show still playing. i told C i'd get up early and talk her to sleep and set the alarm for 8:30, but i couldn't sleep.

the dorm has such an effect on me that i have no clear sense of time after midnight. the light is always on, someone always in motion. even when our apartment is quiet, noise comes down from the apartment above. the whole night can feel like the same hour, enacted over and over again. i awake to the alarm at 8:30 and the 1st thing C says to me is, did you set an alarm? i don't want you to set alarms. go back to sleep. we talk for a while about whether i should set alarms, and then she says she is sleepy too. she says, let's sleep together. i sleep till noon. every time i wake, the thought that we have run out of toilet paper prevents me from getting up. in my dream i follow mom and dad through souvenir stores. they keep asking if i want anything. i'm not sure if i am a child again. after a while i start to read an illustrated short story collection. there's a section titled *sports* and when i leaf through it i see that all the stories are about homoeroticism between professional athletes. i consider if i should stay in the dream to finish the book, and decide against it. 5 almond sea salt crackers. 1 plain bagel with cream cheese and strawberry jelly. need to experiment more on the cream cheese/strawberry jelly ratio.

2. 1 cup of instant ramen (shrimp flavored). realized i haven't had dinner for a while.

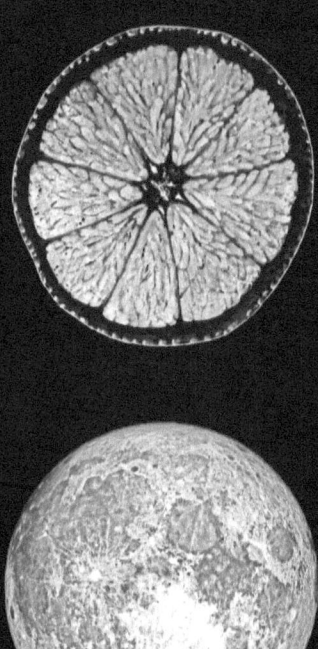

ON ORANGE: ACT I

We open to what appears to be a train car.
Lights are dim, and vaguely we see the interior.
Y and D sit side by side. There is a window to
their right, and they are staring out of it.
We see only their profiles. As they talk, they
never look each other in the eye. Sometimes they
turn their heads to stare straight ahead.

Y: What happened after you got married?

D: We counted the years by rolls of toilet
paper. When friends came over, we'd buy ginger
and sesame dressing so they'd believe we were
making authentic Asian food.

Y: My mother used to dream of toilet paper. She
thought it would be nice to open a cabinet and
see rolls and rolls of perfectly stacked toilet
paper. I think she picked this up from some
TV show. She saw someone open a cabinet after
getting married to examine all their toilet
paper storage for the year. It runs out so
quickly. When I was a kid I would count how many
sections I needed to tear off, 8 for poop and 4
for pee. Now I don't do it anymore, but I'm sure
I still use the same amount every time. It has
become automatic to me.

D: Do you remember the time we took the train
downtown? It was near dusk. The sun was setting.
Mountains were pink under pink clouds the size
of mountains. They looked like pink creatures.

Y: It was the day I got broccoli coleslaw and it

tasted like ginger. It was disgusting. I mean,
all kinds of coleslaw become disgusting at some
point, but broccoli coleslaw especially. The
fiber, you know, it's hard fiber, raw, very hard
to chew or swallow. Bad decision.

D: Even pink billboards, pink billboards against
pink mountains and pink clouds. Then everything
turned red, then it was too dark to see.

Y: But it started off orange. When the sun
starts to set, it beams orange first.

D: Right, orange, pink, red, gone.

Y: Do you want to get pregnant? Have you tried?

D: No. Eventually we'd love to have children,
but now is not the right time.

Y: I think we should start using the word
"orange" more often because it's difficult to be
orange. It's easy to be called red or yellow.
During a sunset when we get orange, it fades and
turns to pink; when you eat an orange, people
will ask if it's a tangerine. Orange is blurry,
fleeting. I feel bad for it.

D: But what can we do?

Y: Maybe just eat more oranges.

(Pause)

D: If I get pregnant there's a 50% chance I'll
crave oranges. If I develop this craving, I know
it'll be a boy. Do you know the saying? Sour for
boys, spicy for girls. I don't want a boy. Can't
stand spicy food, it gives me a runny nose. If
I had to choose between the 2 ... I'd rather
eat oranges and end up with a frightening son
than shovel peppers down my throat expecting the
reward of a daughter. And what if the proverb
turns out wrong?

Y: When you get old, your sense of touch is the
last sense to go. You can't see or hear or smell
or taste but you can still touch. How would it
feel to eat an orange when you only have your

sense of touch left? Someone—a nurse, friend,
or family member—would need to peel the orange
and feed you. They'd have to wedge it into your
mouth. It would be lying on your tongue and
you'd feel its weight, but there'd be no smell,
no flavor. How can you dare to bite? How do
you know it's not part of your palate that has
fallen off? Keep it there for a while and it
picks up your body temperature, which makes it
even more like an expired part of you. Half-
close your mouth and it becomes supple too.

D: I never peel oranges. I always slice them.
It's much more satisfying. You can tell a dry
orange by its shape, the peel shrinks a little
and all the wedges bulge up. You might be able
to dissect it without causing any bleeding. Or
cut in between 2 layers of the thin white film
and keep both sides intact. Then you can eat an
orange with no trace of eating, if you also eat
the peel. It's healthy. Except if I get pregnant
we should get rid of all objects with sharp
edges, the fruit knife would have to go, too.
We'll childproof everything with those labeled
children safe. Now is definitely not the right
time, because we have so many rolls of toilet
paper. We're in the beginning of a toilet-
paper year. If I get pregnant I'll give birth
in October of toilet paper year and by December
the baby will be crawling all over. One of the
last few rolls of toilet-paper could easily fall
out when we open the cabinet. It could hit the
baby in the head, from above, with a speed of
$\sqrt{2gh}$ meters per second. The baby might want to
play with the roll and wrap it around its head
and choke. One should not get pregnant in the
beginning of a toilet-paper year.

Y: During that time on the train you told me you
were getting married.

D: Did I? I don't remember.

Y: You did. You said, "We're getting married.
When are you getting married?" I said,

"Congratulations! I don't know yet. We haven't talked much about it." You said, "Are you going to talk about getting married instead of keeping it nonverbal and suddenly get married?" I said, "Yeah. Now is not the right time."

D: Now I remember. And you also asked if I remembered the time we walked around the block to get donuts. You said you never thought pistachio could be that sweet and not nutty at all. You felt strange because you didn't know how many pistachios were in it and if there were too many you would gain weight and if there were too few it wasn't worth the price. It was winter. I was wearing a scarf and you a hat. I wanted your hat because it had a pompon the size of my fist, which is the size of my heart. We exchanged hat and scarf and shared donuts. You ended up eating a chocolate old-fashioned. We talked about straw wrappers.

Y: That was what we talked about. The block we walked around had a children's hospital. The lobby was some 4 stories high. A children's hospital should not have such a lobby. It scares children, especially those who can't set their heads straight and have to tilt them back to look up. That morning I dreamed of my grandmother. She was on a bus coming to stay with me for several days. She had a white pillow in her arms. For a moment her eyeballs rolled back and I could only see the whites of her eyes. It startled me awake. We went out. A straw wrapper is another thing children cannot handle.

D: We sat on the train eating broccoli coleslaw thinking of everyone who got married and is still married now. Why were we going downtown? I really don't remember much of that trip. Before we got married, I wondered how long I would feel married, or if I would feel it at all. What problems would it solve? How long have your grandparents been married? What did we say about straw wrappers?

Y: My grandmother used to work in the development team for rocket fuel. She doesn't eat fruits, except apples and bananas. Apples are good for you. Bananas are convenient. Everything else either has too much fluid or is too much trouble. At first she didn't like my grandfather. If I drew a curve it would be something like this:

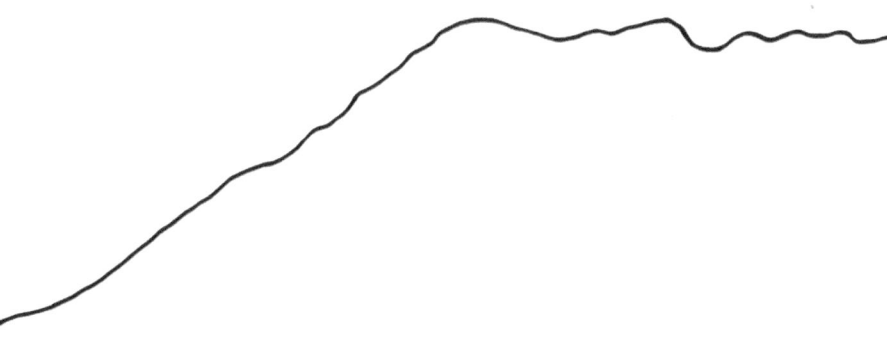

D: It's a pretty nice curve. I hope I can describe my marriage like that.

Y: Describe it.

D: So far it's kind of like this:

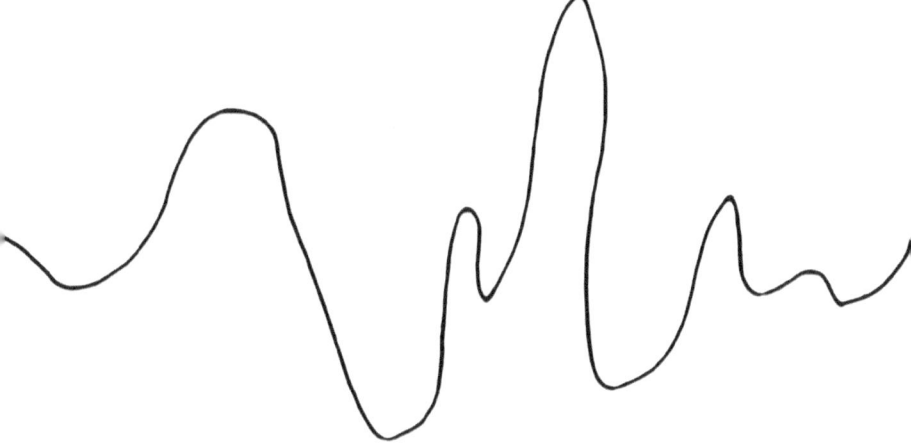

Y: It seems normal.

D: We talked about straw wrappers. You'd always
seen people unwrap a straw by thumping one
end of it against some flat surface, but you
couldn't do that. You thought it was a grown-up
thing but how much more grown-up could you be?
You still have to tear the wrapper to access the
straw, which makes you seem inexperienced. I
can't do it either, but I can cut an orange with
no juice leaking out.

Y: Another skill is to cut a chunk of cucumber
with a plastic fork. Last week I saw a man
struggle to cut cucumber with a plastic fork.
2 days later I raised my fork to a fingerling
potato, which is generally harder to cut than
a cucumber. But to use a knife is more a waste
of plastic and to bite into it without cutting
would be to eat like a dog. In the end we both
gave up.

D: I never really thought about it, how much
strength and how many skills we're in need of.
I never stopped to think about oranges either.
What is holding an orange together? At first
the peel embraces it in a tight grip, but when
you get the peel off you still have an orange.
So it must be something inside, perhaps the
film between each wedge, although it doesn't
feel very sticky when you separate it from the
flesh and touch it with your fingers. Have you
tried placing it between 2 fingertips to see
if they stick together? But the juice on the
film contains sticky sugar and that seems like
cheating. Oranges are hard to figure out.

Y: Like lemons and tangerines.

D: But neither is as round.

Y: Figuring them out could be useful. They're
so proficient at sharing their parts. Sometimes
when 2 people walk down the street they share
arms too.

D: Sometimes when we walk down the street arm in
arm it occurs to me how easy it is to throw the

other person out. You just swing your body and
release and here they are in the middle of the
street. Has it ever occurred to an orange wedge
how easy it is to throw out its fellow wedges?
If it is not yet dry, if there's enough juice in
it, if there's a strong wind, the whole orange
could swing and all the juice inside a wedge
punches the one stuck to it so hard the latter
is sent flying right through the peel. But you
can't teach an orange such things, otherwise
you'll end up with an orange-flavored apple,
because only one wedge would survive.

Y: Then my grandmother would eat oranges too.

D: What is unhealthy or inconvenient about
oranges anyway?

Y: Did I tell you why my grandmother had not
been very into my grandfather at first? My
grandfather used to be skinny, all skin and
bones. My grandmother's parents sold fruits for
a living, she cut ties with them when she was
18. Not that she had anything against selling
fruit. It was not personal. She happened to live
in a larger context of encouraged ties-cutting.
When she met my grandfather she was working
on rocket fuel and he on plastic lunch boxes.
He specialized in plastic. She didn't like
chemistry professors specializing in plastic.
But they got married and have been describing a
nice curve.

D: When are you getting married? I'm so curious
to see your curve.

Y: Now is not the right time.

D: I wonder what it will be like.

Y: After my grandparents got married they
counted the years by plants. A plant year can be
as short as a month. Or else it can drag into 24
years. When my parents got married, they counted
years by mop heads.

D: Have you ever seen a blood orange? Its skin

is not evenly colored. It looks like it's
bleeding under the skin and there's so much
blood it shows on the outside. Like a dying
orange. I don't like to think of it or look at
it. They're expensive too. Ordinary oranges are
just ordinary oranges, they don't need to kill
themselves, because they will likely die soon
when someone eats them, but blood oranges are
extra-ready to die a second time around.

Y: I heard they were bitter.

D: You can always add sugar or put them in
yogurt.

Y: Yogurt is not sweet either.

D: There's sugar.

Y: Peeling oranges is also hard to figure out,
if you prefer peeling. I always press my index
finger and middle finger against it, curl up my
ring finger and pinkie, and insert my thumb into
its skin. If you take away the orange, my hand
assumes a gesture of blessing or sex, depending
on the position of my thumb. These 3 actions
require some coordination. When in doubt, half-
bend the thumb so it can be taken as bent and
extended at the same time.

D: I'm always worried I'll turn into a blood
orange. Think of all the people who have turned
into blood oranges and have or have not survived
that stage, or are still in it. Am I ready to
step into blood-orangehood? I don't feel very
ready. Wish I could dash in and out but that's
impossible. I haven't even learned to thump out
a straw. How can I learn to bleed properly under
my skin? I would also very much like to see
people eating a blood orange when they only have
their sense of touch left. They may appear to
be vomiting blood, but I could be wrong. Maybe
blood-orange juice has the same color as orange
juice.

Y: No, it doesn't. It's actually red.

D: Does it make you feel worse for the orange?

Y: Sometimes an orange doesn't even have an orange color. Sometimes it's just yellow.

D: The size makes up for it, though. Typically an orange fits perfectly in your hand, taking up all the space without being too large. And it's very smooth, very likable.

Y: My grandfather wrote me a letter 2 years ago and it was all in English, which seemed a little strange to me. My mother said, maybe he didn't know how to type Chinese on a keyboard, because he'd only learned typing in English. How could he have figured out by himself a way to apply an alphabetic system to an analphabetic language? That is the only letter I've ever received from him.

D: Do you know how much I hate, hate ginger? If my husband eats it I won't kiss him for 3 days. And it has no practical application except to let you know what a breast-cancer lump feels like. If you feel a ginger-like lump in your breast, you're in serious trouble: that solid, irregular shape. But an orange-like lump can be benign or bad.

Y: Oranges are pretty children-safe too.

D: After getting rid of all dangerous objects, we'll start to purchase oranges on a regular basis.

Y: Sit your child on a flat surface across from you and push an orange towards it. If your child pushes the orange back, then it has normal or even better arm strength.

D: Sit your child on a flat surface and put its hand on the side of an orange to see if the hand slides down. If not, then the child needs moisturizer.

Y: Place your child on a flat surface and wave an orange in front of its eyes. If it does not

respond, it is not sensitive to color or not
interested in orange.

D: If I have a child, I'll feed it oranges as
early as possible to test its sourness tolerance
level. If it has a low tolerance, then vitamin
C pills need to be dissolved in water, so much
water that it tastes only of water, until my
child turns 10. At that point the child must
increase its tolerance and add more sourness to
its diet.

Y: That's probably too late. Regardless of
your child's tolerance level, you can always
roll an orange along its body to cool down a
fever. Oranges are round and smooth with a fruit
temperature, and do you think orange is a baby
color? What kind of color is it? It's the color
of flame, but for rockets and stoves the flame
is white or blue, which seems cooler but is
actually much, much hotter.

D: Once we started to count the years by rolls
of toilet paper, we had more control over how
fast or slow a year went by. But during times of
diarrhea we lose control again. Sometimes I feel
happy about it. Sometimes I get angry with him
and hide all the rolls away and when he comes
home, are we at the end of a toilet paper year
already? No, but you have to look for the rest
of the year by yourself. And he goes searching
for it everywhere in the house.

Y: Where is the rest of the year?

D: I load it all in the car and drive to a
parking lot half an hour away.

Y: Do you remember the time we went to buy rain
boots and you told me how you met your husband?
You were in a mall, walking around, drinking
soda. He came up to you and you didn't know him.
He said, "Your boots have rivets on them. Do
you like rivets? I like rivets too." And you 2
started to talk. I disliked him from that moment
on. We stayed for an hour looking for rain boots

and do you know how tired I felt right then? You were trying on gloves. In the end you bought a vest and we left to get frozen yogurt.

D: Once I made coleslaw and put oranges in it. I served it to all our ginger-eating friends. Do you know the kind of huge glass salad bowl that's transparent for people to see everything in it? I mixed orange wedges into the coleslaw and they scattered all over the place and from where I was sitting, they looked very unintentional, like a bunch of butterfly pupas that somehow ended up among sliced purple cabbages. What did it make us then? We were insects chewing with our mouthparts and it disgusted me. I could have replaced oranges with raisins but they would only call to mind smaller pupas. In general, there are more food items that could be taken as pupas than we'd expect.

Y: My grandfather loves canned oranges. He likes anything sweet, but maybe oranges taste better than any other fruit when they get canned. But my grandmother won't let him eat them because they're unhealthy, with all the extra sugar. She only allows him one can during the New Year. Just think of all the orange cans he could have eaten but didn't because they've been married for 60 years. It's such a long time that at some point they just stopped counting and started to subtract. You haven't reached that point yet.

D: We count 1, 2, 3, ... 50 rolls of toilet paper, 100, 150, 200, pregnancy, baby #1, 300, ... 358 toilet-paper years since the 1st pregnancy. Your grandparents have been married for so long. Seems impossible to imagine your grandmother was once pregnant too.

Y: She managed to find the time. They got married and made my mother, and my grandfather left home for years and came back to make my uncle and left again. During the time when he was gone, my mother and uncle grew up. He wrote

letters and asked them to join him. They wrote
to try to drag him back. In the end he called.
He said, "Either you come now or I'll go home
for good and none of us will ever go anywhere
again." My grandmother won't travel. She doesn't
take planes, nor trains or ships. For the most
part she walks everywhere, if it's a place in
the city. But there's only so far you can get on
foot.

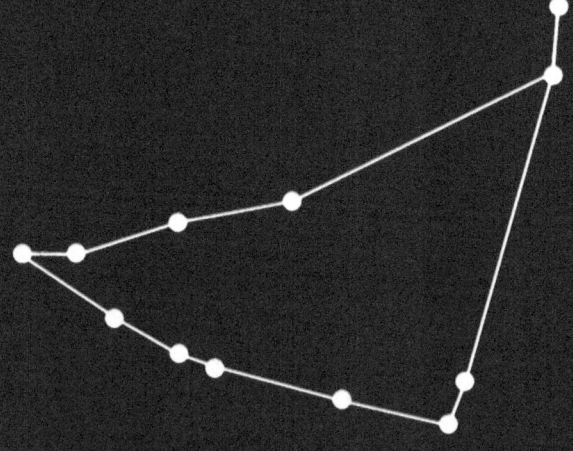

CAPRICORN

12/11

1. dream: massacre in a conference room. 5 almond sea salt crackers.

2. 1 small cup of red curry chicken soup. 1 small cup of green iced tea.

3. 3 eggs scrambled with 3 pieces of bologna. last night before sleep i realized virtual sex is a symbolic act of putting one's body on display for the other, an act that carries no direct sensory pleasure in itself, but C sees it as a necessary proof of love and an act that has the same function as face-to-face sex. tonight after dinner when we make love, i notice she tends to use more detailed descriptions of imaginary actions she does to my body, believing in their ability to stimulate physical pleasure. yet i prefer to use more abstract and atmospherical expressions. i am considering this while writing part of C's oral assignment while kissing her in our imaginary bed. sometimes she says she wants to be my dog and 5 seconds later i am her dog instead. we dog each other in turns and the shift is natural and smooth.

12/12

1. 2 pepperidge farm bordeaux cookies. 2 mini croissant. 1 small cup of 2% milk. C doesn't drink milk. when she was in kindergarten, they had flavored milk twice a week as between-class snack. she always went out into the hallway to pour the entire cup out. her teacher would tell her mother, today your daughter dumped her milk again! and her mother would say, she doesn't drink milk. yesterday C let me guess where she 1st learned the word infinity. i said, car commercial. she said, i

learned it from mit's online mathematics class.

2. 1 small bowl of salad: 7 broccoli, 4 tofu, 12 potato. small matcha (hot).

3. soft fruit candies: 5 peach, 2 strawberry, 2 orange, 3 purple grape. been reading *pictures from home* (larry sultan), which consists of pictures of his parents that are in their 70s and family history narrated by the 3 of them. when i was in new york this spring, mom told me grandma X passed away. [*my grandfather's 2nd wife, i had no blood relation to her.*] all i could think of was the touch of her hand against mine when i helped her down the stairs, the truly happy but somewhat guilty smile on her face when we told her she could eat more and take what she couldn't finish. this past summer dad asked me what i was writing about in a certain story. i said, aging. he said, how is aging worth writing about? it's just a natural process. we'll all be old one day.

12/13

1. last night i sent this whole document to C and she wasn't happy about it. this morning the situation resumes. we both cry until our eyes are swollen, then she goes to sleep and i start my day. tuna melt. medium raspberry iced black tea. finish my sandwich without crying but as i am sitting in the purple rocking chair messaging C, tears come for no reason. i wander around looking for a place to hide and cry, ending up at the far corner of the parking lot, on the edge of a grass slope. from where i'm sitting, i can see the shimmering of a tree. it is tall, its trunk a shiny white, leaves golden green. today the sky is very blue. as i sit next to a black car crying, i see from a reflection that T is climbing up the slope, soon right behind me. he sits down and says, i might have something sweet to offer you. he digs in his backpack for a while and says sorry, i only have chopsticks.

2. 1 mini tangerine

3. C says in my journal there is so strong a sense of distance that she feels afraid. i tell her that's what i'm interested in: the sense of distance between one place that holds my body and another that holds hers, between life as of now and how we want life to be in the future, even between a self and the same future self. 1

slice of cheese pizza. W tells me she is leaving next semester. she plans to find a farm and work there for a while. she also tells me she has a long drive after our night shift and now it feels extra long because she doesn't have an aux cable anymore and can't play music from her phone. we watch an episode of *human planet* titled *arctic—life in the deep freeze*. neither of us expects to see so much hunting, and i am reminded of a javelin accident my father and i witnessed on tv several years ago. that was before they increased the weight of javelins and an athlete threw his really far, so far that it pierced right through a runner's shoulder. we watched the emergency team carry off the runner. now we watch inuit hunt narwhals in a similar way. i tell W i dreamed about her weeks ago. in the dream we were each wrapped in a warm, fluffy blanket, side by side in the middle of a street, napping in the sun. a car drove by and she got up to let it pass and lay back down. she says, maybe i traveled to you in my dream and don't remember. after we say goodbye, i walk down the stairs and find the lawn is being watered. water is gushing out from hoses all over the slope, and one stream lands on my head.

12/14

1. after C goes to sleep, i go back to sleep too. sometime past 10 i force myself to get up, so that i can go to vons before class and buy W an aux cable. while struggling to stay awake, i dream that i hop out of bed in my underwear, run across the street taking off my bra, straight into vons. the guard at the door shouts, you can't get into vons without clothes! but i ignore him and run past. once inside, i slow down and consider putting on some clothes. at that point i wake up and see shadows cast on my wall by the blinds. they look like 3 distant galaxies seen through a telescope, rotating and expanding and contracting. dancing. last night before sleep i wished C could be here with me. i wanted her body against mine, it would have been nice to point out the shadows to her. instead i sent her a short video of it. 1 cheese danish. grande pink drink. is it just called pink drink? C gets back to me in early evening. she says the shadows look like flowers.

2. now that the semester has ended, mom and dad ask what i plan to do before going home. mom says, you should travel around la

and really experience christmas, since you're not going anywhere once you're back. i think that's a little strange, since she knows i'm going to see C. perhaps she is trying to cooperate by not mentioning it. the rationale (i think) is that, if i don't say anything about seeing C now but casually throw it out there when the day approaches, dad will believe it's not planned out beforehand, that i'm not that interested in seeing her. french fries. garlic mashed potatoes. corns. 1 chicken wing. 3 slices of honeydew. 1 double chocolate chip cookie. C had a nightmare. her schoolmates invited her to a new mall. they spent the afternoon there and after they came back C started to show allergy reactions. her father drove her to a hospital, where she saw patients with the same symptoms and different bottles of medication laid out on a desk. she took some pills, but was told they were not the right ones. she had accidentally taken a pre-operation pill that would make her skull crack open. it would hurt so much that she'd want to die. she woke up feeling scared, then fell back asleep. again she found herself in the mall. her ex invited her to go somewhere else and she refused. she ran into her mentor and left the mall. her ex followed her out and asked, women aside, what kind of men do you like? she said, the good-looking ones. her ex got angry and said, how can you be like this? C said, my girlfriend and i are really good together. stop bullshitting about my sexual orientation. they walked on and arrived at a stadium like the one in *coco*, where some performance was taking place. C wanted to leave, but the ground under her feet was too soft to hold her weight and she had to get down on her knees and crawl backwards. then she woke up.

12/15

1. 1 chocolate donut

2. 1 big bite hot dog. large jasmine milk tea with bubbles. going to see *star wars: the last jedi* with A and H. when H texts me the meet-up time i send him a handstand emoji. C thinks most yellow face emojis are ugly, but we are both amazed by the variety of occupations available in this form and how detailed their designs are. example: the female farmer emoji with a straw hat and 2 carrots in her right hand. why do we need to see the

carrots? why carrots? maybe the bright color. once in the writing center we were told to utilize all the markers by inviting students to color-code their papers. but what if someone comes in and we don't know they are color blind? i wonder if there's a subtle way to ask this kind of question. another time we were given a list of grammatically incorrect sentences, and we had to tell which mistakes were made by esl students and which by native speakers. i found it impossible. i was amazed by how much the others were at ease during this task. i wonder if there's a subtle way to say all this.

12/16

1. C and i are still not entirely over the effects caused by me showing this journal to her. there are mistakes and misassumptions that make her uncomfortable, and she senses a coldness in my tone that she dislikes and fears. meanwhile, something is stopping me from rereading what i have written in this diary, and i've since forgotten nearly all of it. when she says i was mistaken in this and that, i have no excuses for myself because i don't remember. and sometimes she doesn't remember what exactly made her angry but has no strength to go back and look for it. on such occasions i get the feeling we're talking about something in midair, up for grabs, but neither of us knows how so we leave it floating. what has been made explicit is the mistake i've made in narrating our virtual sex. now i know that when she says she misses my body and plays with me, she is actually considering my potential physical needs and trying to fulfill them without my asking. she says it is tiring to play with someone, and she's only willing to play with me because she loves me. but i keep misreading it and invent irrelevant/overly rational explanations for all her actions. to me every thought has always felt imaginary, fictional, absurd. by distancing me from myself it is no longer me but something else, a body, 2 generic female bodies far apart yet reuniting in a virtual space. i am canceled and then reinvented. how can i reenter this if i no longer equals i and does not know what to expect? 1 pepperidge farm bordeaux cookie. canned sliced peaches (16 slices).

2. chicken sandwich. tall chestnut praline latte (hot). i shop for a

pair of slippers to wear on the plane, but it is winter and i can't find outdoor slippers, though most people are still wearing t-shirts. i wonder if we should expect to find everything in a supermarket in all seasons. end up buying a pair of winter slippers with faux fur on the inside. after boiling water with my kettle and unplugging it, i'm always afraid there'll be residual electricity on its plug.

3. 1 cup of instant noodles (roast chicken flavor)

12/17

1. last night C was panicking because she overslept and didn't go clean the basement of their department building with everyone else. i couldn't understand why she thought it was so serious. it was just cleaning. she told me the teachers put much value in this and since she didn't go, they'd think she was not hardworking enough, not reading enough papers, not spending enough time in the lab. she decided to write a post to fake menstrual cramps, but in the end she didn't and then really did get sick. this morning she still feels nauseous. i'm going back home in 10 days. she says she hasn't seen me for so long she wonders if i am real. is this real? am i really her girlfriend? are we really together? i tell her i am real and she can pinch my cheek. i consider sending a sticker of a rabbit pinching its own cheeks, but that would make me seem more unreal. she is too sick to write her paper so i write part of it for her. it is about the lake in my home city. writing it makes me homesick. i start to consider moving back, though it's not entirely up to me. 1 chicken artichoke sandwich. grande passion tea lemonade.

2. salad with chicken. 1 orange (peeled). i bought a bag of oranges more than a month ago. now their color has faded. the flesh is a pale yellow that makes the orange look waxy and less enticing. the skin has also hardened. peeling an orange hurts my fingers.

12/18

1. last night i really wanted C but she said she wouldn't have sex with me before i went back. now masturbation felt to me like some kind of practice. dream: i had an ex-girlfriend and she passed away. i was sitting in the classroom with some of my

classmates. i heard funeral music and went out into the front yard. there were people playing all kinds of instruments and dancing a funeral dance. went back inside. someone brought in a textbook of hers and put it on her desk. i started to pull hairs out from between the pages and throw them into the trash can. there were so many. they felt familiar, like hairs i'd touched before, like my own. a boy said to me, she could have lots of hair in her coffin. i raised my right foot to kick him and was surprised i actually did. so i started to kick and punch and hit him every time but was unsatisfied because all the blows were too light. i wished i could hurt him. i wake up and still remember who this boy is. beef and broccoli with fried rice and 2 cream cheese wontons.

2. asian salad with chicken. i don't understand why it is called asian salad.

12/19

1. dream: i scored 126 on a chinese exam, but i couldn't tell if it was good. i sat in the classroom with C sitting to my left. we watched the teacher draw a black goldfish on the board. the goldfish became alive and swam downward. the teacher told us to pay attention to the point of its tail that was still touching the surface of water. he said this was the point we were looking for. i poked C and she got angry because she didn't like to be poked and refused to talk to me. woke up at 3 in the morning. the person living upstairs was pacing around. every time i wake up after midnight, i always hear the same footsteps. i wonder if this person ever sleeps. wake up and C is reading an essay she needs to present tomorrow (later this evening by my time). she shows me a sentence and i can't understand it and the chrome translation function only makes it more confusing. she decides to get up early so she can finish it. bbq salad with roast chicken.

2. G is flying back home and gets to the airport 4 hours too early. she calls me and tells me her dream is to make a lot of money and buy houses until she has no money left and then make more money through selling those houses. i try to recall if i thought that way when i was 20. she says she wants to go back to china for grad school so she can enter the ministry of foreign affairs

and find a suitable husband. then we discuss whether she should get only a burger from five guys or french fries too. 2 pepperidge farm bordeaux cookies. notice for the 1st time that there is a phone number on the package. it says, tell us what you think of our baking. call us toll free at: 1-888-737-7374. i wonder if people actually call this number and if so, what they say, who would answer. how many of such calls are made annually? i google the number and find a website called gethuman that provides online phone service to help users skip the wait on hold. one can also choose "i just want to call 888-737-7374." above the "dial now" button is a paragraph almost begging the users to "at least use our pro tip on how to get a live person fastest: press 4 or just wait on the line."

3. 3 pepperidge farm bordeaux cookies

12/20

1. C is forced to leave school with 2 of her roommates because there is a pungent smell all over campus. one of her teachers has taken them to a movie and when they get back, everyone is coughing due to the smell. no one is spared and the cough is continuous and has no end. she is scared. she tells me it's like the game *resident evil* and they are escaping. the official explanation is tear gas drill but how could it be? a drill in a university city, powerful enough to make the whole school cough, without warning? some people say it's a hydrogen sulfide leak but no one knows for sure. it is also said there will be another drill tomorrow. students and faculty members are advised to wear masks. i feel helpless. don't know if C is going back tomorrow. noodles with tomato sauce, shrimps, frozen vegetables. in the hotel she and her 2 roommates escape to, C has a dream: we were sleeping together; i was holding her in my arms, but she realized there was something not quite right with me. that was when she felt another being lying on top of her. she cursed it away and i immediately turned back to normal.

2. 1 mini apple tart. small cafe au lait (hot). O, my former roommate in chicago, is going to florida. this time she will meet her boyfriend's parents. last week she kept joking about eating

baby alligators to the point that i believed she would eat them. i think this is part of the florida tradition. now she's there eating vegetarian hot dogs.

3. self-made sandwich: 2 pieces of whole grain bread, 2 eggs scrambled with baby kale.

12/21

1. yesterday i came to alla, los angeles to stay with X for a few days. in the afternoon he went to visit a sculptor introduced to him by his friend. sometime past midnight i asked where he was and he said they were drinking. i fell asleep on the couch. at 3:30 in the morning i was woken by a flash of light outside the sliding window, accompanied by a short, explosive sound. i thought, ball lightning! i have seen ball lightning! but it was X unlocking the door with his phone flashlight. at first he thought i was asleep and tried to quietly get ready for bed, but he was tipsy and the couch i was lying on too short so he kept bumping into my feet. it became more and more embarrassing to pretend i was sleeping. then he went to shower. the apartment was designed in such a way that the shower was like an echo chamber and i could hear him talking to himself, so loud and close that i thought he was speaking to me. after the shower, he showed me pictures he'd taken of some go-go boys in the gay bar they'd been to. he told me about the sculptor and said, jokingly, that he should start practicing to be an asian whore and calling his friends bitches. he said the sculptor was married to an anthropology professor and i thought of *call me by your name*, which we talked about that afternoon. there's an anthropology professor in that movie as well, in fact there are 2, but only one is involved in the romantic relationship. X was talking to me and the next second he fell asleep and started to snore. i stayed awake for another hour. before he came back i had been lying in the dark listening to the howl of wind, which sounded like ocean waves, but it couldn't be the ocean. the ocean was too far. 1 egg scrambled with baby kale and roast turkey breast on 1 piece of whole grain bread.

2. 1 cheese burger with french fries and 1 small cup of hot cocoa

3. caught a cold from last night. took the bus to the museum

of jurassic technology. medium hazelnut latte. on the bus back, i overhear a man telling the man behind him, i don't have any family. for me, christmas is just another day. in fact, i was born on christmas. the man behind him kept yawning. yesterday X asked me why i wanted to save money and i told him i was preparing to be thrown out by my parents (my dad, to be precise). he said, if they don't throw you out will you leave voluntarily? i said, of course not. he seemed a little disappointed. today on the bus i try to be worried about the wildfires again but now they seem so far away; even the mysterious tear gas drill/hydrogen sulfide leak is no longer of much concern, although it happened only yesterday. maybe it's my cold maybe not. maybe it's something else all together. i am coughing.

12/22

1. last night C and i made love. it had been a long time (or so it felt) and at first it was strange, unfamiliar, and for a moment i was worried i wouldn't be able to get into it. but in the end it was not a problem, and my cold was cured. i told her i wanted to cook so we discussed what i was going to make. this morning i go to the marketplace to buy salmon fillet and lime. it's sunny and warm. walking on the pavement i feel very basic, the kind of feeling i get when the only thing i need to consider is what to eat and where to go next: the life of a traveler. 1 cheese bagel with cream cheese. while eating i think of the words *suffocating on cheese*.

2. grilled salmon with frozen vegetables, mushrooms, baby kale. 1 red orange. this is my 1st time grilling salmon. i think i might be a talented cook.

12/23

1. yesterday i played with C while X was sitting right next to me, talking. i felt surprisingly calm, like it's the most ordinary setting for virtual sex. 1 piece of whole grain bread with scrambled eggs, baby kale, mushrooms.

2. 1 spicy tuna don. took the bus to the last bookstore. on my way back, a man says hello to me in mandarin and then in cantonese. i ignore him. i've grown tired of strangers greeting me in mandarin.

he backs up and gives me the finger. i try my best not to look in his direction. he gets off after one stop. when he passes the window, he pounds the glass with all his force. i'm scared and feel weak and ashamed for feeling so. i hope he doesn't think he succeeded in scaring me. spent the rest of the ride struggling to recall if i shuddered and regretted not giving him the finger. at the same time, i wish i had an insulting hand gesture that is more original. to a certain extent it is similar to the jerk off situation— there is an equivalent of the phrase *jerk off* in mandarin but no word for *twig off*, as if to exclude female masturbation from casual conversation. because there is no word for it, it feels like an act that is yet to be owned, like a gesture that is borrowed and may be taken back at any minute.

3. 1 yakisoba bread

4. mint chocolate chips ice cream

12/24

1. noodles with chicken, asparagus, mushrooms

2. U, a former schoolmate of X's, comes to pick us up with his girlfriend R. they are going to photograph a man proposing to his girlfriend at griffith observatory. R is visiting U and in the process of her working visa application. they list the advantages of getting married. they say it saves on insurance. it is a sunny day. R wants to take her shirt off but doesn't because U says he doesn't want her to be objectified. i'm not sure if it's a joke but i figure since she doesn't take her shirt off, it's not. we spend a lot of time parking and by the time we get to the spot outside the observatory, the man has proposed to his girlfriend. while we are waiting in line, U does his pee-pee dance, a dance that distracts him from the urge to pee. small french vanilla latte. X and i watch the sunset on the upper level of the observatory. after sunset the far clouds turn a tender orange that makes me want to propose too, so i text C and ask her if she will marry me. we have mentioned this so many times before that it makes this time more excusable and less serious. i also send her pictures of the clouds and the observatory. later she wakes up, sees my messages, and says, if i say i do now, what should i say when you really do propose to me?

3. we drive to a friend's house and make hot pot together. this friend has a dog that X has been wanting to pet for years. the dog has an instagram account. X says, i have seen her grow up from a puppy! hot pot: beef, lamb, tofu, tofu skin, lettuce, bok choy, spam, fish balls. 1 can of beer. red wine. sparkling wine. the dog wanders between our legs. i realize i barely know U and R. the 1st time i saw U was at the school cafeteria in chicago, and i left for class after 5 minutes. then O texted me, U asked if you're a lesbian. i've always wanted to know why he said that. later when we are washing dishes, R announces that U is the most feminist man she's ever known. U is considering offering a course titled *how to talk to a feminist 101*. earlier when R mentions the short conversation they had about her shirt, U says, what a good way to talk to a feminist. after drinking red wine, my tongue turns purple. am i the only one who has ended up with a purple tongue after drinking red wine? i wonder why that is. i search for an explanation online and it says it's either the tongue or the wine. i usually don't drink and when i do, i feel like crying and speaking nonsense to C. now i'm still in my nonsense zone, my tongue still dark purple and the water also purple when i spit.

12/25

1. C had a dream last night: her mother got irritated by her frequent messaging and asked who she was talking to. why are you always messaging someone? what's so urgent? show me your phone. C refuses to tell her but somehow she managed to find out it was me. then she said to C, oh, it's your friend in the states? aren't you 2 really good friends? you don't need to hide that from me. and C thought, no, mom, that's not all there is to it. she had to tell me about this dream when she woke up. she woke up in another dream and remembered she had to tell me about the previous dream. then she woke up. 1 piece of whole grain bread.

2. 1 sweet corn cob. eggs scrambled with diced tomatoes. this afternoon X and i both doze off, he in the bed, i on the couch. but then all of a sudden i am wide awake as if i've never fallen asleep in the 1st place. i hear footsteps outside the window facing the couch and the bed. someone unlocks the front door and a head

pops in. the person seems very surprised and says, i thought you were checking out today. i say, no. X says, no, we are not checking out. the head retreats. before seeing this person, i thought X had gone out and was coming back. X sleeps for a while longer. i sit on the couch worrying if something has gone wrong and we will be forced out. i try to remember the name of the thing a gangster wears on the fist when punching people, but i don't know what it's called. what if the owner of the house comes in and punches us both in the face with that metal thing i don't know the name of? in the end nothing happens and i hear that person settle in the other apartment in the front.

3. 1 peppermint white chocolate. stir fry chicken with celery.

12/26

1. 1 piece of whole grain bread with 2 strawberries sliced in ½. 12 additional strawberries in a bowl. 2 slices of turkey breast.

2. i fall asleep on the couch and dream about reading a newspaper. it features the story of a boy who wanted to be a basketball player but got kidnapped. when his family finally gets him back, he says every kidnapped child gets a new name from the abductor so that their family won't be able to locate them, and there are fortune tellers who can prophesize such a name for a price of 7,600 dollars. in order to find the boy, his family had to get such a prophecy twice. his mother paid for the 1st and ran out of money, so his grandfather paid for the 2nd. reading this, i start to cry in my dream. i cry a handful of tears and say to myself, i should tell C about this; i am crying to newspapers again. then i wake up. i realize that when i consider telling C something, i always consider it by means of messaging instead of talking face to face. it seems i keep the constraint in mind even when i sleep. i wonder what it's like for C but don't dare to ask. salmon and avocado sushi (8 pieces). grande flat white (hot). C wakes up and tells me her dream: she is walking home with some of her high school classmates and sees a group of stout men chasing a thief. they catch him and punch him in the face and his eyeballs fly right off. then she finds herself in another dream and this time she's in a stadium with some other classmates, and it is announced that

a class will be held there soon. when the teacher shows up, she realizes it's one of her teachers from junior high. she manages to wake up before the class begins. X has gone out and we start to make love, but he comes back before an orgasm has been reached. he sees me and asks, why are you in bed again? are you sick? i tell C i'll finish it in the shower, though i don't feel particularly unsatisfied.

12/27

1. curry: asparagus, mushrooms, tofu, tofu skin, 1 fish ball. i've eaten a whole year's worth of tofu skin. 1 can of la croix (cran-raspberry flavored).

12/28 (= 12/29)

1. 1 sweet corn cob. 1 boiled egg. take a taxi to the airport. meet a woman in her 50s and she asks me to help her check in. while sitting there waiting to board, she shows me pictures taken in australia. she tells me kangaroos will pat you on the shoulder with their fuzzy paws and tilt their head to look at you, asking you for food. she says, the australian children were so cute! every time i saw a little child i wanted to hug them, but i didn't dare to because their parents were close by. 1 plain bagel with cream cheese.

2. 1 turkey and cheese sandwich. 1 cup of coffee with cream and sugar. on the airplane i sit by the window. a man comes to our row and greets the woman sitting to my right, and she stands up to talk to him. he looks like D's boyfriend, they have the same standing posture, the same smug air of confidence. i finish watching the 1st episode of *twin peaks* which is more than an hour long and they are still talking. i can't stand people talking in such proximity to me for so long. i consider telling them to go talk somewhere else. reconsidering it, i decide i should say please go talk somewhere else. they talk about the wildfire that the woman "didn't get a chance to see," as if it were some tourist attraction. they agree that the roller coasters in disneyland are not exciting enough because they are designed for kids. a little boy comes by and stares at the emergency exit next to our row. he waves

his arm in the air, mimicking the gesture of opening the door. i tense up, want to shout, where the fuck is this kid's parent? take him away before he opens the exit and gets sucked out. they go on talking. i sit straight in my seat staring at them. the woman tells the man about the times she went skating with her husband. the man says people in his master's program were too laid back and that's why he did his phd. i consider saying to them, please go talk somewhere else, you're giving me a panic attack. the man sitting the farthest out gets up to use the lavatory. another boy runs by and pushes down the man's tray table, making a crashing sound. i turn to look at him. he forms 2 guns with his hands and shoots me. they talk and talk and talk it seems endless, but eventually the man returns to his seat. i regret not speaking up. the opportunity is gone. a rage forms within me and i want to kick and beat and smash everything, but here on the plane there is nothing i dare damage. i reach for an empty water bottle and wring it till it gets all twisted and my hands hurt. i realize i'm shaking and crying. over and over it plays in my head, how much i want to hurt someone, everyone, the woman and the man who have talked in front of me for a whole hour about the most trivial matters, the 2 boys who have been running around thinking it's their right as small kids to shoot others with flesh guns, and how much i'd wanted to hurt D who i loved from when i was 16 to 20 and her current boyfriend who works at a pro-trump think tank and how incapable i've been of hurting them and how capable they've been of hurting me without even trying, without being aware. i feel disgusted and desperate and alone. i can't imagine facing my parents. can't imagine facing C. what if deep inside i am still depressed to the same degree? what if i am not ready? i start to imagine coming out the 1st thing after seeing my parents, crying in the airport, in the car, on the way home. not making the necessary sacrifice for my family, hurting everyone except C. yet i also want to tell her, i hate children, let's never have children together, which is more than anything a way of hurting her without meaning to.

4. scrambled eggs with ham and cheese. 1 cup of hot black tea.

5. rice with diced pork, carrots, onions, mushrooms. 1 cup of yogurt. before sleep i tell C what happened on the plane.

12/30

1. rice cakes with sugar. 1 cup of milk.

2. rice with broccolis, tofu, pork, 1 egg. medium taro milk tea (hot). 1st day home and i've got all the symptoms of rhinitis again. feel dizzy and weak. C is coming tomorrow.

3. dine out with my parents, G and her parents, parents of my other cousin, and yeye. lose track of what i eat. G gets trapped in the elevator right after she leaves home. she calls me from the elevator and says, i need some distraction. let me tell you about my new boyfriend. i say, ok. she says, no never mind. someone from the elevator company arrives in 20 minutes and opens the door.

12/31

1. 2 rice buns with red bean paste. 1 cup of milk.

2. C is coming by train and i take the subway to meet her at the station. we both feel anxious. more than anxious, i feel as if it were a dream, and i was flying, floating without touching the water beneath me. it is for me at the same time an ecstasy and the highlight of self-doubt. japanese barbecue: beef, beef tongue, lettuce, sweet corns, shrimp, salmon rolls (6 pieces).

3. grande black tea latte (hot). we kiss in the fitting room we kissed in last summer. C says she has a feeling we will frequent this mall area when we date in the future. we sit next to a wall of gashapon machines for a long time, holding each other, blue and red led lights flashing. a girl gets a *frozen* gashapon and hands it to her parents, and from the dark pink shell they pour out shiny plastic snowflakes. we laugh at the strange and overpriced hippo gashapons. i feel ill in my stomach but also safe and sleepy. wish we could go home and fall asleep together. the time with C is so short i can't register it in my mind. i wonder if C had a good time. C says it was short but she was happy to see me. lying in the dark, i wait for 12am so i can be the 1st to wish her happy new year, in the same time zone. as soon as it reaches midnight i hear distant cheers and fireworks outside the window. fireworks have long been banned from this city. maybe that's why there are so few.

i remember walking out from the mall and into the chilly winter dusk, the desire to live with C heavy in my stomach. today my stomach is unusually present.

4. pumpkin porridge. 2 oranges.

1/1

1. rice cakes with sugar. 1 pork mooncake. 1 cup of milk.

2. my parents and i go for a hike in the mountains. on the bus an elderly woman tells the person standing next to her about an older man she knows. she says all his children have died of cancer. he is 97 years old now but still, he sleeps with whores every night. people always see him picking up different women. her voice is so loud everyone in the bus hears what she's saying and from every corner emerges the same murmuring, 97 years old! beef, pig feet, tofu, seafood fried rice, eggplant with chicken and oyster.

3. 1 pear

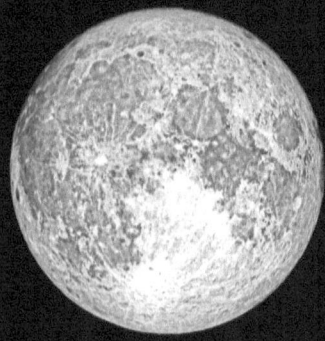

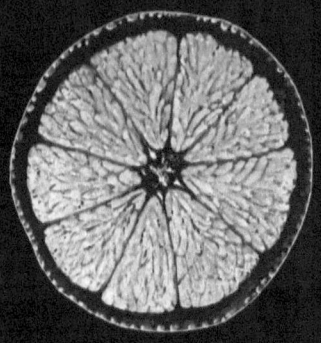

ON ORANGE: ACT II

D: What if I use blood oranges instead? They
look like oranges that have been punched by
other oranges, the weaklings in the world of
oranges. Their skin seems covered with bruises.
What if I punch all the oranges before cutting
and putting them into our coleslaw? Nobody will
notice. Punching makes oranges tastier. Some
blood oranges look the same as ordinary oranges
once they get peeled, you can't tell from the
inner flesh.

Y: When was the last time you got bruised?

D: After we got married I went to a hospital
to get my hormone level tested and the nurse
had trouble drawing my blood. She inserted the
needle and shifted it under my skin to find a
better angle, but it didn't work so she pulled
half of it out and shifted it again and inserted
it in further. I still wouldn't bleed so she
pulled the whole needle out and tried another
vein and kept shifting without pulling back.
She'd asked me if I wanted to watch and I'd
said yes, so I felt it would be disappointing
if I looked away. She said, "Are you just not a
bleeder? You should have told me." Afterwards I
got a bruise the size of my fist which was the
size of the pompon on your hat on the day we'd
gone to get donuts.

Y: How was your hormone level?

D: It was normal.

Y: Is it still?

D: I'll check again when we decide to have children.

Y: Before my grandfather left home and saw a keyboard for the first time, he and my grandmother had been dispatched to the countryside to grow sweet potatoes. The meat of sweet potatoes, if you've ever noticed, is sometimes orange. It's the kind of orange that turns exhausted and depressed after boiling. They grew and ate what they grew and at night slept on the same bench in a room full of shared benches on which sweet-potato growers slept, growers who specialized in plastics or rocket fuel or genetic engineering, which were all useless for sweet potatoes. They were always hoping they'd get the ones with orange flesh because those were sweeter. It's hard to imagine my grandparents were once bruised like blood oranges.

D: It can't be easy being an orange. Any kind of orange, I mean. It has a warm color, warm color wrapped in warm color clustered with more warm color, so much warmth inside out. It must feel deadly hot in summer, like lying on a bench all day with 9 other people hugging and hugging and sweating into your sweat, except it's orange juice. Sometimes when we sleep too close to each other I feel we make up part of an orange, body against body under an orange-peel comforter. If I get pregnant I'll become a stand-alone orange and my husband an orange tumor growing inside me, or am I the tumor? There has to be a period when I am gaining so much weight that I absorb him, transferring part of him onto the baby. If I get pregnant, I'll be more easily bruised, but my interior will still be intact, or will it? How do I know I'm not bleeding on the inside? I don't feel ready for it.

Y: But if you are only walking ...

D: Then there's always some space in between,

even when we share arms. We can separate and fall apart.

(Pause)

D: I guess you're right.

Y: About what?

D: Do you remember the time we took the train downtown and went to the lake?

Y: Which time?

D: A different time.

Y: The sun was setting, the sunset in its orange phase. The sky and the lake were darkening, but your face caught the last glimpse of sunlight and was warm and soft against that cold, hard darkness. To see your face was like standing in front of an aquarium and seeing a jellyfish emerging from deep down, warm and soft against the bottomless seawater. Then it was gone.

D: It would be nice to go to the lake again. If we don't go now, winter will come and the lake will freeze. But a frozen lake is also nice to see.

Y: Years before I was born, the lake in my city froze over one winter. It was unusual and everyone went to go see it. The more daring ones walked out on it and started skating. My parents went there too: not yet my parents, not yet married, 2 young, warm bodies wrapped in their winter clothes connected by a hand and a hand clenched together. My grandmother had long before left to start teaching. My mother had long before ruined her singing voice by standing on the balcony every day after school, calling my uncle home from half a mile away. From where my parents (before they were my parents) were standing, they saw the sun setting and it was so orange, the most orange sun they'd ever seen, and it remained orange all the way till it disappeared behind the faraway mountains. It burned 2 blue-green holes in their eyes. They

felt marked and trapped. They left the lake and
went home. That was the first and only time
either of them has seen the lake frozen.

D: When I open the cabinet and see all those
rolls of toilet paper, I feel trapped. But is
it possible? Once a roll runs out, immediate
replacement is required. From the direction
the new roll is facing, you can tell who has
put it on the bar. My husband always leaves
the tail close to the wall, but I like to have
it facing outward. Not that I'll bring it up
or argue against his habit. I don't know how
much attention should be paid to these sorts of
things and in my mind I'm already counting: me
reloading t.p., him reloading t.p., me reloading
t.p., me reloading t.p., me reloading t.p., him
reloading t.p., me reloading t.p., me reloading
t.p. ... Should I tell him to do it next time?
Is it even worth mentioning? And once we have
kids I won't be able to count anymore because at
least 2 of us will reload t.p. in the same way.
It's like counting the wedges of an orange while
it's in constant rotation, and I am one of the
wedges. I rotate and count, and I lose track. I
am trapped within the space under the skin of an
orange and one by one by one we stick to each
other and rotate like a satellite.

Y: Only that you're not in outer space.

D: We could be.

Y: The first time I threw up, I was 5 years old
and had just eaten an orange. I was traveling to
another city by bus with my grandparents. The
half-digested orange rising through my throat
felt warm. I mistook its taste as the universal
taste of vomit. It would take another 3 bouts
of vomiting for me to realize I had been wrong.
Later, my grandparents took me to a restaurant
where they met with former colleagues. Outside
the main entrance was a water fountain. In the
lobby I slid down the short slope beside a

3-step staircase and climbed up to slide down
again. I remember seeing many older people, but
don't remember them seeing me. After that I had
trouble associating names with faces and avoided
oranges for a long time.

D: Maybe I'd vomit too. I'd rotate and stay
pregnant and vomit twice as much. My vomit
would taste like either oranges or ginger, sour
or spicy. Then I'd start to resemble an orange
too. But once an orange becomes an orange it may
not want to turn back into non-orange and even
if it wants to, it doesn't know how. How does
an orange come into being? Do all its wedges
grow at the same time? Does the skin hurt when
they're inflating underneath it? If the skin
expands too slow it may hurt, and if it's too
quick the wedges won't feel protected enough.
How do they know they're supposed to grow? Maybe
they're really trying to push everything around
themselves farther and farther away without
knowing how futile it is. Do they grow into
different sizes too? Me, my husband, the dog,
child #1, child #2, etc., etc. We rotate between
rolls of toilet paper and grow fat and when I
vomit, I vomit into the skin above our heads.

Y: I could go on and on.

(Pause)

Y: My grandfather invented plastic wrap. They
were sent to grow sweet potatoes because my
grandmother said Marshal Lin was bald like
Khrushchev, which is true if you check their
pictures from that time. Was it about the
baldness, or who it made him look like?

D: What would it matter? She could have just
said his hairline was receding.

Y: I've always wondered if she would have
preferred staying home handling oranges,
arranging them into perfect pyramids in winter,
hands soaked in the sun, dried up by the wind.
It's a southern city but not southern enough to

escape those 3 months of coldness. After sitting all day in a store, an orange will freeze, then thaw if brought into the bedroom where a fire is burning, and liquify and go bad because of this excessive warmth that comes too late in too little time. Would she have preferred that? Would she have preferred a husband who had invented plastic wrap, can type English on a keyboard, is as bad at growing sweet potatoes as her, is not afraid of taking planes but hasn't done so in the past 40 years, because once the necessity is gone what's the point? Would she have preferred to relate to oranges as someone who could eat them but chooses not to?

D: A baby could not choose because it doesn't know enough. It could choose between yes and no but it could not say, "I don't want this because I want that." It's either this or not-this. A baby must be shown there is also a that and actually multiple that's. In order to make a choice, it needs to learn its options fully, otherwise it may end up crying or vomiting. Maybe that's why a baby is always crying or vomiting.

Y: I am most scared of vomiting. More than diarrhea. More than anything.

D: There was a time when my husband would vomit often and we were both scared. But have you seen a baby vomit? It looks very natural and the baby doesn't seem to pay much attention to it, like it's something that ought to happen when you're not as aware of or familiar with the boundary of your body. If a baby doesn't like baby food it cries and pukes it out and maybe they feel the same about crying, they emit tears to eject the hated thing itself. When asked what it wants, a baby can't answer. You must wait till later, years later. How can you fill up these years of waiting?

Y: Despite them growing sweet potatoes and

looking more and more like blood oranges, the
point was my grandmother always cut oranges
up to see if they were rotten inside. My
grandfather would always peel. Then they both
learned to eat an orange in its totality and
an orange seemed more and more like an edible
color, as if the color was ripeness in itself,
and whatever was orange they would grab and
swallow. My grandmother hasn't eaten any oranges
since, but she brought 2 to keep me occupied on
our trip. As much as I liked and wanted them, I
threw them up. It's not a good idea to give your
children or grandchildren oranges if you know
they'll get carsick.

D: The day we got married, we drove to the
place we would get married in and then drove
back. It was not a long drive, but at one point
I was sure I'd be carsick. I opened the window
so the wind could slap me in the face, but it
made me dizzier. He asked me if I was hungry,
if my blood sugar was low. Suggested I climb
into the back and elevate my feet. So I climbed
into the backseat and lay down with both feet
resting on the windowsill. I asked him why they
should be elevated and he said it helps with the
circulation of your blood. Lying there, racing
forward at 70 miles per hour, I felt something
was about to come rushing out between my legs,
like how most people on their wedding night
probably feel. Nothing really came out. The next
week revolved around dinners. There were so many
guests we had to reload toilet paper every day,
and it felt like a month had passed though it
was only a week. Then the marriage slowed down.

Y: I don't know when we're getting married or
if we ever will. And if we want children, we
would very much like to be an orange. I mean, of
course we can't use apomixis through nucellar
embryony, regardless of whether we understand
it or not. That's how oranges reproduce. They
duplicate themselves in the closed space they

are given and in a sense, that's how you
reproduce too. Everything happens under the skin
of yours, which can be the boundary of your
house or bedroom or the blanket or comforter on
your bed. We have to break the skin and go out
in search of an outside seed. Do you remember
the time you told me you didn't feel prepared
enough for blood orange-hood and I didn't even
need to think about it? And we talked about
straw wrappers and plastic forks and everything
we didn't feel prepared for instead. Most of
them we have managed to avoid.

D: I don't like peeling oranges because without
all that white stuff, the flesh looks so naked,
so raw, almost bleeding, and you realize there's
nothing else in an orange except that which
could bleed straight out. Sometimes I have no
choice and I feel bad for it. If all you have
in you is something that could easily flow
out, how can you stop others, inside and out,
from peeling your skin off? You're right, it's
difficult to be an orange, which can't count the
years by anything and is usually dead by the end
of the first year. But even when I feel the most
like part of an orange, I still count and count
and count.

Y: I could have been like that. We could all
have been keeping track of toilet paper because
plants can die and come back alive and mop heads
are just too enduring. We could all have been
oranges of different sizes rotating in the same
way.

D: It could be tiring and it is. It's
exhausting. The longer it stretches, the harder
it becomes, and why hasn't that warm-colored
skin exploded yet?

Y: When they first started to buy toilet-paper
rolls, my grandparents were not familiar with
those brands. So they picked the cheapest one.
My mother found it too rough for her liking.

Sometime, along with the rough toilet paper and fights with my uncle, she learned to type from my grandfather. Then she got married and learned about the black market, where she could change their money into foreign currency. Maybe that wasn't enough. She was prepared to not see my father again, but it didn't happen. Maybe you only get to see your lake frozen once if you live in a southern city, frozen like really, really frozen with no corner left unfrozen, so frozen you could walk straight across to the other side. Then it would never happen again, as expected, because the weather never gets quite as cold as in that winter.

D: That wouldn't be so nice anyway. On the other side are just mountains and the sun has set. After sunset it's too cold, and would you stay in the mountains overnight or walk back? Either way it requires a lot.

Y: I wonder if my grandmother was prepared to not see my grandfather again. She had been prepared to not see her parents again and that was indeed what happened. How many people can you be prepared to see off forever?

D: On the rare occasions when I peel an orange, I let the parts I'm not eating sit beside me and watch. It's not a very nice thing to do. Maybe I should cover their eyes or set them farther away, on top of the fridge. But if part of it is missing, the remaining parts will know. Maybe they'll just bleed juice and say nothing. What would they have to say anyway?

Y: I guess you know what it's like.

D: There really is nothing different on the other side of the lake, but you can always make use of an orange so bring one with you when you set off. Although your children need to increase their tolerance level of sourness at age ten, don't let one shout out from the balcony for the other lest they can't sing anymore. And if

you find yourself in a meeting after work, a
meeting of any kind, don't say anything related
to someone being bald. If you heed this advice,
you are likely to become a successful part of
an orange. Sometimes you feel like throwing
everyone in your arms out. Sometimes you make
coleslaw and add ginger into everything and feel
fine. Maybe even most of the time. Fine, intact,
protected; overheated in summer. But it's hard
not to be, oranges or not.

Y: I have never dreamed about my grandfather.
Not that I can remember. I wonder why that is. I
wonder if part of him was left at the other side
and he never came back intact, and we've never
said anything. What could we have to say anyway?
Plastic wrap is nice but rocket fuel is too.
When you step into orange-hood what you actually
step into is an orange Mandelbrot set and
small oranges graft onto you and they in turn
reproduce smaller orange buds. Then we start to
count the years by generations of oranges.

D: Which look like molted butterfly pupas and
can't prevent coleslaw from turning disgusting
at some point.

Y: But could be cut and peeled and passed down
to keep your child entertained, if you have one.

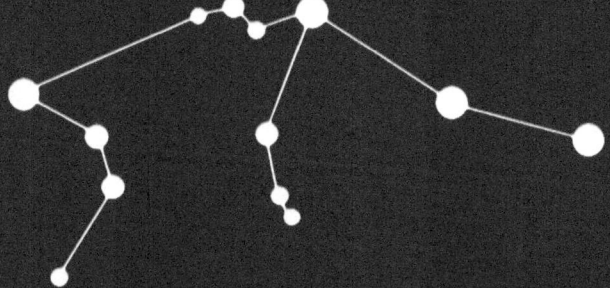

AQUARIUS

1/22

1. flew in yesterday and skipped dinner. had trouble falling back asleep after waking up at 4 in the morning. mom called me abnormal again, nothing's changed. i feel she took back the understanding and approval she had once given me. then i sleep past breakfast and lunch. G calls and tells me she had a fight with her boyfriend because he promised her mother he would not have sex with her before they got engaged. she starts off by saying how angry she is and ends up telling me how satisfied she is with her boyfriend in every way, asking if i agree. 1 blueberry bagel with cream cheese and blueberry jam. i finally got C's postcard, though i already knew what's on the front, a deer that looks like a cartoon hedgehog with antlers.

2. asian slaw. 4 tofu cubes. chocolate and vanilla ice cream. i wonder if i should ask D what she is writing me. 2 days ago she asked for my current address. i told her i'd just dreamed about her: we passed each other on the escalator, she was telling her colleague how the camera should move in the documentary film they were making. now that i think back on that dream, i realize we were both going upward, but my escalator was faster and i surpassed her. after giving her my address, i asked if she was writing me a postcard. she said, i'm writing you more than a postcard. what else does she have to say to me?

1/23

1. yesterday mom reminded me it was dad's birthday. i messaged him to say happy birthday and he told me to go eat something nice. i said i didn't want to eat anything. sleep past breakfast and lunch again after reading ⅓ of a book about chinese women in the

countryside from the 1920s to after the great leap forward. in my dream a woman is hiding from a psychopathic killer with her little daughter. the killer has killed her husband. she manages to find a ramshackle single-room apartment near a market place, but there is no way to get in except sitting in a basket and having the landlady pull them up to the window. the woman makes up her mind not to rent the apartment just as her daughter is about to climb into the basket. i wake up and drag myself out to have my 1st meal of the day. pulled pork sandwich with seasoned fries and broccoli slaw. 1 small cup of coke. C has been having trouble with her lab work. all their results turn out wrong and no one knows what the problem is. this has happened many times before. they don't know what to do except to keep trying it again. i feel useless because i understand nothing about her field and can do nothing to help.

1/24

1. last night i only slept for 4 hours. i thought about pain. i haven't experienced any severe physical pain, but it seems impossible to live one's whole life without getting a serious bodily injury. so i have been waiting for it to happen. when i visited C over the winter, we went to a mall and again into a fitting room to kiss. then C actually tried on a coat. it was a light moldy green. she handed me her coat and shoulder bag and put the new coat on in front of a mirror. she said, it's too short, i wish it was longer. seeing her standing under the bright fluorescent light, a sharp, piercing strangeness rushed over me. i thought, i have never seen her do this before. we had been to multiple fitting rooms, but had mostly used them as temporary spaces of intimacy, or as a private room where we could spend time prior to the next separation. the lights in a fitting room were often dimmer. this was the 1st time i saw her try something on in a semi-public space. i felt she was far away from me. this strangeness, this sudden distancing, i felt them in my body. last night i thought of this moment and physical pain. i thought back to when i was 4 or 5 years old and rubbed the ankle of my left foot against the bamboo bed mat so hard, for such a long time, that i broke the skin on my ankle and started bleeding. i remember the exposed, muddy redness. i thought i could see my bone, but it could not have been, since i

was not bandaged. i remember resting my foot on the rim of the bathtub so the wound wouldn't get wet. but i don't remember any pain, so it doesn't count. 1 small bowl of salad: bow-tie pasta with blue goat cheese, sweet corns, 5 tofu cubes. the blue goat cheese is the strangest cheese i've ever had. small mocha (hot). i chafed my right thumb while pulling out toilet paper from the container.

2. 1 chicken breast. 11 baked potato chunks. grilled squash with cauliflowers and broccolis. S emails everyone about the new hair situation in the shower. B adds that the shower is covered in mold. the 1st time S and i ever talked, she asked, *do you have friends in your cohort?* after i said yes, she said, *are they immigrants too?* i said, *no.* i thought i might have heard her wrong. between the 2 of us, she is the immigrant and me an alien and wondered why she thought to ask me that question.

1/26

1. dream: i'm back home and all my family members are in the same room eating strawberries. the dining table is covered by strawberries. i wander around taking pictures of them. in one picture abu and diadia are looking down at a washbasin full of strawberries. after waking up i am surprised i don't feel scared, since i'm easily scared by the excess of food and overeating. but now that i think back, i realize i never actually see the act of eating in that dream. C says she is too emotionally manipulative and wants to change herself. i tell her i don't think she's manipulative and she says, it was in the tarot card. when i went back she gave me a small, fabric-covered notebook with an embroidered crocodile on it. last night we video-called and watched each other cry. she kept asking me if i was unhappy and eventually said she missed me. i told her i had been unhappy 2 days ago but now i was fine. i showed her the new toothpaste i bought that afternoon. there was a rabbit on the bottom right corner of the package. C said, it's cute. i said, it says *never tested on animals.* then i reflected on whether this could be perceived as indirect proof of my depression. 1 beef burger with mushrooms and lettuce. 1 small cup of coke. served by the cafeteria worker i am most scared of.

2. 1 dumpling with beef goulash and steamed broccoli. served by the cafeteria worker i like the most. C sent me a link to a website that lets people read a simple sentence to determine whether their accent is american or british. it's a strange sentence, it reads: *please call stella and ask her to meet bob the frog at the store with 3 small red plastic bags.* my result is 94% american and 6% british, same as C's. when i do the test, C is in the bathroom and doesn't hear anything. she wants me to re-read the sentence, but i can't bring myself to. when i was in 3rd grade and had just started learning english, dad asked me to read my textbook to him. at the beginning of each term, every student was given 2 tapes they were supposed to listen to on their own time, so that they could sharpen their listening skills and learn the right pronunciations. i never opened any of my tapes. i still have more than 20 of them in my drawer back home, since mom says she will learn english with these tapes one day. not yet, she says. as a child i wouldn't read anything to dad. that demand always caused a strange rush of shame and unease within me. to read english, which is not my 1st language, to others whose 1st language is also not english, seems unnecessary and slightly absurd. it is a way of communication that does not actually communicate anything except the sound of me reading/speaking a foreign language and the (dis)fluency reflected in it. if someday i can figure out exactly what makes me uncomfortable, maybe i'll be able to get over it. but right now i can't re-read a sentence as short and simple as *please call stella and ask her to meet bob the frog at the store with 3 small red plastic bags.*

3. 1 orange. L has picked oranges from his friend's backyard and gives them to T, E, and me. his friend doesn't like oranges. neither of them knows why there is an orange tree.

1/27

1. last night i had trouble sleeping. i want to find a summer internship in shanghai and was too worried to sleep. i talked to C about random things like a tv show that had been popular recently and how heavy the snow was in her city. again and again the same realization keeps coming back to me: as long as we are not living together, i will never be fully in the present; i am always

living in my expectations for the future, and my whole being is in the future tense. this is the case for both of us. small matcha (hot).

2. spicy avocado shrimp rolls (8 pieces)

3. 2 mini chocolate wafers. 66 blueberries. 8 mini chocolate wafers. drive to town center with H, A, and P to get sushi. spicy tuna rolls topped with avocado and cream sauce (8 pieces). wicked lady sangria. H tells everyone the story of A and him going to a bar with a girl A was trying to sleep with. A talks to everyone at the same time and no one in particular and keeps saying, what? H says he once saw B's mattress on our shared patio. B told him she got rid of it. one day, at the beginning of last semester, B showed me her room and said she'd moved her bed so it was against a different wall. H says, does she know how heavy our bed is? is she on steroids? later we play exploding kitten at H's dorm. this is the 1st time i ever hear of this game. all the while i am texting C. she tries to convince me it's ok to not have a paid internship at this stage. somehow i don't feel as stressed as yesterday. i come back to my dorm through the door on the patio. H says, we were all surprised when you walked all the way around to change shoes. just use this door! i tell him i am scared of this door. one day i saw someone (one of my roommates, as it turned out) standing outside the door and it was dark so i could only see his contour. this door makes me feel insecure. in the end i use it anyway, it's convenient.

1/28

1. dream: i am pretending to be a man's girlfriend and live with him and his boyfriend. his mother shows up unexpectedly and the 2 men are sitting next to each other on the floor, while i am alone on the sofa. his mother realizes i am not her son's girlfriend and he is actually in love with this other man. my mother is there too. i grow infuriated at my fake boyfriend's mother. wake up at 7:30 and make love with C. afterwards she goes to sleep and i do too. dream 2: i'm waiting for the bus with abu. at 1st we are on the subway, then a bus comes and parks nearby. we are hesitant. eventually we get off to catch the bus, but it closes its door

before our eyes and drives away. we are left at the station, with no subway, no bus. a drizzle starts to fall. abu smiles and says, we have missed the bus. we walk around the block and see the bus at the next stop. run, abu says. but i feel weak and don't want to run. 1 chicken quesadilla. 1 small cup of iced green tea.

2. medium cafe au lait (hot). before i had the dream about living with a gay couple, C dreamed she was having dinner with a straight male friend of mine who, in her dream, had a boyfriend he kept ignoring. the boyfriend was a good-looking monk from tibet. after some further interaction, C found out he was also a graduate of harvard university. that made her even angrier at my friend for not walking together with his boyfriend.

3. 1 sugar glazed donut.

4. 34 blueberries

1/29

1. wake up to the alarm at 8:30 and see C said she was going to sleep ½ an hour ago. tonight there's no heating in her dorm and it's freezing cold. i had some terrible dreams i don't remember. i start to panic and cry out for her, which is to say i send her 3 crying alpaca stickers. she also said there was a loud ringing sound in her ears that made it hard for her to sleep. she hadn't realized it was so loud before because of the noise of the heating system. i lie in bed half asleep, worrying, wanting to cry. then she shows up. she says, i know you have an alarm set at this time although i keep telling you not to set alarms. 3 mini chocolate wafers

2. eggs scrambled with vegetables, hash browns. 1 small cup of chocolate milk. today i get an influx of messages from G about her boyfriend's expectations. i still can't come to terms with romantic relationships between men and women that are based on suitability calculated by preset standards. seems like a privilege. i'm probably jealous that she can talk to her family about her boyfriend with ease and have him call her mother. she is considering visiting him in singapore this may. it reminds me of how much fight i had to go through last month in order to visit C, who lived in another city, 1.5 hours by train from mine.

3. 1 drumstick, scalloped potatoes, spinach. C says she was very afraid last night. says, i wish you could sleep beside me. i want to hear you breathe.

4. 59 blueberries. 5 mini chocolate wafers.

1/30

1. last night D told me her dog was going to be euthanized. at first his liver stopped functioning. last week he stopped eating and today he started to have seizures and couldn't breathe. it was too torturing for him. they had no choice but to euthanize him this afternoon. i tried to calculate his age and decided not to ask. i met him several times, more than 7 years ago. he was a strong dog who liked to dash towards everyone who came into his sight. sometimes D or her parents would block his path with a bicycle. C was telling me about the ringing sound in her ears and i checked the flight tickets back for this weekend. she said she was afraid to go to the hospital alone. last night after checking the flight tickets i cried. i didn't want C to turn around and comfort me, but she did anyway. she promised to go to sleep early from then on. today i wake up at 8 to say good night to her. i fall asleep quicker than her. i think i've been spending too much time sleeping. 3 mini chocolate wafers.

2. 1 small cup of minestrone soup. in my mind i keep calling it milestone soup. medium mocha (iced). 1 saltwater taffy. someone in my class is giving out saltwater taffies and everyone else is surprised that i've never had them. it doesn't taste much different than toffee. it's chewy and sweet and in the end i realize there are crushed peanuts.

3. 1 cheeseburger with mushrooms and 2 slices of tomato. 1 small cup of coke. tonight the moon is hanging low and bright, large like the sun.

4. 11 green grapes. L sits next to me in a poetry workshop. 1 white chocolate animal-shaped cookie. we agree on the polar bear, but there are other animal shapes we can't figure out. later some more people gather near the food table and comment on how good the cookies are. someone else reaches into the bag and says, oh, a mammal. then they flip another cookie around

and say, another mammal. i write something like a poem and consider sending it to C, which i haven't done yet. it reads:

> we went to a mountain that was unmistakenly a mountain
> perhaps there was no rock that
> was younger than either of us
> perhaps there was no rock that
> was older than the 2 of us combined
> there came a drizzle that
> washed some of the mountain away
> we asked each other,
> were you washed away too?
> let's do the calculation again
> because of that we started to sweat
> we wanted to eat a tiny bit of the mountain
> it would keep our teeth firm

we are supposed to tell someone else a moment when we felt strongly the power of language, whether the moment was positive or negative or even destructive. L tells me a stranger kept kissing him and running away at the halloween party last year, when he was drunk. he followed that person out of the campus and came to a pause, alone, under the northern wall. there he received via text one of his favorite poems. i tell him i went back home for winter and one day i was on the way to the hospital with my mother. we were crossing a busy street. i was still trying to get used to all the cars and bikes and pedestrians, dodging them in the rain, worrying if i had a tumor in my ovary (i'd been missing periods). my mother was asking me about C, but i wasn't prepared to answer her right then and there. then she said, maybe in the end you'll both meet men you like, and the 4 of you will become good friends. i remember coming to a halt in the middle of the street, not wanting to take one step further. while i paused, i thought about what to say. am i being too theatrical? am i overreacting? should i laugh? the situation started to seem funny. i said to my mother, don't you think that's not a very nice thing to say? she got irritated. she said, it was just casual talk. why do you have to take it so seriously? i tell L this is my moment and he says, the biggest christmas drama i've had is a debate between my father and i over whether i should go canoeing; he has strong feelings about it.

1/31

1. dream: a doctor diagnoses me with an impossible disease. he says i will lose all my memories and the ability to think at an age when it shouldn't be happening yet. after he announces it, i begin to find evidence in favor of this diagnosis. i am heartbroken and cry hard till i wake up. i feel my face. it's damp, but i'm not actually crying. i want to tell C about my dream, but she has gone to sleep. 3 mini chocolate wafers.

2. 1 small cup of sweet and sour soup

3. medium matcha (iced). 1 piece of chicken breast, spinach, kugel. don't know what kugel is. it tastes like potatoes with eggs and onions.

4. 72 blueberries

5. 10 mini chocolate wafers. C goes to the hospital for the ringing sound in her ears. she says everything's fine. the doctor tells her it might be because of the snot. she says to me, i was thinking, if you were really really old and your wife had passed away, and you went to the hospital alone and saw an old couple walking by hand in hand, how sad would you be? i say, maybe they come hand in hand so that they won't slip and fall. you won't go to the hospital alone. someone will wheelchair you there.

2/1

1. 3 mini chocolate wafers

2. 1 small cup of soup: beef, farro, onion, celery, carrot.

3. medium chai (iced)

4. chipotle: white rice, steak, diced tomatoes, sweet corns, lettuce, shredded cheese, guacamole, sour cream. sit in the classroom listening to the introduction of a new writing center initiative. they've selected 10 students who come to the writing center on a regular basis and made a diagnosis for each of them, so that when

they come in, the tutors know what to focus on. i wonder how the selection process was carried out. while listening to others speak, i consider whether my occasional feeling of unrealness actually comes from familiarity. even now, sometimes when i realize C is my girlfriend, i am almost startled. if i wake up after midnight, i am equally startled by the factuality of my body being my body. after sitting there for a while, i forget which language i am hearing, reading, or speaking. now that C has become part of me and my daily life, maybe i have trouble separating her role as my girlfriend from her whole being.

2/2

1. dream: i'm back home and take the bus with my parents to my grandparents'. it is warm. mom and i are both wearing skirts and over-the-knee socks. we plan on going out to see the festival lanterns. abu says she won't go because otherwise she'll miss her bedtime, which is 7pm. wake up not liking the dream. i think it might come from my friend telling me his grandfather will soon turn 85. he says he's relieved, since it's often said that if someone lives safely past 84 they'll live on for at least another 5 years without a problem. i tell him my grandmother will turn 84 towards the end of this year, and my grandfather is a year younger. 3 mini chocolate wafers.

2. sandwich: 2 pieces of whole wheat bread, tuna salad, 4 slices of pickle, 3 slices of lettuce, 1 slice of cheddar cheese. 1 small cup of chocolate milk. G calls and says her roommate blames her for not cleaning up the kitchen after cooking. she says her roommate is very biased in picking on her while assuming their other roommate, who is from the states, does the cleaning every time. after talking to her roommate, she goes back to her room and reaches for the ibuprofen bottle. she holds a pill in her palm and stares at it for a long time, but in the end, doesn't take it. she says, i can't go on like this. my boyfriend is so patient, so nice, i don't want to disappoint him. today for the 1st time, i realize the word *sweetheart* is imprinted on the plastic cup lid.

3. 1 small cup of clam chowder soup

4. 91 blueberries

2/4

1. C is going home today. her mother told her to buy new clothes for the new year, so she bought a grey coat. her mother said she looked like a little mouse in it. last night before i went to sleep, she said, sleep now; tomorrow morning we'll play for a while and go home together. i started to imagine i was really going back home with her, and felt she was talking to me as if i were a child. white rice with korean minced turkey and steamed broccoli. medium black tea lemonade.

2. frozen yogurt, flavor: original. toppings: mochi and hot fudge. it's sunday and i have to take a bus that doesn't go directly back to campus. the driver says he writes science fictions and tells me in detail about a novel he is writing, which involves a male protagonist living simultaneously in 2 separate worlds, one just like the ordinary world, the other a utopian world where the residents do not work for personal gain, but for the happiness of the society as a whole (he uses the word socialist) and are always helping each other. i stand beside him. as we drive out of the transit center, he gestures towards his seat and says, you can sit down. come and sit with me. i say, i'll just stand here. he asks me what i am. are you japanese? i thought you were japanese. what is the difference between the japanese and the chinese on the face? what's china like, full of people and motorcycles? he stretches his arms forward and grabs his imaginary motorcycle, lowers his shoulders and sways his torso like dancing, while mimicking the sound of an engine. i tell him now in many cities you can't ride motorcycles on the street. he seems surprised. he asks how old i am. he says i look like i'm only 17. i was thinking the other day that, when C reaches my current age, i'll be 26. when she graduates at the age of 25, i'll be 27. where will we be at that time? C once said she thought coming out should be easier for women because if the parents wanted grandchildren, we could do the job. if it is really so, when would be the best time for this to happen?

3. spicy shrimp inari sushi (6 pieces) with green onions on top. someone walks by, reciting to her friend a text message she's received, *my tummy hurts, frown face*. why did he write out the emoji? her friend says, sometimes i write out emojis too. i will write out *smiling face*.

2/5

1. salad: cabbage, celery, carrot, edamame, chicken breast, mango. run into W at the writing center and tell her she says *oh* a lot. she says now she'll be conscious every time. sitting through my shift, i recall the bus driver from yesterday asking me what i'd do after graduation. he said, are you going to do restaurant work or teach? i said i'd probably teach. he said, no restaurant? i wondered if i'd heard him wrong. he also told me about his encounter with a guy who worked for warner brothers. he said, the guy told me i'd be rich; i'm crazy, i got imagination.

2. small coffee with 2% milk and brown sugar (hot).

3. 1 plain bagel with cream cheese. took a b.c. pill yesterday and decide to quit today. i'm always on the verge of b.c. pills. during the time when i have trouble sleeping, seems to me such a mystery that people are actually capable of falling asleep. now it is just as mysterious that so many get their periods regularly. i've never had that kind of regularity since i got my 1st period 9 years ago. now that i'm with C, maybe i shouldn't be so happy about my low probability of getting pregnant. otherwise i'd feel bad, almost guilty, for my own malfunction, my failure to carry out a task that shouldn't even include me trying.

4. 40 blueberries. 2 mini chocolate wafers. this week's blueberries have a strange texture and sourness that remind me of apples, which i dislike very much.

2/6

1. dream: mom comes to pick me up with a helicopter. she is wearing a police uniform and gives me one too. it is snowing heavily. once we've landed, we see 2 policemen standing on the pavement, chatting. we crouch down to avoid being spotted and walk home. another dream: i am watching a commercial for a potato pie. the slogan says: *a potato pie that pacifies your sin of bad cooking.* my friend wants to tint the left iris of an octopus and then extract it. he throws bait (an eel's head) into the sea, but the octopus doesn't bite. it snatches the bait and swims away with a smirk. i wake up at 7 in the morning, talk to C for a minute, and fall back asleep. she says she can watch movies from the tv she has at

home. lying in the dark, i start to wonder why sex is complex but pleasurable, not painless and pleasureless, physically boring. just as any other feature of humankind, it must have happened purely because of chance, coincidence. but still, what if the evolution of sex had taken a different route? then there would only have been sex for the purpose of reproduction; what we now know as sex for pleasure would not have existed. consequently, a relationship like the one between C and me would have been asexual because if there's no fun in it, why waste the time? in winter we'd spend those long nights sleeping. sex solely for pleasure means desire and wanting. if it is taken away, maybe there'd be an even more absolute division between the status of queerness and that of long-established normality. i do desire having sex with C; it's hard because it takes a lot of time to understand the physical needs of your partner and also yourself, but it is part of our relationship and i'd like to do it every day, not sleep through 3 months of coldness in the dark. scrambled eggs with hash browns.

2. beef chili with cornbread, sweet corns and broccoli. small hot chocolate with whipped cream. made by that actor kid who always makes bland matcha.

2/7

1. last night i told C i took a b.c. pill 2 days ago. i got a feeling she thought i was being careless and immature. she said, when you went to the hospital last month you didn't ask the doctor how you should be taking b.c. pills. she told me not to have coffee drinks too often because they had too much sugar and fat. and, she said, no milk tea. i said, ok. she was quiet for a while. then she asked if she was being didactic and over-restricting me. i had typed in no, but deleted it and said, just a little. she sent me a sad rabbit sticker. she said, ok, do what you want. we're so far apart anyway. i told her i understood and would follow her words. while saying this i started to cry. the sense of being blamed and talked to like a child made me feel vulnerable and incapable. she tried to comfort me. eventually we both calmed down. 3 mini chocolate wafers.

2. salad: lettuce, black beans, sweet corns, carrot, 4 grape tomatoes, mango, mixed cheese. yesterday morning, sitting in

the cafeteria eating before work, i realized i was probably just moving money around within the school: out of the department funding, where my paychecks came from, into the profit made by this cafeteria. i thought of the word *currency*. what if i could have them deposit my paycheck directly to the cafeteria and come and eat like i am somehow entitled to free food?

3. medium peach black tea lemonade. C wakes up early. she says the ringing in her ears is especially loud today, and is afraid. i start to worry too. i feel strengthless. we talk for a while before she goes back to sleep. G calls and says she is angry at her boyfriend because he spoke in a condescending tone when telling her to go to bed early. then, in an effort to straighten things out, he jokingly told G her roommate was standing behind her. she got scared because she knew there was no one else in her dorm, and was vulnerable due to her nerve issues. she's angry but calls me and asks for my opinion on whether she should be angry and for how long she should not talk to her boyfriend. she also says her father wants to have a son. her mother is over 50 years old, so he would need to find a younger woman willing to bear his son. G says, he thinks he's still capable. he thinks he has high-quality sperm. i say, but sperm quality doesn't determine the sex of your child. she says, my father believes he will have a son. he says if there's someone else at home, my mother won't drag him out for walks along the river anymore. and without a son, he has no heir. listening to her, i think of the time when mom told me dad had always wanted a daughter, since a son would cost the parents too much when he got married. my mother wanted a son and, judging from her symptoms, thought it would be a son. fries with ketchup and ½ an avocado. so it almost equals avocado fries! a luxurious appetizer. C wakes up again and calls me. she dreamed a huge white cat bit her and she had to get vaccinated. she had another dream of burying bombs, another of brushing teeth for a long time, and another of going to school on a rainy day. she says her mother urges her to find a boyfriend. her mother says, i don't have any requirement as long as it's a guy; don't always nitpick on what you don't like about someone, no one's perfect. we don't want you to bring anything when you come back for holidays, just bring a boyfriend. briefly we talk about when she'll

come out to her parents. she says this coming summer, and i'm worried that might be too soon. then we discuss which laptop i'm going to buy. apple this, apple that. her mother comes back and we end the call.

4. the other ½ of the avocado

2/8

1. dream: i am in a taxi with 4 other people and we are being sent to the front to fight invading monsters. we all know we may die and don't want to go, but we have no choice. i wake up. i tell C i don't want to go and fight deadly monsters. 4 mini chocolate wafers.

2. 1 pizza puff. medium matcha (iced). the pizza puff is a very laughable object. it looks like a chinese bun and has a round piece of baked flour on top, like a sun hat. i'm not sure from which side it should be eaten, so i eat it from the bottom up.

3. V says to me, i have a weird question. then asks if i have a chapstick. thinking that question not weird at all, i decide she is asking for chopsticks and tell her no, suggesting that she ask T, who offered me chopsticks when he saw me crying. it takes me some time to figure out she really wants chApstick. coincidentally, i was wondering the other day whether T had actually said chapstick or chopsticks. A lent V his chapstick. she says she used to have the same brand. the flavor was peppermint. A's is fruity. it's nice, she says, layering balm on her lips over and over again. sandwich: sourdough, roast beef, cheddar cheese, lettuce, pickles, mayonnaise.

2/9

1. dream: dad finds out about C. he scolds me and demands us to break up. after he leaves, abu comes in. i start to work up courage to tell her i have a girlfriend, thinking she'd take my side. but i wake up before saying anything. 4 mini chocolate wafers.

2. small bowl of salad: cabbage, cauliflowers, 4 tofu cubes. medium cold brew with half and half. tell the barista to leave some room on top. sitting in the cafe, i get an email saying i have

a package from D. she's sent me a recipe book of singaporean dishes and a new year card. i sit down beside A and open the book. the pictures in it are collages of ingredients such as ginger, raw meat, purple and green onions, potatoes, and all kinds of spices. there is one picture of whole bulbs of ginger collaged into a single strip across 2 pages. A glances and says, what is that, worms? i tell him it's ginger. he says it looks like worms. i say, no, it looks like shit. A stares at me. he says, you said it. i feel outraged, and this rage almost embarrasses me. is it shameful to still get angry after so many years, to tell others i once tried to cut myself with a knife because of this person? so many years have passed and D still sees me as unable to take care of myself, saying in her card, *remember to eat every day*. i tell A, at least she's not getting married. later i see L and E sitting outside on the patio. L is trying to write a haiku on birth certificates. E is writing a novel and tells us about her dream: it is the apocalypse and she is driving on route 4 with her sister. because it's the apocalypse, there's no electricity. they're completely buried in darkness. E's sister criticizes her driving skills. they arrive at a factory where a gay willy wonka character demands everyone to dress in alice attire. we end up watching music videos from the '90s because they are trying to show me the american fashion around that time period and express their lack of understanding towards this trend they've once witnessed and even participated in.

3. chicken breast with sausage and peppers with sliced purple potato. ice cream with chocolate chips. C sends me pictures of hens and roosters from her grandfather's backyard. i ask her about the ugly dog she told me about last year, and she goes to ask her elder cousin. he tells her it died because of food poisoning. she says, my grandfather never could keep a dog for a very long time. when she was 5 years old, her grandfather had a small white dog that she grew really fond of. when she was 5, C had been a wild little girl. once she chased her mother up and down the stairs with a knitting needle. she says the knitting needle was her best weapon. i would love to see it, even though it means i'd have to risk being stabbed.

2/10

1. dream: i am in a large room with some dozens of other people; the windows are open. i stand in front of a fridge. we get bombed and the heat wave of explosion rushes in from the windows. people start to scream, *close the window! close the window!* soon after another bomb lands closer to the building. we are crawling all over the floor, looking for a place to hide. again and again bombs are dropped till we are clustered in the remaining ¼ of the original room. then an army marches towards us, led by 2 villains specialized in crushing open barred doors. i manage to wake up before they do. i message C and she responds after 8 minutes, which is not a long time at all but is at that moment quite scary. i can't really fall back asleep afterwards and drift in and out of dreams instead. when i finally decide not to sleep anymore, C messages me. perfect timing. yet again i wait for more than ½ an hour before she sees my next messages because she forgot to turn on notifications. during the time when i'm waiting for her, instead of questioning her existence, it is my own being that i start to doubt. i feel a suspicious serenity in my body, in its lying posture, as if my figure has morphed into a form too thin, too transparent. after saying our good nights, i take the train to la to buy several things C has told me "can help you get your period." spicy salmon don. i realize i am far more familiar with little tokyo than chinatown, which can be an intimidating place. there is always the possibility that language may fail me, since i don't know cantonese and in some stores mandarin and english don't work. but isn't that also possible in little tokyo? maybe i feel a certain expectation of me knowing cantonese but not japanese. after asking someone in a tea shop, i find a small market and get red dates, fructus lycii and haw slices (all dried). though i don't have too much belief in them, successfully acquiring these dried fruits brings me unexpected joy.

2. sea salt black tea (iced). for no obvious reason, i want a rosary from the cathedral of our lady of the angels. i climb up the slope. a bunch of middle school kids in uniform are distributing bottled holy water. i go to the cathedral store but feel no connection to any of the rosaries, so i give up. and i'm also thinking, C said she didn't like religion. i didn't ask her if she meant abrahamic

religions, and i know she's read greek myths. small cucumber lemonade.

3. 1 curry croquette bread. once Z referred to *sleeping* as *getting horizontal*. multiple people have used this expression since, and when Z laughs now i doubt if she still remembers she introduced me to the phrase.

2/11

1. last night i sent C a barcode leading to a simple webpage game where one could collage provided materials into family portraits. i got very into it and made 3 portraits of C and me and our 2 dogs. when C played with it, she added 2 cats. today G asks me for the link and then sends me her version of her and her boyfriend. i tell her the figure doesn't look like her. she says, i'm bad at drawing, especially lacking the sense of perspective, so i can only look at colors and the overall result. looking at the 5 collages (i made 4) together, the family portrait C made is the warmest and most symmetrical. if one draws a vertical line dividing the picture evenly into 2, on either side will be ½ of a window, ½ of the table on which dinner is set, one of the 2 women sitting behind the table. in either character's lap lies one cat. beside either character stands one dog. the only thing that lies outside this symmetry is a potted plant at the far left corner of the picture, almost touching the border of the frame. but since the dog on the right is bigger than the one on the left, its weight is balanced by that of the smaller dog and the plant combined. the sizes of some objects are enlarged a little so that, even though it doesn't have that many elements, the frame looks quite occupied. none of my family portraits are symmetrical. i put the window on the left, a small table or a chest on the right, pot plants on either side. even when the 2 characters are sitting together on the sofa, their dogs (and occasionally also cats) won't be stationed along the same invisible line. G's is very different. she makes the window very small and puts it on the upper left corner, a place neither of the characters is able to reach, even standing on the sofa underneath the window. the characters themselves are out of proportion. it seems she didn't try to choose a hairstyle that matches her own, the girl looks nothing like her. both characters

are standing, with a small distance between them. it resembles a couple greeting someone outside the frame, the viewer, instead of a random scene captured in their daily life. looking at it makes me feel uneasy, awkward. today before i wake up, C says she is thinking of the past winter break, when i went back, visited her, and accompanied her to the hospital because she got a fever. it was the flu season. almost all her schoolmates got sick and the hospital was packed with sneezing, coughing patients. she says when we slept at night i'd wrap myself around her and place my feet on hers to keep her warm, and she liked it. i tell her my feet are almost always freezing cold in winter but when she was sick and felt cold, they happened to be warm. i was secretly very happy. cheese burger with mushrooms and 2 slices of tomato. by now i have grown a little tired of mushrooms, but i don't like any other topping and without toppings the price is still the same. medium peach black tea lemonade.

2. 1 plain bagel with 1 avocado

2/12

1. roast chicken breast with roast tomato, baked potato, spinach. today G tells me that—although she told me her boyfriend went to a brothel during his depression—it ends up he went on a regular basis, almost once a month, for a year. it was a total of 10 times. she is telling me now because this morning her boyfriend says he wants to go to the brothel again. he has been busy for quite a while and feels exhausted, and he can sense the wicked flame of desire burning inside him. i don't know what to make of it. i start to remember the times when i felt his words were too contrived, almost too perfect, while detouring around or avoiding the actual question posed to him. the 1st time i went out for tea with him and G, he said he liked reading novels in his spare time. yet when i asked him what kinds of novels he preferred, quickly he said, but of course that's when i'm especially free. usually i go to art shows on weekends.

2. chicken fried rice with steamed vegetables: squash, mushrooms, onions, green beans. 1 small cup of chocolate milk mixed with nonfat milk. as i go up the stairs, i see A sitting behind

an orange table outside the cafe, holding the leash of a cat. the cat is sprawling on the table being petted by someone else. i ask him what he's doing. he gives me a death stare and groans, *cat-sitting*. i say, oh. then he tries to show his affection and reaches for the cat's head. fiercely it turns towards him and hisses. he backs up in his chair and waggles his finger. no! he says.

2/13

1. when i wake up, C has gone to sleep. the ringing in her ears is still bad, but a little bit better than yesterday because she's taken some medicine soup that's supposed to help. she says the key is to not remain lying for too long. she also sent me a picture of the river close to her home. i was strolling along the river this afternoon, she says, and it was very warm. we can go together next time. 5 mini chocolate wafers.

2. sandwich: sourdough, tuna salad, cheddar cheese, pickles, lettuce.

3. 1 maple glazed old-fashioned donut. C wakes up when i'm in the middle of my class. she says it's too loud she can't stand it. she barely slept. i think of what i can do which is essentially nothing. she tells me not to worry. i tell her i love her. what's the use in knowing what she already knows? it can be a vulnerable statement, like a magnetic field, weakened by increasing distance. sometimes i feel that i am operating in 2 separate realms simultaneously. despite knowing i can't be, it also feels true: i am here and also lying beside C, sending virtual hugs and kisses that actually land on her face. every time i say such things, they feel more real than i expect them to be. but maybe *i love you* is too abstract, since it's not a single action. its abstractness cancels the reality of other more concrete expressions of love and desire. every time we say it, it brings the distance back. but i can't think of other things to say. C says she'll try to sleep now.

4. 1 baked drumstick, baked cherry tomatoes with garbanzo beans, baked cauliflowers.

2/14

1. dream: walking to the left of abu holding her arm. mom is a few steps ahead. we are on our way to a hospital. abu turns her head to talk to me. i sense she is happy. wake up at 7. light rain, almost a drizzle. C has taken some medicine her parents insist on her taking, and she doesn't think it's helpful. i try to reassure her, telling her there could be a lack of zinc, maybe magnesium and vitamin b also. last night she was telling me ducks ate chicken bones too. she said, they can't chew the bones up because they don't have teeth, but they keep sucking. when she's gone to sleep i stay awake for another 3 hours before finally deciding to sleep again. as i flip the comforter, my phone falls into the gap between my bed and the wall. to retrieve my phone i have to 1st remove the mattress and then pull on the wooden bed frame, since the 2 combined are too heavy. then there comes an impulse to change the bedsheet. i don't feel sleepy anymore. 1 slice of pork parmesan pizza. medium mocha (iced).

2. beef burger with 2 slices of tomato, lettuce, sour cream. not very sour. 1 small cup of coke.

2/15

1. 5 mini chocolate wafers. been waking up at 7 every day. today is the lunar new year. i wake up at 7, exchange happy new year and good night with C, and go back to sleep at 10:30. waking from a dream, i want to tell C. i grab my phone and find myself late for class. i jump up and run to the classroom without changing. halfway through it, i wake up once again, not late for class. the dream is so real that i can't believe i haven't been back in reality until now. feels like a narrow escape. i tell C my dream when she wakes up. she says it's so terrible she can't sleep, worse than before. now i can no longer call it a ringing in her ears; it's her tinnitus. doesn't seem like something that will go away on its own. 1 slice of meatloaf, baked potato, sweet corn on a cob. eating my lunch, i realize i've been avoiding this word, tinnitus, even though i look it up online every day, as if i can escape the truth of this piercing noise by not using its name. at night i find it hard to sleep. i'm constantly worried: about C's health, abu's health,

my protruding front teeth, the summer internship i need to find but have to wait since it's still too early to look. i am generally happier at night, but everything becomes more worrisome at the same time. C says she wants to live in a place where she can go to the hospital whenever she needs to. in her town there aren't any sophisticated doctors. she's going to the hospital on the 1st day of the new year. yesterday she told me her parents insisted on her taking some useless medicine, and suddenly i found myself crying. i was angry, partially because of how her family reacted to her ear condition, partially because i hadn't had enough sleep. i felt my pillow damp against my cheek but i couldn't stop. i kept crying. that's when i accidentally dropped my phone into the gap between my bed and the wall and had to move the heavy mattress.

2. 1 small bowl of chinese sweet and sour chicken soup. not sure what's chinese about it. 1 chocolate sprinkle donut. i see a pink flash in the distance outside the window i'm facing. at 1st i believe it to be a firework, then i realize it's the reflection of a paper cutout hanging somewhere behind me, swaying under a vent. 2 students are singing *a rose is a rose is a rose is a rose*. C is angry at her family because they keep telling her the tinnitus is not real; they say it's a psychological problem instead of a physical one. she says, how can i not know if my ears are actually stuck? but they won't believe her. it's the lunar new year, they say. there's no doctor in the hospital. there's no one in the hospital, they say. don't go to the hospital.

土狗

LITTLE BEE'S KINDERGARTEN

Last week I called my grandmother and asked her to come run the kindergarten with me. She said she didn't want to. She didn't know how. "It's simple," I said, and went on demonstrating to her how the kindergarten would be run. I decided on the name *Little Bee's Kindergarten*. It would be fairly small, with a total enrollment of 10 to 15, situated on the mini train track in the courtyard of Westfield Mall. She said she didn't want to know because even if she knew, she wouldn't be patient enough to run a kindergarten.

Last night I dreamed of my grandmother again. I was walking beside her, walking her to the hospital, holding her left arm. It felt warm in my hand. She turned her head to talk to me, and I thought she seemed happy. Waking up, I feel unsure. If we were really walking to the hospital, how could she be so happy? Maybe it wasn't a hospital. Maybe it was an old-folks home. Would that be a more suitable destination, one that could make her smile on the way? The only thing I know for certain is that she knew where we were going and she felt prepared, content.

Every time before I fly back to the states, I always go visit my grandparents one last time. If I'm not careful enough as to leave no gap between this visit and my departure, my grandmother will come knock on our door the next day. I can sense it when she is coming. While we say goodbye after dinner, I can look at her face and tell if she'll show up. I'll tell my mother, "We can't go out today. Grandma is coming." "How do you know?" my mother will say. "She didn't tell me." "We had eye contact yesterday," I'll say, "when we were waving goodbye."

Last winter I realized I'd become taller than my grandfather when we both stood up straight. I felt ashamed for putting on that pair of boots with thick soles. I felt ashamed for wanting to be taller than I was.

Little Bee's Kindergarten is a toy train in Westfield Mall, Santa Clarita, California. The tuition is collected on a daily basis and the rate is 20 dollars per day. Included in it are the costs of 2 meals (breakfast and lunch; dinner is optional), technology fee, book fare, toy fare, and maintenance fee. On each day 1 kindergarten staff member (my grandmother or I) will remain close by, right beside the train track, to sound the horn, distribute books and toys, and keep the children safe.

Once when I was in the kindergarten, I shat my pants. That was the only time I remember and, I am sure, the only time I actually shat my pants. I was around 3. My grandmother came to take me home. I didn't cry at all, and she wasn't telling me it was all right, or it was natural, or it was something that would happen when you were 3. Maybe because of that, the lack of conversation, of sounds in general, I don't remember the whole walk from the kindergarten back home. What I remember is the angle of my right arm, which was pointing upwards, away from me, ending in my grandmother's left hand. The only way for me to walk beside my grandmother is to walk on her left.

There were chances when I could have ended up unborn. My grandmother wasn't going to marry my grandfather because she didn't like how he looked. He was scrawny, though she herself was too. Most people were anyway. She didn't want to marry this man, though she had accompanied him every morning to the soccer field, where he finished his morning jogging. It was a duty but also an honor bestowed on my grandmother, who had been leader of the Party branch at their college. My grandfather was weak, slow at running. His mental and physical health had both become my grandmother's responsibility. Then he wanted to marry her and she refused. Then, after graduation, she was dispatched from Hangzhou, Zhejiang, to Taiyuan, Shanxi, an inland city far up north, 883 miles away. A few months later, he arrived at her door. Three years later, they got married (end of the 1st chance of my unbirth).

Yesterday was the Lunar New Year. Today I wake up and see 3 family portraits taken on a phone. My parents, my grandparents, my grandfather from my father's side, my mother's younger brother and his wife, my father's elder brother and his wife: all standing in front of the restaurant where they have just had their New-Year dinner. My grandfather is the only one with mouth hanging open. His face assumes a bemused expression, almost surprised, like he is not yet ready to be photographed. He is the 2nd tallest person in the picture. Looking at it, I wonder if any of my worries about my grandmother are grounded in reality. She hasn't changed, or so it seems, since 8 years ago. Maybe it's the magic of a photograph. It suits certain people especially well. I can make this comparison because there is another family portrait in my parents' bedroom, taken 8 years ago when my grandparents celebrated their golden anniversary. Everyone else in that picture has changed in their own way, but my grandparents appear to remain the same. Maybe when one gets older time starts to take a different approach: 1st it changes your face, then it leaves your face alone and marches down your spine, crumpling it up so you are shorter and shorter, doubled, almost. Then eventually it returns to your face. Maybe my grandparents have been in the spine stage. It's hard to determine how long the stage will last.

Little Bee's Kindergarten is a necessary move towards the improvement of kindergarten education. Children in kindergartens are prone to unfair treatment, such as bad meals, lack of versatile toys, forced afternoon naps, impractical and thus useless learning, unreasonable blaming, etc. Among all the possibilities, it is unreasonable blaming that hurts children the most.

Here is an example:

Once when I was around 5 years old, our teacher showed us a model rocket and a book that came with it. She told us the name of each part and what its function was. She opened the book and held it high for us to see an illustration of how a rocket was shot into space. All the children sitting around me were nodding, so I nodded too. I don't remember at which point I started to apply a rhythm to it. I was nodding so fast everything in my vision turned to a blur. Then my eyes were closed for a while. When I reopened them, the teacher was staring right at me. She said, "I've been watching you the whole afternoon. You are not behaving. Do you think I didn't see what you were doing? I've been watching you all the time." She kept staring at me a little longer before resuming her lecture on rockets. I stopped listening. Thirteen years later I learned that my grandmother had worked in the development team for rocket fuel. So she had been a Party branch leader and one of the people working towards building a rocket. But what were we supposed to feel when we were confronted with that model rocket at the age of 5? What did they want us to remember? Why had the teacher been watching me the whole afternoon? Had she really? I was always the one kid who needed the least watching. I was good at doing as told. I barely talked. She couldn't have been watching me the whole afternoon.

There is very little shame in shitting your pants in kindergarten because almost everyone will do it once or twice, and you are even rewarded for doing it: you go home. Most of the shame comes from being called out, being recognized in the middle of some inappropriate behavior, sometimes pressed to account for it too. I propose that the best solution to this problem, this sudden, unreasonable blaming and the surge of negative emotions it causes, is to minimize direct interactions between teachers and the children. Little Bee's Kindergarten, therefore, is designed as a kindergarten where the presence of the teacher is rarely sensed.

Once my mother said, "30 years later I am 80, your grandmother is 110; 70 years later I am 120, your grandmother is 150." My mother is also 30 years older than me. When I was 5, I thought women could only bear children at the age of 30.

Yesterday I drew a tarot card for my grandmother's health this year. I sensed an intense energy on my right-hand side but couldn't settle on a card. Finally I drew out Death, reversed. Yet in this context what difference would the reverse make?

The basic structure of Little Bee's Kindergarten is like this:

```
screen1                                              screen2
t r a c k t r a c k t r a c k t r a c k t r a c k t r a c k
k                    train →                                t
c                                                           r
a                                                           a
r                                              train ↓      c
t                                                           k
k                               changing                    t
c                               settings                    r
a                               with                        a
r                               fake                         c
t                               animals                      k
k                                                            t
c train ↑                                                    r
a                                                            a
r                                                            c
t                    ← train                                 k
k c a r t k c a r t k c a r t k c a r t k c a r t k c a r t
screen3              gate (teacher's station)        screen4
```

As can be seen from the layout, at Little Bee's Kindergarten there is no classroom per se: children will spend the whole day onboard a toy train circling the track, which is built in the shape of a square around changing settings with fake animals. Installed at every turn of the track is a screen the size of the average projection screen used in a classroom. The content shown on each screen changes 5 times daily. In the morning when the children 1st board the train, the breakfast menu of that day is displayed on the screen. After breakfast, it changes into a selection of books and toys, and the children can choose 1 or 2 of each. Later, the lunch menu comes up. After lunch there come all the choices of afternoon activities, including reading, playing with a toy, free drawing and writing, and getting off the train to play with the fake animals in the center of the track. Little Bee's Kindergarten also provides 1 additional meal to those who can't go back home for dinner, and the menu is the next thing shown on the screen. Eventually before being dispatched, the children can make a final selection and decide which setting and which animal they would like to see tomorrow. The seats are equipped with buttons so the children can indicate their choices easily. Teacher's Station is the place where the teacher (my grandmother or I) will stay for the majority of our day at the kindergarten. It is from here that breakfast, lunch, dinner, and books and toys are delivered to each child. This is also the spot from which we will give our words of encouragement to the children and sound the horn. When the toy train passes Teacher's Station, the teacher is going to hold out their hand and pat everyone's shoulder, saying, "Well done!" Then the horn will be sounded twice, followed by a warm "Goodbye!" Such is all the interaction that is supposed to happen between teachers and students.

Last time when I went to Westfield, the setting in the center of Little Bee's Kindergarten was a small bamboo forest with 3 fake giant pandas. It was almost the Lunar New Year. The temporary teacher on duty that day had dyed her hair blonde, and now it was a color that resembled calcified bones. In order not to make her aware of my presence, I observed her from behind a pillar on the 2nd floor. She seemed to enjoy sounding horns quite a bit, but fell short when it came to encouraging the little passengers. Instead of patting them on their shoulders, she stretched her fingers wide open but merely tapped them in the palm. The worst was when children not enrolled in the kindergarten showed interest, she sold them tickets and let them board the train. This should be strictly prohibited at all times. It should also be made explicit that some children don't like being touched in the palm, since palms can be ticklish.

It is very hard to imagine any part of my grandmother's body being ticklish, although there has to be at least one. Or does there? I remember once, after going to my grandparents', my father said to me, "You must like your grandmother a lot. You always smile when you see her and so does she." Having a ticklish body part means to have a body part that, when tickled by someone else, makes you laugh uncontrollably. Once you have acknowledged that, simply recalling past experiences of being tickled should be enough to make you laugh too. My grandmother has ticklish grandchildren but not really ticklish children. Within our family the most beloved photo of her and me shows her holding the 2-year-old me in her left arm, giving me a huge peeled apple with the other hand. I appear to be laughing, astonished by this round, pale yellow object that could cover half my face and is edible at the same time. My grandmother is laughing too. Our mouths open towards each other. That was around the time when she had told me that "Grandma" was too complicated a word and she didn't have the patience to wait long, so she invented a simple word and spoke it to me every day. Ever since day 1, I address her as "abu." It's so simple and easy that my mother wasn't convinced I was referring to my grandmother. She believed it had only been a random word I produced as an infant, up to the point when I finally realized "abu" equals "grandma." Years later it became a word that brought me much shame. None of my friends addressed their grandmother this way. It's not even the word for "grandma" in any dialect.

In Sumerian religion, Abu was a god, though only a minor one. He was a god of plants, 1 of the 8 deities born to relieve the illness of Enki, the god of water, knowledge, mischief, crafts, and creation. Abu is father of plants and vegetation.

My grandmother is the only one in my family who has a green thumb.

Shanxi is a province famous for its coal-mining industry. Both of my grandparents studied chemical engineering, and they were in the same class; otherwise my grandmother wouldn't have been assigned the task of watching my grandfather jog around the soccer field. After graduation, my grandmother was assigned to Shanxi, to one of the coal factories in the rather deserted plateau, and my grandfather was assigned a teaching job at the university. Besides being scrawny, another common feature of their life was being assigned: from position to position, from place to place. It wasn't their choice to accept or decline. From here the story takes on 3 possibilities:

1. My grandmother had not intended to move that far and only took it on as a test for my grandfather, to see if he loved her enough to go after her and propose again. If this is the truth, then she had liked my grandfather from the beginning and was confident he would come for her.

2. My grandmother was very excited to be assigned to such a remote place because she had never been that far from home. Yet after 3 years, the excitement wore out and the reality sank in, and she started to regret leaving. When my grandfather showed up, she agreed to marry him because once they were married, she would be allowed to relocate to where her husband was.

3. My grandmother accepted this assignment as merely another assignment and didn't think much about my grandfather or his proposal. However, when he repeatedly showed up during a time span of 3 years, she was moved because it was indeed a long distance, especially when there was only the slowest train running between those 2 places. So she reconsidered and accepted his proposal.

I grew up hearing only the 1st version of the story, but one day my mother made a slip and mentioned Possibility 2. The reality, of course, would have been a mixture. There are 4 possible ways to make a mixture: 1+2, 1+3, 2+3, 1+2+3. So we have a total of 7 possibilities of why my grandparents got married.

There are many who don't think much of kindergarten education, such as my grandparents and my father. My father didn't attend kindergarten and there was no kindergarten at my grandparents' time. I don't remember learning anything useful during that time period either. If we are to improve this situation, it will be crucial to determine what exactly should be taught to children of that age. At Little Bee's Kindergarten, every child needs to design its own spacecraft and finish the blueprint by the time of graduation.

My grandmother was born in Nantong in 1934, Year of the Dog, and my grandfather in Suzhou in 1935, Year of the Pig. Both cities belong to Jiangsu Province, a province in South East China, though not so east as to border the sea. This year is again Year of the Dog. It is my grandmother's year. She is turning 84 in December. A friend of mine once said, "If an elder person can live past 84 safely, they can go on living for another 5 years without a problem." I don't believe that. I believe it's just a myth that you will always have bad luck in your year. In fact I have just passed my year, Year of the Rooster, and it turned out to be my favorite year thus far. As the only daughter of my parents, I started a relationship with a girl shortly before my 24th birthday.

When I was still in kindergarten, I remember finding it funny how my grandmother's Chinese zodiac sign is the fierce dog and my grandfather's the gentle, amiable, ultimately edible pig. I'd always seen dogs as male symbols, which at that time meant I would choose the pronoun "he" when I pictured a dog in my mind. It also happened that my mother's younger brother was born in Year of the Lamb and his wife Year of the Horse, which played out to me like an accidental gender reversal. My own parents brought this reversal to a whole different level: my mother's sign is the dragon, my father's the rabbit. When I was little, simply remembering these facts was satisfying. I believed I had a special family.

Learning to place her own family into a social class, my grandmother for the 1st time came face to face with the word "bourgeoisie." Her father had a small fruit store. Starting with bourgeoisie, words flooded towards her: wealth, capital, means of production, landlord, corruption, working class, cutting ties. She went to a female-only high school. Her parents had wanted her to go on to a female-only university and study to be a teacher. They signed her up for the exam. On the day of that exam, my grandmother escaped home and jumped onto a train bound for Hangzhou, the capital of the neighboring province, Zhejiang. She never went back home. She never saw her parents again.

If your family is not special in a positive sense, why keep a family? If your kindergarten is not special and does not satisfy your expectations, why attend kindergarten? I hated my kindergarten but loved my family on the same ground, the precondition of being or not being special. My kindergarten was ordinary. I believed my family was special because my grandmother ran away from her family, which had been special to her in a hazardous way, and became a female professor at a top-tier university. And I used to feel so fortunate that she'd escaped; otherwise, I wouldn't even have been born (end of the 2nd chance of my unbirth).

Once, we all gathered in the auditorium, every student and teacher at my kindergarten. There was a thunderstorm. Every so often, I saw lightning against the darkening sky. We were given toys. We sat playing in the auditorium seats, guarded by the teachers pacing about. It fitted almost too perfectly into the monster phobia I'd developed from watching *Ultraman*. Then my grandmother walked in.

To this day I still don't understand why the teachers had thought it necessary to settle us in the auditorium. Was remaining in the classroom not safe? Was a window leaking? Sometimes I'm convinced it's only a dream, even though I know it is not.

In designing a rocket, the biggest challenge lies in accommodating all the passengers. The rocket needs to be divided into cabins, and assigning each cabin can be quite an exhausting task. Children in Little Bee's Kindergarten are faced with this task every day. For this purpose, the train which is in itself a major part of the kindergarten must be reasonably spacious. Each car should be wide enough so that drawing tables can fit in easily, leaving space for the children to wander around, immersed in their thoughts. There also needs to be doors that make it possible for them to enter different cars, should they find it helpful to discuss with their friends an idea or a problem they encounter. The train has no dining car, but in the last car are 10 beds for them to take their afternoon nap undisturbed. Out of sanitary consideration, no toilet is installed aboard the train, but a bathroom is easily accessible if one steps off the train and takes the nearest turn. The kindergarten is, after all, in the Westfield Mall courtyard. It is important that the teacher on duty establish it concretely that they should not go window-shopping casually as they wish. An unusually long bathroom trip will be counted as either a ½ absence or an absence, depending on the length.

When they are studying, the children at Little Bee's Kindergarten devote much of their time to practicing combinatorics. Here is an example of the kinds of problems they deal with:

1. My mother has 1 sibling.

2. My father has 2 siblings.

3. The 3 siblings each have a daughter. Together there are 4 daughters.

4. Three of the 4 daughters live on the same continent.

5. Only 1 daughter can be reached by train.

6. The daughter of the youngest sibling lives the 2nd farthest from home.

7. The oldest of the 4 daughters lives the closest to home.

8. I am the 2nd oldest and the 3rd farthest from home.

9. My grandmother does not take planes. My grandfathers from both sides do.

If you are to design a rocket, how many cabins does the rocket need and how should the passengers be arranged?

Rockets, when they are carrying people, are called space shuttles, or spacecrafts. So it should be stated that most children in Little Bee's Kindergarten are trying to design their own spacecraft. It is not obligatory. A satellite is an option too.

Even in terms of jogging: my grandmother runs faster than my grandfather does, though she is less than 5 feet tall and he's 5 feet 6. Jogging was crucial, directly related to how a student's performance would be evaluated at the end of each term. The thinking was, by jogging every day and running faster and faster, you were building a stronger body. A stronger body was critical because it demonstrated your willingness to serve your country. Therefore, my grandmother was leader of the Party branch, while my grandfather was a weak-bodied and thus weak-minded boy in need of her help.

My grandmother still had a few relatives alive in her city, so throughout the years my grandfather kept trying to get her to go back. She always said she had nothing to say to them.

Waiting for my mother to pick me up, I would overhear my grandparents get calls from "over there." The caller was referred to as "someone from over there." After answering the phone, my grandfather would give my grandmother a summary. Once someone was getting married. Once someone died. The calls were infrequent, but felt like cracks through which I could glimpse this other world. I looked forward to them. I imagined my grandparents were spies getting contacted by a central base. Direct phone calls are not a safe way to make contact with spies, though.

One summer I went back home and filmed my grandparents. My grandfather had just returned from a wedding in Suzhou. He brought wedding candies for my grandmother—a variety of chocolates, chewy fruit candies, peanut candies, candies shaped like corn cobs, etc.—all wrapped in several red fabric bags. My grandmother poured all the candies out onto the dining table. They formed a pile that couldn't be circled by her hands. She picked up each one of them and said either "This is bad" or "This is good." I filmed her sorting through all the candies and putting them into 2 piles, one for bad candies, the other for good candies. Then she offered me some. Many of them had the symbolic meaning of "bearing a son soon." She asked me if I wanted any. "The chocolates," she said, "are good." They had no meaning to me, they were just sweet. Most candies that ended up in my grandparents' apartment came from weddings, and they always took the train to these weddings. Why were the candies not melted? My grandmother thought I was young and herself old. Now I am still young, but she's older. Have I not aged? I wonder how it feels to watch your children and grandchildren grow older. If I am quick enough, my grandmother will be able to hold her grandchild's child. This is considered a form of the highest happiness. We ended up with 2 piles of candies and since neither of us wanted any, my grandmother mixed them up and put everything away.

Law of physics: if you are an object capable of accelerating, as you accelerate closer and closer to the speed of light, you will become heavier and heavier because you are not supposed to be as fast as light unless you are light. So eventually you can no longer accelerate, and if you are in outer space you will proceed at that speed, which is quick, but not quite enough. If you are light and you accelerate, since you have no weight you can surpass the speed of light and then time will start to flow backwards and you will shine into the past.

The most enviable thing in the world:

When humans had just built their 1st towns and cities and lived in them for several decades, it was possible to remember everything that had ever happened. As history grew longer and longer, gradually it became impossible to remember everything. This also applies to individuals only a few years old. Keeping records is still viable. Yet most children let the opportunity slide out of their hands because they just aren't aware. We need to tell them about this on the very 1st day they board Little Bee's Kindergarten, lest they lose their chance and attempt later, in vain, to reach the speed of light. They will have to accept the fact that none of them is light and none of them or their spacecrafts can be quick enough to travel into the past. If they try too hard, there is the risk of being crushed.

Some of the things I learned when I was in kindergarten (but not *from* the kindergarten):

1. My grandmother doesn't like most fruits, which enables her to feed me apples and peaches without temptation.

2. There is a TV hidden inside the bookshelf in the main bedroom.

3. My grandparents have nothing against watching TV while eating dinner.

4. My grandmother doesn't like noodles. She makes noodles for my grandfather twice each week.

5. My grandmother did not know how to cook when she got married. She would boil everything.

6. Just like the word she's invented for "grandma," the word I use as "grandpa" is also my grandmother's invention.

After dreaming about walking my grandmother to the hospital, I woke up and thought it might be a bad omen. I dared not tell anyone. Then I thought it might actually be the opposite. Then I thought I identified more with my grandparents than with my parents and that might be why I dreamed about the former more often.

In terms of identification:

Sometimes it can be hard for children to decide which animal they want to see on the following day. Sometimes you made a decision yesterday and today all of a sudden you are repulsed by your choice. When the train is circling fake bamboos and fake pandas, some of the children arrive in the morning and say, "Oh, Panda Express!" Panda Express is a restaurant chain serving American Chinese food and, less well known, it has a sister restaurant called Panda Inn, which is supposed to be a higher-end, sit-down restaurant serving Chinese food that is less American. Yet it is easier for the former to ring a bell, since Little Bee's Kindergarten is on a train, which can also be called *express*. Gradually all the animals will be addressed in the same way and we will have Elephant Express, Seal Express, Dog Express, Catfish Express, etc. It is a tendency to watch out for because the children may come to enjoy saying these phrases too much and eventually abandon the original name of the kindergarten. Teachers must keep in mind the fact that this is 1st and foremost a kindergarten, not an express.

When my grandmother arrived at her college, she felt liberated for the 1st time. In fact, the collective feeling of liberation was pervasive. It was only 4 years after the official establishment of the People's Republic of China. She graduated in 1957. On May 23, 1958, the Great Leap Forward started.

When I graduated from college in 2017, 60 years after my grandmother's graduation, I was the same age as she was back then. February 25, 2018, I woke up at 3 in the morning and saw a message from my girlfriend. China's Communist Party had proposed removing the 2-term limit for its President and Vice President from the constitution.

In Little Bee's Kindergarten, milk should be provided in abundance. Unless a child is allergic to milk, roughly 16 oz should be distributed to the child every day. Milk is rich in protein and calcium and benefits the development of the brain. A train full of fresh, young brains. Noisy brains. Without the sound of the friction, it will be unbearable for anyone to stay at Teacher's Station for more than 5 minutes.

My grandmother has a habit of drinking milk every day. In the morning, she says, "See? I drink milk every day. I've been drinking milk every day for more than 5 decades. It makes me healthier. Did you drink milk before you came?"

My grandmother has a habit of drinking milk every day. Before lunch, she says, "See? I drink milk every day. I've been drinking milk every day for more than 5 decades. It makes me healthier. Did you drink milk before you came?"

My grandmother has a habit of drinking milk every day. After lunch when she reads the newspapers, she says, "See? I drink milk every day. I've been drinking milk every day for more than 5 decades. It makes me healthier. Did you drink milk this morning?"

My grandmother has a habit of drinking milk every day. Before dinner, she says, "See? I drink milk every day. I've been drinking milk every day for more than 5 decades. It makes me healthier. Did you drink milk this morning?"

My grandmother has a habit of drinking milk every day. After dinner when I tell her I'm leaving, she says, "See? I drink milk every day. I've been drinking milk every day for more than 5 decades. It makes me healthier. Will you drink milk tomorrow morning?"

Then she walks me to the door.

In the 1970s, milk was still a luxury. My father had never drunk milk before marrying my mother. My mother grew up drinking milk because it was delivered to my grandparents' door every morning. They both worked in the chemistry lab. Milk was supposed to help treat possible chemical poisoning.

I ate a lot of sweet pickled garlic in kindergarten. Sweet pickled garlic kept children from getting the flu. Every day after lunch we were each given one clove. The most desired piece was the heart. Unlike the cloves, which you had to bite and chew, a garlic heart was something you could hold in one hand and suck with ease. It was also sweeter. Only the best-behaved child got the garlic heart.

Regardless of how much I want it to change, my relationship with my grandmother is founded on my being fed. Apart from daily meals, she encouraged me to eat fruits and bread as snacks. Cookies, too.

In kindergarten, it is important that we try to conceal the fact that most parents send their children here merely to be fed. Knowing this is the most effective way for the children to feel worthless. Thinking about the rocket that powers this spacecraft can keep them occupied, motivated and confident.

These are the basic parts of a rocket:

```
                    n
                   ose
                  cone
              f fuelfue f
              r lfuelfue r
              a lfuelfuel a
              m fuelfuelf m
              e uelfuelfu e
              f elfuelfuel f
              r oxidizerox r
              a idizeroxidi a
              m zeroxidiz m
              e eroxidize e
              f roxidizer f
                r pumps r
                a pumps a
                 m noz m
                 e zle e
                  finfin
                 finfinfin
               finfin finfin
             finfin    finfin
              fin        fin
```

And it has 4 systems: structure system (nose cone, frame, fin),
payload system, guidance system, and propulsion system (fuel,
oxidizer, pumps, nozzle). The Space Shuttle is significantly
different and also more complex. The Space Shuttle system
consists of: 2 Solid Rocket Boosters (SRBs), the External Tank
(ET) that feeds fuel to the 3 Space Shuttle Main Engines (SSMEs)
during launch, and the orbiter, which is where the crew lives and
also the main focus of the children at Little Bee's Kindergarten.

At the age of 83, my grandmother has lost all except 2 of her teeth. She refuses to get a set of porcelain teeth implanted because she's afraid of the pain. She has dentures, but there are only 2 teeth for them to attach to. She dislikes dining out more and more, since she can't chew anything up thoroughly and is prone to diarrhea because of that.

During the years when my grandfather lived in the states as a visiting scholar, my grandmother ate bags of cookies every day. Preparing breakfast and hustling the kids off to school left no time for her to eat before work. She rode a bike to her office and ate cookies on the way. In the evening, she'd come back home from work hungry and there'd be nothing to eat but cookies. She ate cookies standing in the kitchen while making dinner. She tells me she had eaten too many cookies in those few years and had no chance to brush her teeth in between. This is why they have all fallen out. They rotted into dark holes and then they were gone.

When my grandmother had just married my grandfather, she applied to be an adjunct professor. The university informed her that in order to be an eligible candidate she must learn either Japanese or Russian. She picked Russian. She learned Russian while cooking and eating cookies, hunched over her gas stove.

We all knew what my grandmother did (she worked on and succeeded in developing rocket fuel), but we couldn't articulate it. While in the middle of it, she was not supposed to tell anyone, and once the work was done the details were no longer important. It must have been a distinguished role because right after the arrest of the Gang of Four (which marked the end of the Cultural Revolution), someone from the Ministry of National Defense was sent to visit my grandmother at the apartment where she was living with my grandfather and their 2 children. My mother and my uncle were both around 10. Neither knew who that person was. My grandmother would not tell.

Wouldn't it be interesting if one ancient human in some way recorded everything that had ever happened, and made it a tradition of their family/tribe to carry on? Then there would be a special tribe, like how the Levites were a special tribe, but that's not quite what I mean. This person would have been able to start with the very 1ˢᵗ possibility of the very 1ˢᵗ historical event. Now, unfortunately, we have lost our chance of a complete history.

To count the fake pandas in the center of the courtyard:

There are 2 adult pandas, one on the left, the other on the right. Each of them is holding 2 child pandas on their knees. 2 other child pandas crawl in the middle, making for a total of 6 pandas. They all face the same direction, which means most of the time everyone on board Little Bee's Kindergarten sees only the backs or profiles of these pandas. Naturally, there is great excitement when the train makes a left turn in front of Screen 1 and the panda faces are gradually revealed, as if we are on a plane flying across the dividing line between day and night.

To recall my 1ˢᵗ memory:

Of being pushed by my grandparents and my mother, in a stroller, to a park with an artificial pond, which had dried up due to lack of rain. It was a winter afternoon. The trees were a shimmering gold. As we paused in front of the pond, I saw, standing on the rock island in the middle, 3 deer made of bronze. I can still see their antlers. They, too, were golden in the sun, even though they were covered in rust. It was the 1ˢᵗ time I'd seen fake animals that were set up to mimic real animals in their habitat.

In order to acquire a complete account of all the events that have occurred throughout time, in Little Bee's Kindergarten it is necessary to establish that "everything" truly means everything. In order to practice the preservation of everything, we can start by making a list of the animals we see every day and what we notice about them, what we feel towards them. Such a practice should be titled *Animal Stimulated Response in Children: Reception, Observation, Emotion.*

Nitric acid, dinitrogen tetroxide, UDMH, liquid fluorine, liquid ozone, ClF_3, ClF_5: which ones are supposed to dissolve in milk, to be tamed, to repent and finally behave?

There is something else I have inherited from my grandmother: her liking for milk skin, or lactoderm. The transition and translation from Latin to English to Chinese (not to say that the Chinese word comes directly from English) are quite literal: lacto, milk, 奶; dermis, skin, 皮. During the years when I lived with my grandparents, my grandmother let me drink milk every night before bed. Mug in hand, we would stretch our tongues and try to reach that thin layer of protein. By then the living-room lights would have been turned off. The only light came from the kitchen, which had its own door to lock in the greasy air, and a small window. The light was tinted, a color like that of our skin.

Wouldn't designing a rocket or spacecraft be a nice exercise in learning the names of shapes and colors? Little Bee's Kindergarten itself should be constructed with this purpose in mind. Each car will be painted a different color, each table and each bed a different color and different shape. With 10 to 15 total enrollment, it will be reasonable to order 6 cars together with 10 tables and 10 beds. Here, another exercise can be added:

With your pencil, connect as many dots as you want to make an enclosed 2-dimensional shape, which will be the shape of your table.

· 2   · 15

· 1

· 18   · 12

· 17   · 6

· 4

· 3

· 16

· 8   · 11

· 5

· 14

· 10

· 7

· 9

· 19   · 13

· 20

Once you have finished, take another sheet of this exercise paper and make a new shape for your bed.

Once you have your 2 shapes ready, press the button to signal the teacher, who will in turn deliver you a box of crayons. Color your shapes as you wish with the crayons.

I lived with my grandparents during my kindergarten years. There was a game that my grandmother often played with me:

1. Take a deck of cards that have a variety of animals printed on the front and the same geometric pattern on the back. The same animal would only appear on 2 cards, which was called a match.

2. Lay the cards down on the table face up.

3. Look at them and try to memorize the locations of each animal pair.

4. Flip all the cards face down.

5. Start by flipping a random card and try to recall the location of its match.

6. Find as many matches as you can from memory.

It was my favorite game of all time: slow, quiet, uncompetitive. Growing up, I realized that when I memorize a word, it is the shape of it, rather than the actual letters, that I remember.

(We don't even need cards! Give each child a calendar and ask it to circle the days when the same animal is installed in the courtyard.)

(Those who write down everything are more likely to get it right.)

Geography:

· **Taiyuan**

· **Nantong**

· **Suzhou**

· **Hangzhou**

My grandmother does not have an enclosed shape, because she refuses to go back to Nantong. She draws her line from Nantong to Hangzhou, then to Taiyuan, and then back to Hangzhou—2 lines with no enclosed area. She would have failed the exercise and ended up with no table and no bed.

Though my grandparents got married 3 years after college, my grandmother didn't move back until more than 2 years later, around 1963. The university could provide only a limited number of permissions for faculty spouses to relocate. A year later, my mother was born; then in 1967, her brother, my uncle. The Cultural Revolution officially started in 1966.

By 2016, Xi had been president for 3 years and we realized we would have to spend another 7 years under his reign. Now we are not sure how long it might be. I wonder if this was the same fear my grandparents felt in the 60s and 70s: of a regime extending into eternity. Yet compared with those around them, it would be a stretch to say my grandparents were oppressed during that time, and I have hardly suffered anything at all. I wonder if the lack of suffering makes one less valuable as a witness.

THE NUMBER OF CABINS IN MY SPACECRAFT: AN ESTIMATION

My grandmother has always had her own room. It is her bedroom and study. Most of the time she doesn't take afternoon naps, but on the rare occasions she does, she will go to her room and shut the door.

My grandmother's room is small, somewhat hidden. Here is a map of the apartment where my grandparents live now:

Enter through the front door. In front of you, you'll see the dining room and the kitchen.

Turn left at the dining room and see the living room, where the TV is.

Walk across the living room and see a short hallway.

To your right is the bathroom.

Take 3 steps down the hallway and to your left is my grandmother's room.

Take 1 more step down the hallway and to your right is the study.

At the end of the hallway is my grandfather's room.

Connected to my grandfather's room is the balcony.

My grandfather's room is the largest room in their apartment. The living room is about the same size. My grandmother's room is smaller than the study and larger than the bathroom. The bathroom is about the same size as the kitchen. The dining room is larger than the kitchen.

If you go solely on the information above, it will be impossible to deduce whether my grandmother's room is larger than the dining room.

Before they moved into this apartment, they lived in another apartment right across the street. Clustered with that 5-story apartment building were other identical 5-story apartment buildings. All those were faculty dorms of the university. Back then my grandmother had her own room too. The size was almost the same as that of her room now.

It's nice to have a room of your own, but how large do you expect it to be? Not that my grandmother has ever wanted something bigger. She is small. She is short and thin and that was how she was in her youth too. Every time I go into her room and see her asleep on her small bed, head turned to the left, arms stretched, legs bent, I always find her like an aged, dwindled good witch in a fairy tale. Even standing at her door, I can picture myself as Alice entering a room where everything has turned so small she has to become miniature as well.

Setting foot in a kindergarten as a grown-up feels like this too.

I hate moving. I didn't want my grandparents to move from the faculty dorm to their new apartment, though the latter was so much bigger. I didn't want to move from the one-bedroom I was living in with my parents to our new apartment, though the latter was so much bigger and had a much better location. Neither did I want to transfer from one elementary school to another. I hated moving. I wanted to stay at the old place forever. Problem solved: at Little Bee's Kindergarten, we are simultaneously moving and fixed to where we are all the time.

Years after they moved, I'd still dream about them in their old apartment. Sometimes I would be living there with them too. Never in my dreams have they been situated in their current home.

What could a short, thin, newly graduated 24-year-old female do in a coal factory? She couldn't be a simple worker; that was not the expectation for her. She might work in the design department, on the chemical processing of coal, which would then be transformed into coke, which would then be used to manufacture water gas. My grandmother spent most of her working life with fuel.

One thing I just realized:

I have not mentioned my grandmother's name or the name of any other character. Here is my grandmother's first name:

遗 (yí)

梅 (méi)

"遗" means to lose, to leave, the lost, the left, the forgotten, or the rest; "梅" means plum blossom. My grandmother is the youngest daughter who was almost not born into this world. She had 6 elder brothers.

Here is my grandmother's family name:

陈 (chén)

As a family name, "陈" indicates possible ancestry from Henan Province, Jiangsu Province, or ancient Kucha (now part of Xinjiang Province).

Put my grandmother's full name into the search engine:

You will see that she sued the Property Owners' Committee and the Estate Management Service Office in 2011. It was around the time when she would lock herself in her small room all day, calculating and recalculating on sheets of paper spread across her desk how much each family was paying for the management service. It was not an annual sum. She broke it down to the unit of yuan per square meter per month. That was the 1st time I'd seen her handwriting.

You won't be able to access the verdict online, but my grandmother lost. She didn't want to pay for a lawyer because it would be expensive and she was confident in her calculation and reasoning. However, when she stepped into the court she got cold feet. She was unable to speak. It was during that summer I thought that maybe I could come out to her. Of all the people in my family.

To differentiate a rocket from a spacecraft:

Names. The latter carries names; the former doesn't. What is a spacecraft? A powerful plane that takes 1 or several names into outer space and, it is hoped, brings them back intact, breathing, unbroken. It's a cruise ship for names.

So, when the teacher takes attendance in Little Bee's Kindergarten, it should be easy for the children to imagine that they are onboard an early spacecraft.

When my grandparents went to those meetings every day after dinner during their college years, it was easy for them to imagine that they were onboard a spacecraft.

The teacher waits.

The train (kindergarten) comes close to the Teacher's Station.

The teacher takes out the roster.

The train starts to drive past the teacher.

The teacher inhales deep and slow.

If a child happens to be moving about, its attendance might not be taken. The teacher might fail to notice its presence. It might fail to hear its own name. The other children might fail to remind it. The other children might intentionally pretend its name has not been called. It becomes antimatter. How do we house it? Design a cabin for antimatter.

My grandmother went to the group meeting in one of the classrooms. She arrived early, and the instructor was not there. She sat down beside some other girls and they started chatting. Back then there were always portraits hung on the front wall, right above the blackboard. Looking up, she saw:

Lin Biao Lin Biao	Mao Zedong Mao	Nikita Khrushchev
Lin Biao Lin Biao	Mao Zedong Mao	Nikita Khrushchev
Lin Biao Lin Biao	Mao Zedong Mao	Nikita Khrushchev
Lin Biao Lin Biao	Mao Zedong Mao	Nikita Khrushchev

Thinking that anything said prior to or after the meeting didn't count, she remarked, "Marshal Lin is bald, just like Khrushchev."

The next day she was declared an anti-revolutionist and sent to the May 7th Cadre School with my grandfather and their 2 kids. It was the year 1971. Later that year, Marshal Lin died in a plane crash. The following year, they moved back.

If it is an exaggeration to say that my grandparents had suffered, how should it be named? If a spacecraft is named, is it one step closer to suffering from radical friction and subsequent burning? If someone, something, must be sent into orbit, why not build a robot? Under extreme changes of climate, pressure, and altitude, a robot undergoes transformations too. Equip it with artificial skin, veins, and organs, and monitor its vitals from Earth. Burn the robot, it doesn't matter in the least, it will even make the spacecraft happy.

(Teacher's notes: It is very sweet of you, but a better world can be built only upon flesh and bones. Yours is a design that does not meet graduation standards.)

When I was 5 years old, the scariest thing was to wait for my mother to pick me up. There was always a chance she might not come. One day she was late, and it had started to rain. I curled into a ball on a sofa chair. Instead of a regular dust cover, the sofa had a dark green blanket on it. The blanket was wrinkled. One of my favorite games was to pretend the blanket was a tiny lake in which I could swim and never drown. While I anxiously waited for my mother, time seemed to have been elongated, and with it came the presence of my grandmother. My grandmother became a thin long thread all wrapped around a spindle for me to unwind and unwind and unwind. If I lost patience, no one else would pick her up.

More than a decade later, I was again prepared to lose my mother. The whole family was to gather for dinner. My father and I were waiting for the bus. My mother was still at work. We called her over and over again. She didn't answer. We tried texting. We tried calling again. We switched back and forth. Then her phone was shut off. It was early winter, with gray clouds rushing by like it could rain at any minute. I thought my mother might have been abducted, my mother might have been in an accident, my mother might have eloped with one of her colleagues. My father cursed the weather and the bus that just wouldn't show up. We waited without moving. She was my mother. Was she gone? Was my mother prone to sublimation?

My grandfather ran after my grandmother for 3 years. When she was young, my grandmother was very beautiful. She was beautiful in a way that would make people say she was beautiful even when she was no longer young, when she was almost 80 years old. In the past year I noticed a decline in other people's tendency to make such a statement.

In the summer when my grandmother was preparing for court, she told me about a friend of hers from college. She said, "We were so close. We were always together. We were so close that our classmates called her King, and I was nicknamed Queen. We were assigned to different places after graduation and only saw each other again after several decades. I thought I would be really excited, but when we met again, I felt nothing." All the while, I was leaning against the wall of her room. There was that feeling of nothing, the end of another chance of my unbirth? How can you tell love from love, a comrade from a comrade? Maybe my grandmother, of all the people in my family, would understand.

Also in that year:

The 1st section of my grandmother's right little finger began to bend towards her right ring finger. It kept bending for a while and stopped at a certain degree. They said it was due to her excessive calculation by hand. Now when she points at a plant with that finger, it seems as if the finger might fall off and land beside the pot. Rather than a little finger, it resembles curved tweezers.

About Dog, Pig, Dragon, and Rabbit:

If you have 4 animals, you can have them line up and make an orbit too. But around what? How would you like to line them up? You have 24 choices. Try and explain why you prefer one arrangement in particular.

Dog, Pig, Dragon, Rabbit   Pig, Dog, Dragon, Rabbit

Dog, Pig, Rabbit, Dragon   Pig, Dog, Rabbit, Dragon

Dog, Dragon, Pig, Rabbit   Pig, Dragon, Dog, Rabbit

Dog, Dragon, Rabbit, Pig   Pig, Dragon, Rabbit, Dog

Dog, Rabbit, Pig, Dragon   Pig, Rabbit, Dog, Dragon

Dog, Rabbit, Dragon, Pig   Pig, Rabbit, Dragon, Dog

Dragon, Dog, Pig, Rabbit   Rabbit, Dog, Pig, Dragon

Dragon, Dog, Rabbit, Pig   Rabbit, Dog, Dragon, Pig

Dragon, Pig, Dog, Rabbit   Rabbit, Pig, Dog, Dragon

Dragon, Pig, Rabbit, Dog   Rabbit, Pig, Dragon, Dog

Dragon, Rabbit, Dog, Pig   Rabbit, Dragon, Dog, Pig

Dragon, Rabbit, Pig, Dog   Rabbit, Dragon, Pig, Dog

While Little Bee's Kindergarten is running on the track, it moves like the ball in the hammer-throw sport. It circles round and round, waiting for the final moment of release. It becomes the satellite of the animal in the middle. When you first see Little Bee's Kindergarten, it is a panda satellite. The pandas launch it into the space around them. You might think it's the teacher (my grandmother or me), but it's not. If the mass of the animal in the middle is not great enough, the balance can't be maintained and the kindergarten will detach from the orbit and start to flow into outer space (Westfield Mall, Santa Clarita, California). So cast your vote with caution.

I was once nicknamed Queen too. King was a boy who was said to be in love with me, though I never liked him in that way. He was one of my best friends. With 3 other friends, we established a 5-person republic that existed solely in the form of a blog. The republic consisted of that King boy, a 2nd boy (who would go live in Australia), a 3rd boy (who would become a straight cross-dresser), my cousin (aka the daughter in statement #5, list #2), and me. I still have the voice recording of the 2nd boy declaring the official establishment of our republic. I remember the bio of our blog. It read: There is a pentacle on the dark land.

Except for my cousin and me, we no longer talk to one another. When a boy and a girl are nicknamed King and Queen, there comes an expectation, within and without, easily failed. To this day I still feel guilty that maybe I have torn the pentacle apart.

If that was the case, how could I expect more from my grandmother? Why did I imagine her carrying her nickname through, why did I wish she could have been just a little more excited?

Once a spacecraft is launched, it becomes a matter of how it carries its body through space and how long it will endure. Here is a free-body diagram of a spacecraft in orbit:

$$\text{spacecraft} \quad \rightarrow \qquad\qquad\qquad \text{center}$$

∴ a spacecraft moves in orbit around its center (star) because it has a centripetal force.

Here is a free-body diagram of my grandmother during the 1st few years after graduation:

$$\text{ground support}$$
$$\uparrow$$
$$\text{my grandmother}$$
$$\downarrow$$
$$\text{gravity}$$

∴ how my grandmother carried her body through space can't be explained. She should have remained still. Yet she roamed at random.

The May 7th Cadre Schools were labor camps established throughout China. The 1st such camp was founded in Heilongjiang Province in May 1968, in order to celebrate the 2nd anniversary of the May 7th Order.

The May 7th Order was a letter written by Mao Zedong to Lin Biao on May 7, 1966. In the Order, Mao proposed that soldiers, as well as workers, farmers, students, and those in charge of the management of the Party, should all attend collective schools where they would not only labor physically but also deepen their political understanding. The intellectuals, especially college professors, were regarded as the most in need of such a reeducation.

Lin Biao was the general who commanded 2 of the decisive campaigns in the Chinese Civil War. After 1949, he was active in politics and was named Mao's designated successor, the sole Vice Chairman of the Communist Party of China, in 1969. On September 13, 1971, the plane carrying him and some of his family members crashed in Mongolia. After his death, Lin was labeled as a failed assassin of Mao who had intended to defect to the Soviet Union.

A total of 106 May 7th Cadre Schools were established in 18 provinces. After Lin's death, a majority of those "students" were released. That was when my grandparents and their 2 kids moved back. Their reeducation began near the end and ended too soon. It was nothing but another accidental orbit.

After a while, it all turns clear and boring because every child thinks it has its rocket figured out. This is when we introduce lunch. After lunch, we launch those that feel like it onto the fake animals so they may play. Here the most attention should be paid to the roundup process. Once our children are launched, aside from keeping an eye on them, we need to start considering how we will round them up. Common methods include: roundup by promised rewards, roundup by promised punishment, roundup by conditioned response, roundup by peer pressure, roundup by magnetic field, roundup by Morse code. When a child enrolls in Little Bee's Kindergarten, have it select its preferred means of being rounded up.

When I was in kindergarten, the afternoon nap was a requirement. Every day after lunch, we were given small blankets and put into small beds lined up near the windows. I never slept. I would always stare out the window, though there was nothing to see. Only the salmon-pink facade of a tall building across the street. It seemed so natural to me that its facade should be pink. Though no one told me so, I believed the color had been chosen because it was suitable for the eyes of kindergarten kids. When I stared at the facade, the other kids fell asleep, and a silence overcame the classroom. The silence, the unusual lack of motion, the still, faded, pink facade: this was something too immense for me to grasp. It was under such a circumstance that one day I shat my pants. It made me feel smaller than what I was. I thought I had grown past that stage by refusing to take my afternoon nap.

If a child selects roundup by magnetic force, it should feel extra fortunate because now it can also select the preferred route of being rounded up: from the fake-animal playground to either its desk or its bed. This way to round up is simple: install a strong magnet on the child and, when the time comes, activate the other magnet placed on its chosen destination. The child will be collected within seconds.

What is the fun in being a child? Yet I had always wanted to remain a child, to never grow up, to never reach the point where "it's too late." I wanted to remain a child who could memorize all the animal cards on the table, did not cry on the 1st day of kindergarten, and saw no need for an excessive amount of sleep.

In Little Bee's Kindergarten, extra credit should be given to the children who pay special attention to the recycling of their spacecrafts during the design process. It would be nice if they could recycle valuable parts, data and logs, and passengers. Be sure also to remind them it is extra credit, meaning that not everyone can succeed and it does not matter if they don't. Be sure to tell them it is optional, so that they won't feel too much pressure.

My mother had 1 C-section. My grandmother had 2. It was true that I didn't cry on my 1st day of kindergarten, which surprised my mother because I used to cry a lot before I turned 3. Before she turned 6, my mother would cry every day. My grandmother once said, "Your mother cried so much as a child. She must have been scared by the C-section."

The May 7th Cadre School my grandparents were sent to was located to the west of Hangzhou (recall the geography, refer to map on page 130). My grandmother was 37, my grandfather 36, their 2 kids 7 and 4. While the parents fed the pigs and planted sweet potatoes, the kids ran around playing in the village. Sweet potatoes were often stored in baskets hanging from the beams. Sometimes they'd climb onto a table and steal sweet potatoes, as most other kids did. It was a place for reeducation as well as resettlement, and adults brought their kids along if they were too small to manage. Every time a pig or a calf was slaughtered, the kids gathered to watch. Later my grandparents were assigned to help build a reservoir upstream from the creek flowing through the village. They helped carry bricks and mud. The reservoir was about 40 miles to the west of the school. The school was only about 18 miles away from the university and the faculty dorm. While assigned the duty of building the reservoir, my grandparents moved farther west with 30 other May 7th soldiers to live closer to the construction site.

Compared to my grandfather, my grandmother believed more. She listened to everything that was taught to them, and she defended it. Now she doesn't listen to anyone else but insists on what she's said. She doesn't listen in the sense that when we talk to her she always smiles like she has just caught a child lying.

Imagine how that smile would play out in a kindergarten!

My father once said the institutional structure needed drastic change. He said kids should start dating and forming serious relationships in kindergarten and get married before they graduated from elementary school. Afterwards, with this responsibility out of the way, their time could be devoted solely to learning. I wondered how my grandparents or parents could ever have gotten married in that case.

My grandparents' marriage certificate is a single piece of paper. It looks like an award letter from elementary school, something you would glue to your bedroom wall alongside other similar pieces of paper. In their wedding photo, they both seem unhappy. They had just had a fight. Then they sat down to have their photo taken. On the left: my grandfather, mouth clamped shut, eyes looking down, with high cheekbones that make him appear angry, as if he is still distracted by their argument. On the right: my grandmother, lips falling short of a smile, staring straight at the camera. I grew up with this photo placed on the bookshelf. I have realized, by looking at it and comparing this young couple with my grandparents, that in this photo my grandfather has his default facial expression, but my grandmother doesn't. Maybe that's why my grandfather doesn't seem to have changed a bit, while my grandmother is much different. Neither of them remembers what they were fighting over (their obliviousness ended another chance of my unbirth).

While being photographed, my grandfather doesn't smile, my uncle doesn't smile, my father doesn't smile, I don't smile. My grandmother, my mother, and my aunt: they are the ones who always smile in a photo. Look at my photos from kindergarten. I am not smiling in them either.

I first developed my monster phobia when I was 4. I read an *Ultraman* picture book and started to worry that, when we were asleep at night, a monster's foot would crush the roof and tromp us to death. Afternoons, while lying in bed, the silence became unbearable with the possibility of danger, and a nap could hinder the potential escape. Listening to the teacher lecturing on rocket structures, I was struck by waves of fear. I didn't tell anyone. They wouldn't be able to stop such a gigantic monster anyway, nor was there anyone who could predict its arrival. I waited for the monster to happen. As much as I believed in the existence of monsters, I never believed there was some hidden Ultraman ready to offer us all protection.

When the children in Little Bee's Kindergarten get off the train to play with their fake animals, the kindergarten looks like this:

```
screen1                                              screen2
t r a c k t r a c k t r a c k t r a c k t r a c k t r a c k
k                                                          t
c         .                                                r
a                                                          a
r                   .                                      c
t                              .                           k
k                   .              changing                t
c                         .     · settings                 r
a                         · ·    with   ·                  a
r                             .      fake   .              c
t                                   animals                k
k                             .    .  .   .                t
c                                                          r
a                                                          a
r                                                          c
t                              traintraintraintrain        k
k c a r t k c a r t k c a r t k c a r t k c a r t k c a r t
screen3            gate (teacher's station)          screen4
```

Each dot represents a child. The train comes to a halt. The teacher observes from Teacher's Station. In this diagram there are a total of 15 dots (children), and some of them may be erased at random to represent the kindergarten with a smaller enrollment. On the day of their graduation, all children should stand in lines on the fake-animal playground and launch their spacecrafts one by one. The teacher should take notes on whether the launch is successful. If not, the child will not be allowed to graduate from kindergarten.

Here is a sample chart of what to look for:

Name:

Age:

Name of Rocket:

Dimensions of Rocket:

Angle of Launch:

Curve Described by Rocket:

Maximum Height:

Maximum Distance:

Recycled: Yes   No

(Applicable Only to Spacecrafts:)

Number of Cabins:

Number of Passengers:

Passenger Roundup: Yes   No

Number of Passengers Collected:

Status (Mental and Physical) of Passengers Collected:

In any given year, any given child shall be granted the certificate of graduation only when its chart has passed final evaluation.

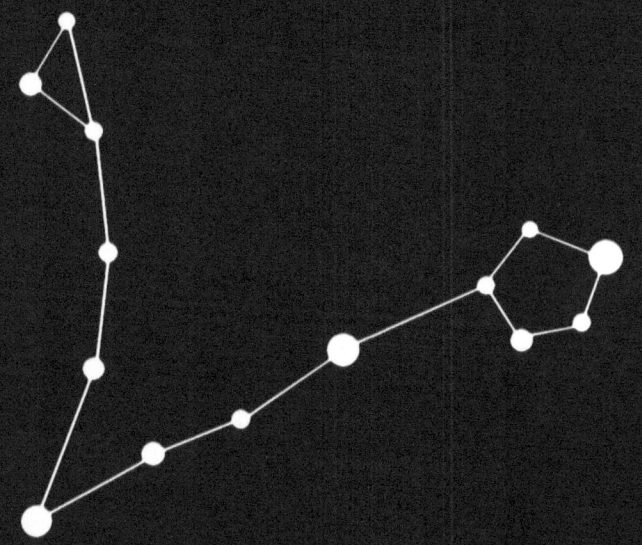

PISCES

2/16

1. today C doesn't seem as worried, nor does she say how bad it is. now that it's in both ears, she says, it feels more balanced and less annoying. i wonder if she's trying to free me from my worries too. after saying good night, i sleep almost through the morning. lying in bed yesterday i was sure there was a ringing in my ears too. today i can hardly discern it. sandwich: whole wheat bread, tuna salad, sriracha, 1 slice of ? cheese, lettuce. i've heard people saying the word *sriracha*, but only recently have i realized what it is, that popular thai chili sauce with chinese instructions printed on the bottle. 1 small cup of chocolate milk mixed with nonfat milk. G calls me to say how happy she is with her boyfriend, but her statements are always followed by a question, a need to be confirmed, reassured. do you think so? does he really love me? i'm not being silly, right?

2. 1 tea-leaf boiled egg. 1 can of brown sugar congee. C hasn't woken up yet, which could be a good sign.

3. 1 tea-leaf boiled egg

2/17

1. couldn't sleep last night. i wasn't thinking or worrying about anything in particular; just couldn't sleep. reminded me of the time before i met C when i couldn't seem to understand the act of sleep. C tried her best to calm me down and i managed to doze off after 2, waking up at 8. today she doesn't mention the ringing in her ears. 1 can of brown sugar congee.

2. G's boyfriend went to visit her mother yesterday and talked with her for 4 hours. G calls and says her mother really liked

him because they shared the same opinion on multiple issues, including when G and him should have sex (after they get engaged). G and i talk on the phone for 1½ hours trying to figure out if her boyfriend likes her as much as he claims he does. as i'm sitting in the sun talking to her while reading a textbook, it occurs to me that maybe he is frustrated that their relationship hasn't functioned in the way he's wanted it to. G says this hypothesis is too much for her to bear. maybe i should refrain from speaking to G about her boyfriend. turkey meatball sandwich with fries. medium passion peach tea with honey and milk (hot). today C hasn't woken up mid-sleep either. after she gets up and has lunch her father drags her out for a walk. later she calls me while walking across the city to see her friend. whenever she comes to a crossroad, she tells me she's going to remove the phone from her ear, so she can't hear me. then she crosses the street.

2/18

1. this morning i wake up and say good night to C but fall asleep before she does. when i wake up again, she's sleeping in her parents' room because there's a numbness in her hands and she gets afraid. i feel guilty for not seeing her messages in time. 2 pieces of white bread with nutella and fried fish powder. G says she's decided not to devote her whole heart to her boyfriend. if sometime in the future she meets someone better, she'll leave her boyfriend for him. i ask her why she has changed her mind so fast. she says, when he went to see my mother she gave him a box of baked tea and he just took it. he didn't start by saying he couldn't take it; he didn't even say thank you. i say, but how do you know? she says, i was watching them and talking to them over video call the whole time. yesterday i finally got my period and today, after multiple tries, i succeed in inserting a tampon. the trick is to not be afraid of using your fingers.

2. 1 bag of instant noodles with 1 tea-leaf boiled egg. shouldn't have added the egg into it. take a nap in the afternoon since i'm going to see *uncle boonmee who can recall his past lives* at 9:30pm. lying in bed, the small noise in my ears sounds like someone has turned the tv on. after i wake up, mom tells me to eat vitamin c pills every day. the picture she sends is of bottled

chewable vitamin c pills, the ones that look and taste like candy. she says it's good for one's skin and organs. C says she returned to her own bed after a short while because it was too crowded, sleeping in the same bed with her parents.

3. small hot chocolate.

2/19

1. dream: i am with my parents and we see 2 squirrels, 1 with a normal tail and the other with a tail twice as long. i slip under a comforter and the squirrels start to attack my parents. i tell them i'm fine but they ignore me. as soon as i've said that, the squirrel with an extra long tail jumps on me and bites my right hand. now it looks like a person in a squirrel costume, with its teeth sunken deep into my hand. it hurts bad. i kick it and step right on its face but it won't loosen the grip. i wake up scared. i look at the phone and see that C has come back from her walk. it's windy, she says, tomorrow the temperature is going to drop. i tell her i had a nightmare. she talks me to sleep. scrambled eggs with hash browns. small earl grey tea with 2% milk. tastes like soap water. today i also try to mail my tax return papers but the post office is closed in observance of presidents' day. walk around the hill to buy pads. G's mother won't allow her to go to singapore, saying it's not yet the time for her to visit her boyfriend. her father says it'll lead to a reduction of her self-worth. once a teacher of mine asked me if the chinese used the term *yellow pearl* when referring to women who were getting older and not yet married. it took me a minute to really remember the phrase. it was indeed *yellow pearl*. G's mother tells her, there's no need to hurry. she still has much time before she yellows.

2. 1 slice of veggie pizza

3. 1 can of brown sugar congee

2/20

1. last night C taught me some phrases in the dialect of her hometown. she taught me, did you eat? what did you eat? do you want to eat? who are you? here's a dog, here's a cat, i want

to sleep, you're really silly, you're a little silly, you're sillier, and how to say someone is silly without using the word *silly*, which is to say, someone is a sweet potato. she also taught me things like pumpkin, pig feet (which has no *pig* in it), pig, butt, friend, and fuck your mother. today i am woken by mom's call. she says she dreamed i was ill and wants to see how i am. she also accidentally sent me a message intended for dad which reads: *just got out of shower. i almost froze, luckily you let me leave.* i ask her what it's about. she says they were at yeye's for dinner, and it started to rain. the temperature dropped. icy winds blew in through the door, which was kept open throughout the terrible weather. she felt cold. dad told her to go home though the dinner hadn't ended. she went back home, took a shower and reaching for the phone half asleep messaged me instead of dad. the message and her sudden call almost scare me out of sleep. sandwich: tuna salad, pita bread, shredded cheese, sour cream. today i finally succeed in mailing tax return files. they might smell of sour cream since i walked down the slope eating the sandwich with sour cream all over my hands. one clerk at the post office congratulated the other for being selected as the clerk with the best customer service. i've been wanting to try a sour cream old-fashioned donut. there seems to be a number of food cults, like those centered around coffee, donuts, pizza, tacos, avocado, etc. personally i like most of these and have had much fun eating old fashioned donuts because of the shape alone. when i met W in the cafe the other day, i told her i was deciding if i should get a donut. immediately she said, i think you should, it's a good idea. but why was it a good idea? what if i shouldn't be eating donuts (then of course i'd be responsible for controlling myself)? on that same day, i looked at my classmate's shirt and asked A, are those pink donuts on that shirt? A turned to look and said, yes, it's a pink donut shirt.

2. 1 small bowl of black bean and chicken soup. 1 sour cream old fashioned donut (not sure if it really is). i'm wearing a shirt saying *vast and boundless* in chinese. A asks me what it means. later i want to show him the chinese dragon on the back but can't find him. G tells me she still thinks her boyfriend is not at all good-looking. she says, if i'm angry, looking at his face makes me even angrier. but my ex-boyfriend, i took a look at him and

was instantly half less angry. i try to convince her that her ex-boyfriend was really much worse looking because he always had a dispirited look, but how can you demonstrate such a thing? at some point i pause and wonder if what i'm saying is true. i start to see a vague resemblance between these 2 boyfriends. examined closer, however, the resemblance soon wears off.

2/21

1. yesterday was like an explosion. C said she woke up after midnight and the ringing was so loud, occupying her whole brain, that she felt isolated from the world and trapped in her own head. every day she's afraid of going to sleep. and i thought she was getting better. i felt silly. while telling her not to worry, i start crying. then i think, is this real? are we really going through this? it could have been a dream from which we'd soon wake up, quick and sudden, like how it started. right now we're just waiting. trying to endure this unrealistic reality that made us feel equally defeated. she called me before i went to bed and i took pains to hold back my tears. she said, am i going deaf? why does it sound so low? i said, no, i'm just speaking low. i set an alarm this morning to get up some time after 7. after C goes to bed, i fall back asleep and, lying half awake, hear Z talking with her friend who slept over last night. i realize how loud and clear she speaks. now G has once again changed her mind and believes her boyfriend really loves her because he tells her he knows how to manipulate and hurt her but he isn't doing any of that. he says, i could have let you sex talk to me while i jerk off. today especially, i find the whole conversation about her boyfriend depressive and want nothing but to run away. i'm infuriated. i want to tell her that to me what he said sounds downright horrible but if she accepts it as a proof of love i don't even care. sandwich: chicken breast, ? bread, spinach, mushrooms, cheese. i tell W i've always thought 1 of our teachers looks like santa. C wakes up when i'm eating lunch. i talk to her briefly. i tell her i love her. later when i run into A we shake hands and he says, after withdrawing his hand, that my hand is soft. he asks if his hand is soft. he got drunk yesterday and painted his nails violet because: african loyalty. i tell him i don't have much knowledge about hands. i tell him his hand is

medium well. waiting for my drink, i keep trying to do a ballet stand in my boots, which proves to be impossible. so i just do a continuous jump. small chai (hot). i ask mom if she can consult a doctor about C's tinnitus. she reminds me to take vitamin c. she says, it has to be purely natural vitamin.

2. 1 slice of cheese pizza. 0.5 bag of lucy's brownie crisp (2 pieces). C tells me about the time when her parents and her cried together at home. it was after her maternal grandmother passed away. at first they were just chatting in the living room, and before she realized it they had gone to cry in different rooms: her father to the bathroom, her mother to the bedroom. looking back at it now, she says, it actually seems funny. i remember once when i told her i was going to my grandmother's, she said, i wish i could go to my grandmother's too.

2/22

1. last night i wanted to have sex with C but failed. we had not done it for so long that, especially over the phone, i was at a loss for the starting point. it felt like a complete defeat, thinking that i needed to learn it all over again. then i dreamed we went to the seaside. from the balcony of our hotel room, the ocean was emerald green. i told her how green it was. i said, you should come and see the ocean. she said, let's make love in front of the mirror. i woke up every 2 or 3 hours throughout the night. the last dream i had was of teenage boys fighting in the hallway. we say good night twice, since i keep waking. afterwards i manage to sleep till 11. 2 pieces of lucy's brownie crisps. 1 small cup of black bean and beef soup. i believe there's a single nibble of bacon in it. later i run into V, and she tells me she wants to spend her summer in hong kong and learn cantonese. at the cafeteria the sign reads, *pork butt*. she asks the staff if it's a mistake but they confirm it is indeed pork butt. she is disgusted but has already ordered that. we go out onto the patio. today is cold, as it has been. immediately V throws a scarlet scarf around her head. she takes a bite and frowns, looking like a grandma dancing around her pork bun. she says, keep talking to me. i don't want to think about this butt. after finishing 1 of the 2 buns, she says, now i'll have pork butt inside me forever. i tell her she can just go and excrete. she

says, not so quick! we sit there imagining we're working the butt down and out of our digestion system. she says, maybe i have pork butt in my butt. i'd like it to be true, but i don't think food goes through one's butt. later she says she'll go and debutt. we see E and L downstairs and L tries to make a point that actually 80% of a pig can be called pork butt. standing there listening to him, i almost dislike him for taking away the butt laugh (though he doesn't succeed). medium china green tip tea.

2. baby back rib half rack with fries and asparagus. sparkling raspberry lemonade. mini salted caramel pizookie. it's my 1st time seeing this. it's H's birthday dinner. E misremembers the date and comes in late from her thai massage. while driving me back, she tells me the 2nd half of the pork butt incident. she went to the library with L after V and i left. as soon as they sat down, L went upstairs and got a pork butt bun from the cafeteria. then he came back, sat down in front of E, and started to eat. E asked him how it was. with his face half-buried in the bun, he said in a muffled voice, *i think this is delicious.* when i get back it's almost midnight and i'm afraid C might be worried and/or angry. but she is not. she says, i know you're just at school. we talk for a while then she has to leave for dinner. she is going to eat shrimp at her grandfather's. she says it requires both hands, so we say good night before i actually sleep.

2/23

1. yesterday i kept thinking it was friday. i had trouble sleeping because the heat was on too high and i had a slight migraine. dreamed of being in a protest and trying to explain to others sometimes i wanted to have multiple copies of myself. wake up at 6:40. maybe it's because i'm determined to make love to C before she goes to sleep. she senses me trying to lead her and i feel a bit embarrassed. without actual touching, what is the subtle way to indicate physical desire through words? maybe i could have just said i miss her, which risks being taken the other way around. maybe there really is nothing wrong if she senses me trying because otherwise, how can we ever start? salmon salad sandwich. medium matcha (hot).

2. 1 tea-leaf boiled egg

2/24

1. dream: i take the bus to a hospital and many get off with me. as soon as we enter the hospital, the floor starts to sink and it sinks all the way underground. then a man says, why hasn't the millimeter of mercury changed? that's not logical. the truth is the outer walls of the building have flown away. once he's said it, the outer walls fly back and the hospital looks just like before. wake up at 6:40 and tell C about my dream. she says i always have silly dreams. i say, it's not silly, it's scientific. she says it's silly scientific. spicy shrimp roll (8 pieces).

2. 1 donut: chocolate glazed creme filled. medium cold brew. this afternoon i happen to see the debate on whether ravioli is a kind of pop-tart. i like to press my fingers together and clap my palms. A asks what i'm doing; i tell him i'm making sounds. he tries it. he says it is like the sound in your ears when you cover them with your hands. C is going back to school tomorrow. i remember hearing 2 people singing a chinese song, *our mother nation is a flower garden*, in the cafe, and the girl said it was the 1st dance she learned in kindergarten. C said she remembered the dance too. i had no memory of learning either the song or the dance.

2/25

1. woke up at 3 in the morning and C told me the news: the communist party of china central committee proposed to remove the expression that the president and vice-president "shall serve no more than 2 consecutive terms" from the constitution. i had trouble sleeping and only slept for 2, 3 hours. and suddenly, i recalled the weight of my comforter at home. this morning C says she has a headache. she is going back to school soon and her father urges her to join the Party, so that she won't be at a disadvantage when it comes to certain academic and career opportunities. she doesn't want to. she says, if i join the Party, will i be forced to marry a man and have children? i tell her i think homosexuality is considered disloyalty to the Party. she says, maybe we should make some plans for our future. i say, yes, but not today. it's getting late where C is, already past midnight. i hear Z saying good morning to S. not until this moment have

i realized our worries are irrelevant to the world at large. beef briskets with baked potato and steamed broccoli.

2. this afternoon i see a hummingbird right outside my window. it has red and yellow feathers. for a moment i think it's going to enter, but then it flies away. mom asks if i've seen the news. she says it feels like we're back in the '30s and she's worried. she didn't sleep well last night. tossing and turning in bed, she decided to wire me all the us dollars they had right now, and divide their savings and deposit it into several different banks. she says the climate can change in an instant. i ask her what dad thinks. he doesn't think it will be so quick, but agrees with her plan. i ask mom about abu's past. she answers without asking why i asked. she says that when dad first went to visit her family, abu told him mom was really short-tempered and he'd need to bear with it for maybe the rest of his life. he said, but i don't feel that way. then they got married. there was a time when they would get into fights and dad would say, your mother told me you were like this, and i didn't believe her. why didn't i believe her? california roll (6 pieces).

2/26

1. now C is back at the university. yesterday she went out for dinner with several friends because the birthday of 1 of them is today. again she woke up after midnight. i've been feeling a stronger tendency to tell her *i love you* and wonder when we'll drain the power of even this sentence. sandwich: sourdough, tuna salad, cheddar cheese, sriracha mayo, sweet pickles. medium english breakfast tea with 2% milk. G tells me about her conflicts with her roommate who thinks she is too noisy in the morning. she says, my roommate is a gemini and you're a gemini too. how come we get along so well but my roommate thinks i hate her? i say, maybe she's sensitive. she says, how can a gemini be sensitive? you're not sensitive. A texts me to borrow some laundry detergent. later i have a session with a chinese girl i've met before. halfway through looking for the assignment on her phone suddenly she says, my size of this pair of shoes is sold out! i was planning to buy it next month! she tells me all her shoes are worn out and it's too expensive to buy shoes here, so she wants to buy something

online and have it shipped overseas. i'm fascinated by the way life proceeds, its casualness, its velocity. things can happen on the other side of the world while we sit here considering if that pair of shoes is worth paying for. even when things are going down there will always be pleasure in acquiring things we like and maybe going down with them could be more or less bearable. of course there is nothing wrong with buying shoes, especially when you don't have any left. i am thinking about my own desire to buy a rather useless pair of summer sandals.

2. 3 teriyaki wings, 1 potato mash, boiled sweet corns and diced carrots.

2/27

1. dream: keep repeating, in my mind, a series of numbers (376362216). woke up and wrote it down. fell back asleep. dream: a man chases C with a gun. i hold C from behind and push her forward and we run. the man pauses and shoots himself in the chest. blood oozes out from a gaping dark red hole. he exits the room through the front door. this morning i notice something itchy on my labia and, not knowing what it is, rush to see a nurse. the nurse tries to tell me where the labia starts and ends, but there's no picture or illustration in the room. she leafs through all the printouts and handbooks on the desk. she says, they have some nice things, but they don't have what i'm looking for. she says, there used to be an illustration on the wall then 1 day a male officer came by and said, ok, this is enough, and we took it down. later i go to urgent care 3 blocks away and find out it is just heat rash. the doctor suggests empson salt, which she says can always be found next to witch hazel (?). C wakes up because the heating is off and it is cold. i tell her what happened and she says, it's just a minor allergy. i wish i would have asked her before going to a nurse. 1 small bowl of salad: macaroni, small cucumber, spinach with mushrooms and raspberries, 5 tofu cubes. small apple cider with whipped cream (hot).

2. spaghetti with ground turkey, 1 small piece of garlic bread, roasted vegetables: broccoli, cauliflower, squash. C is going to the hospital in the afternoon. she didn't sleep well last night. when

she calls she is still on the verge of falling back asleep. i tell her i heard 2 chinese students talking about the proposed constitution modifications and, when they were about to leave, 1 of them said, now i'll go back and make some chinese food. last night i tossed in bed for over an hour too. someone was putting away what sounded like several plastic bags in the living room and the noise, especially at 1:30am, was piercing and unbearable. C decides to sleep for a while longer. we hang up.

2/28

1. A still hasn't done his laundry, neither has he come by to pick up his reserved laundry detergent. yesterday i dreamed that he sent me a picture of himself holding a laundry basket, implying to me that he needed this laundry deter. this morning i see him but he shows no intention in doing laundry. i am slightly disappointed. 1 small cup of black bean and beef soup.

2. ground beef topped with cheese, spinach with goat cheese. feel sick in the stomach afterwards. write a short fanfiction for C and feel happy. go to my playwriting class and hear others read the play being workshopped this week, which includes an opening scene of a man doing a puppet dance with his penis. last night before sleep i wondered if this was part of the reason why i wanted so much to pair one young, male idol with another. maybe it makes me feel safer, like the possibility of male-to-female aggression avoided, if only temporarily. i've been thinking of how the physical pleasure described in my fanfiction pieces can be transmitted into that felt between C and me or evoke such desire, especially when it is a pairing we both like.

3/1

1. waking up especially early. C has not done her routine exercise before bed. we go on mute video talk so i can watch her and her roommates doing ballet without being noticed. at one part she says, this posture looks like little roosters. 1 tea-leaf boiled egg.

2. sandwich: sourdough, tuna salad, sriracha mayo, lettuce, tomato, pickles. without meaning to, i start to recall what happened during winter break. yet i realize i have no desire to

chronologize all the events, nor does there seem to be such necessity. i've scattered them up and tossed them into different journal entries. what i remember most vividly is the day i came back home from C's university, thinking dad had found out about our relationship. he acted as if nothing had happened in such a way that we all knew something had happened. during those few days after i got back, he was so gentle to me, tender even, his expressions always considerate and protective. he cooked me what he thought i would like to eat. he never even once blamed me for anything. when mom was mildly angry at me, he spoke against her. those were probably my softest memories of dad thus far, and i was anxious, restless, thinking i would rather he'd have been severe to me, expecting everything to fall apart sometime soon. he managed to keep it up, though as the date of my departure approached, he started to talk to me about finding a boyfriend. every several days he'd say, you ought to hurry. if there's someone to take care of you, we won't worry about your safety anymore. the only slippage he made was a half joke: you're different from your cousin (G); you never tell us anything.

the 1st day i went to visit C, she got a fever at 11:30 that night. we spent 7 hours in the hospital for her to finish the iv. finally, back at the hotel, the sanitation of which now seemed suspicious, we decided to sleep for a short while, check out, and go back to C's dorm. we collapsed on the bed without undressing. then, after what felt like 10 minutes, i was startled awake and saw 5 missed calls, 2 from dad, 3 from mom. i remember sitting there staring at the screen. i had a hunch something was happening and when mom messaged me to say dad had found out, i took a split second to take pride in foreseeing this. she said, your father saw your text messages on the ipad. he was very upset. neither of you are talking to me! i told her i had been sleeping. i considered if i should make it clear that sleeping really meant *sleeping*. i thought, ipad, of course. i didn't want to wake C up but ended up doing it because i was shaking and crying, though i was surprised by how little i was crying. days later we took a taxi to the subway station and, upon exiting the taxi, i finally answered dad's call. he talked to me as if to a kid. it was a voice from the long gone past. my parents both believed my homosexuality was a result of their negligence during my childhood, though they weren't sure how they failed. i was at the same time moved and terrified. i thought, so this is dad's attempt to make up for his mistakes.

3. chili dog and curly fries. at dusk the clouds are pink again.

3/2

1. pork chop with rice and brussel sprouts and mushrooms. 1 small cup of chocolate milk.

2. small matcha (hot). C says she dreamed she brought me home and tried to kiss me at various places. 1 small cup of thai chicken soup. i'm 100% sure it's actually clam chowder. H asks me about the most butchered way anyone has ever said my name. i tell him once i was called *urine* by someone in the school cafe. things are happening in china. forums are being shut down (temporarily, to be examined and reconfigured), accounts are being deleted on social media. not being there has enabled me to not think much about it. however, if i am to speak with as much sincerity as i can afford, i have to admit i feel a bit of excitement deep down, the excitement of witnessing illogical events that might or might not be the foreshadowing of something terrible, of living in what seems like a pivotal moment in history: the possibility of *happening*, of the unknown, of catastrophe, all mixed up in an excitement that makes me feel ashamed and guilty.

THE BABY-CHANGING TABLE

There were giants in the earth in those days; and also after that, when the sons of God came in unto the daughters of men, and they bare children to them, the same became mighty men which were of old, men of renown.

—Genesis 6:4

By the age of 6, I already knew my mother was a shapeshifter. She always transformed into a dragon before a shower, otherwise the water would be too hot and hurt her skin. One should take care of one's skin because it is the human organ with the largest surface area, everywhere equally prone to injury and bleeding. It is very risky to walk around in your skin, even more so when you're holding an infant, since they have a considerably smaller surface area. So she would bathe me in the tub first, and then risk going into the shower alone. When she turned into a dragon she became huge. She said, "I am a dragon and I weigh 70 kilograms," which had seemed an unthinkable figure when she was a younger shapeshifter. "After giving birth," she said, "I became larger and heavier. Sometimes I feel as if part of you was still inside me. Did I deliver you in whole? I must have, because nothing is missing." My father was a shapeshifter too. When my mother became a dragon, he shifted into a tiger. Then the 3 of us would play a game on our only bed called Tiger Beats Dragon, throwing blankets and pillows at one another. As the name suggests, the tiger always wins. I always sided with the tiger. My mother was born in Year of the Dragon, my father Year of the Rabbit. For the first few years of my life, I always thought tigers were the only predator of rabbits.

Long before he married my mother, my father was caught in a rare thunderstorm. The streets were flooded, water rising up to his knees. He was on a business trip, rushing to the station to catch his train. Standing at the crossroads one block away, he realized the wind had blown down most of the telephone wires, and the loose ends were now buried in water. It was impossible to see where each wire ended, and there was no alternative route to the station. Today I might die, my father thought. It is very possible for me to die. He walked into the water. He prayed like this: "God, if I can reach the train station alive, I will admit that you exist." Years later he married my mother. Once when he was drunk, he sat down on the floor beside the couch, held my mother's hand, and said to her, "You're an angel. God sent you to save me. You're the best gift He has ever granted me."

Thinking back at this, I realize the electricity must have been cut, probably due to the storm. Otherwise my father would have died regardless of whether or not he touched the wire, since water is conductive and with so many wires it would have been like walking directly into a pool of swimming electricity. And why God? Why not Buddha or Durga, or divinity in general? No one in his family is religious, including him. I wonder why that word sprang to his mind.

When I ride the train downtown, again I see the baby-changing table. It is a small, foldable, plastic table in the lavatory. It is where you change your baby, if you have brought one with you. The maximum weight of a baby placed on the table is 35 pounds, or roughly 16 kilograms, which is less than ¼ of my mother's weight. Were I to lay her down in the lavatory on the train, I would need at least 4 baby-changing tables. But it is also a matter of volume, of surface area. I think they ought to include those figures as well: what's the maximum volume of the baby? What's the maximum surface area? If your baby resembles a disk, sufficiently light but overly flat, it still risks tumbling over the edge. A proper model needs to be established before we go on to perform the task of baby changing.

As a kid I got changed very often, sometimes on the table, but mostly on the bed. Our bed was my changing table and it could take much more weight, it could withstand me and my parents lying down together. At night we slept in the same bed and in the morning they were gone, and it was up to me to change myself. I would change into a shark, or a peacock, or a sailor fallen into the stomach of another shark. When I was 6, I was tall but weighed too little, wearing children's clothes that didn't fit but we hoped would as time went by and I grew bigger. I wished they would never fit so I could stay on the changing table forever.

The magic of Chinese zodiac signs, to me at least, is that once you know someone's sign, you automatically liken the person to the animal and sometimes even substitute the latter for the former. This explains why, when I was a kid, I often felt I was living on a farm: my grandmother was a dog, my grandfather a pig, their son—my mother's younger brother—was a sheep, his wife a horse, their daughter an ox, my father was a rabbit, I myself a rooster. My mother's sign was the only animal that wouldn't belong to any ordinary farm, had it existed in the 1st place.

As soon as she went back to work, I felt my mother's absence and believed it to be final. My early childhood was characterized by me crying for her in my father's arms, so much so that he became too embarrassed to hold me. He would say, "Do you not like me? Your mother is working. She'll come back soon." I couldn't understand him so I kept crying. Whenever he took me for a walk, he was worried that someone would call the police, thinking I was not his real daughter. It was fortunate that we looked so much alike. The 1st time my father caught sight of me, when I was wrapped in a blanket and carried out into the hallway by a nurse, warm and soft as freshly baked bread, he knew right away this was his child. It was like seeing himself as an infant, being delivered to his own hands. Even my crying—when my father was a toddler, he would cry for his mother too. In the end I got used to my father. When I was 6, he went to Singapore. It was his 2nd and final attempt to migrate.

Yesterday I went to work at a dessert place. I wiped tables and arranged chairs and reloaded ingredients and washed dishes for an hour. Before washing the dishes I put on a pair of bright-yellow plastic gloves. When I reached into the sink, the glove was pressed tight against my skin. I thought of water pressure and how much force was hidden even within such a shallow body of water. I thought of my father. He went to Singapore with his elder brother, to make their fortune, and eventually they worked as construction workers. They lived in a shipping container, one of many recycled and lined up for workers like them. Before they set off, my mother ironed my father's shirts so he could wear them to his interviews. Fifteen years later he took 1 out while sorting through his old clothes, held it flat with both hands, and showed us a line of grease stains. He said, "Look, the oil splashed when I was cooking." I thought of those stains while rinsing trays and bowls and spoons, throwing them into a final sink filled with disinfectant. When I reached in, this water pressure resisted, refusing my hand, trying to push it away, above water, disconnected. When I pulled my hand out it became heavier, dripping, as if the water had changed its mind and wanted it back. I paused in the middle. My hand was wet and without touching it was already part of the liquid yet drying, little by little, returning to its original hand state. Point zero on this horizontal axis. I thought, my father would never have foreseen this, his daughter washing dishes in Chinatown.

Above everything else, I recall distance: distance, time, separation. I thought my family was the standard model of all families. I thought parents would never have sex again after childbirth because there was no longer the need to. My tiny body had been the 1st thing to set boundaries between my mother and father, followed by walls, streets, the ocean. Now it has gone back to walls. Now sometimes they sleep on the same bed again. My mother often wakes up at midnight, lying in the dark, listening to my father's snoring. When it gets too loud she shakes him awake because she's afraid it will come to a sudden halt. If it never reaches the climax, it will never stop.

How many children have imagined their parents having sex? How many have heard it, or even caught a glimpse? The only time my mother mentioned it, she put it in the form of negation: We seldom slept together after you were born; it helps me stay away from a lot of gynecological diseases. So sex was never talked about, theirs and mine alike. My father has encouraged me to have children. He would say, "2 is ideal. You should at least have 2." No beginning, no middle, just the result, as if children could grow straight out from me and my boyfriend/husband would merely need to watch, to gasp in awe.

Last time when I made a video call to my parents, they said the government was going to lift the restriction on having a 3rd child. I thought of the time when C joked that non-heterosexuality might soon be called treason. I thought, if that's the case, the only official way to make atonement would be to seek help from your straight siblings and/or cousins. A communal baby-changing table would need to be established. Given that every woman between the ages of 25 and 35 should have an average of 2 kids, and also that:

1. My mother has 1 younger brother (my uncle) who has an only daughter;

2. My uncle's only daughter is non-heterosexual;

3. My father has 2 elder brothers, and they each have an only daughter;

4. One of their daughters is heterosexual;

5. My father's 2nd eldest brother's wife has an elder sister who has an only daughter;

6. The daughter in #5 is heterosexual;

7. My father's eldest brother's wife has a younger brother who has an only daughter;

8. The daughter in #7 is heterosexual;

we can conclude that there are a total of 6 daughters in my extended family, 3 of whom are straight. In order to make up for their cousins, they should divide between them the task of giving birth to 12 babies. Then we can gather all the babies on the baby-changing table and assign 2 of them to every daughter. In this way, my father's dream would be fulfilled. I would beget children without laying myself open.

Before she met my father after college, my mother had been in love with a boy in her high school. When I asked her what he was like, she said, "It's hard to put into words."

"What's so hard about it?" I said.

"He was good-looking," she said.

"Did you like him because he was good-looking?"

"Yes."

I wanted to see a picture of him. My mother couldn't find any. She said she would take one next time, if he went to their school reunion. She said, "He's fat now. He has become a grandfather, the 1st one in our class." He had been her 1st love but the 1st time she ever talked to him was long after graduation. She said, "When I was in junior high, boys and girls didn't talk. It was forbidden. I was the most typical example of a bad student."

"But you didn't approach him," I said.

"It was wrong to even think about boys," she said.

At the age of 7, I was in love with the boy sitting to my right and one night before sleep, lying in the dark between my mother and my father, I whispered, "I love [name of the boy]," which was one of the tiny confessions I'd made to my mother during those years. My other confessions included: I crawled under someone's bed to pick up a purple plastic grape; I hid my math practice book under the lunch mat in my drawer; I hid my Chinese practice book in my sweater after my father delivered it to school per my teacher's request; from 1st to 6th grade I had fallen in love with 3 different boys in school, but the person I loved the most was the girl sitting in front of me. With each confession I felt clean again.

On the morning of her wedding day, my mother went to a salon to get her hair and makeup done, as well as to receive a full-face threading. It was still early when everything was finished, so she bicycled back to her parents' place, her hair sculpted and piled high with the help of hair wax, her face painted anew, following the standard regulations for the face of a bride. Back then she was living near the lake with her parents, and the salon was near the lake too. She bicycled along the lake shore for 20 minutes. Everyone who happened to see her during those 20 minutes knew right away they were seeing a bride, though it was mysterious that she was on a bike by herself, in her everyday winter clothes, not wearing a rented white gown or cruising the street in a car. I wonder what they were thinking when they saw my mother. Is she getting married? Why is she alone? Where is her limo? Did she escape from her wedding? Was she abandoned by her bridegroom? But she seems happy. She seems to be getting along well with the situation, whatever it is. How would they begin to decipher this woman?

Translated literally, word by word, the Chinese term for full-face threading means to open the face. While my mother was bicycling back, her face had been opened and transformed into a none-face, a void where personal features were cleared out, making space for the symbolic bridehood. That was the only purpose of a bride's hair and makeup, not to make her look beautiful, but to make a clear announcement of her bridehood. If I were to see this woman, I would have called her a bride, not my mother. I would not have realized she was my mother. I would have loved her because, how poetic it is to see a young bride riding a bike alone alongside a frozen winter lake.

Once I asked my mother what a full-face threading was, and she said it was the procedure to remove a woman's facial hair before her wedding. It used to be a conventional step, one that symbolized the transition from girlhood into womanhood. It was no longer required but still practiced quite often. Then she turned to look at me and said, "See, you have facial hair. You're still a girl."

"Does it hurt?" I said.

"Just a little," she said.

"But how much is a little?"

"As much as when your hair is pulled out. A piercing feeling."

So, when your hair is pulled out, it hurts in the same way as when a needle is pushed in.

Before he met my mother, my father had been in love with a girl in his college. He never dared to tell her, and then she moved to another country. He said he would sit in the hallway every Friday, watching the sun set. The dorm was nearly empty. Most of his schoolmates were from the city where the college was situated, and they usually went home for the weekend. My father would stare at that now harmless sunlight, a warm orange stretched across the floor, and think, another day has passed. When he told me this, he said, "Now 30 years have passed."

One year after my parents got married, my father decided to go abroad for his master's degree. He had a dark-red, palm-size dictionary and going from A to Z he memorized every word in it. He didn't have much to do at work, so he studied for his tests every day. My mother borrowed her father's typewriter and typed out all the application letters. Back then currency exchange was under more strict control, and she learned to secretly get US dollars from the black market. I had always imagined the black market as a real market with dim lights and the smell of fungi. In the year 1991, if you wanted foreign currency for personal use, you would bike to a certain bank and wait near the front gate. Someone would approach you, walking their bike, and say, "US dollars?" And then you'd just follow them.

The 1st time my mother went to the black market, she was scared. She was afraid to get caught, to be taken away, to ruin her parents' reputation as academics. She thought of the son of her father's colleague. He had broken into someone's apartment through the window, intending to steal. On his way out he slipped, fell down and died. "How are his parents supposed to take this?" her father's colleague had said. My mother got her illegal foreign currency and quickly went home. All those times nothing ever happened to her.

I am very bad at telling each year apart in my memory because there are only so many events I can place into specific years. 1971 was the year my grandparents were sent to the May 7th Cadre School, but they came back home soon after, following Lin Biao's death. 1987 was the year my father crossed the flooded street and didn't die. 1989 was the year my father's elder brother almost went to Tiananmen Square in the beginning of June, but changed his mind and went to Tianjin instead. 1991 was the year my father scored in the top 5% on his GRE but failed the visa interview 3 times in a row and refused to set foot in the consulate ever again. 1992 was the year my mother almost lost the 1st embryo inside her that would later become me. 1999 was the year my father went to Singapore and my mother was prepared for him to fall in love with someone else, like what she had expected 8 years before, and he came back only 1 year after. We were always off a little bit, always missing the center of the chaos, always surviving the storm. It must have been some rare good luck, yet it is so close to feeling like guilt. My family is chronicled by things that almost happened, or halted in the middle of happening; the shame is of almost being in sync with some major catastrophe but only coming close, ending up on the safe periphery.

A classic Chinese math problem:

Some rabbits and roosters are locked in the same cage, and together they have 35 heads and 94 feet. How many rabbits are in the cage, and how many roosters?

A math/psychology problem I once encountered, approached by a college student doing research:

Imagine a family of a father, a mother, a 4-year-old son, a 16-year-old son, a 10-year-old daughter, and a 12-year-old daughter. If they only have 1 bed, how will you arrange them from the outermost to the innermost? Increase the number of their beds to 2, 3, 4, 5. Which ones should be sharing the same bed and why?

In the end my father got full marks for math and logic. He is proud of it and likes to give examples. He'll say, "It was something like, the person living in the house that is not white does not wear a green tie," though he's never recalled a problem in whole. Again and again he was refused a student visa because he didn't have enough funding. My mother says he felt so angry and disappointed. "Ever since then," she says, "he has not taken his work seriously again, not even for 1 day."

The 1st time my father went to visit my mother's parents, my grandmother told him, "My daughter is a shapeshifter. If you marry her, you will need to bear with it for maybe the rest of your life." He said, "But I don't feel that way." Then they got married. Now sometimes when they have a fight and my mother accidentally turns into a dragon, in his frustration my father still says, "Your mother warned me you were like this, and I didn't believe her!" Then he will try and fail to transform into a tiger because we moved years ago and the changing table is gone and without it, he can't shift shapes. He can no longer beat the dragon with pillows and blankets and my help.

Why write out an equation when we can easily count the heads of the animals, given that rabbits look quite distinct from roosters? Maybe we can't because instead of rabbits and roosters in the cage there are multiple fathers and multiple copies of me, which are rabbits and roosters that look very much alike and impossible to tell apart. Together with my mother, who is a dragon and an angel and a shapeshifter, we have 36 to 38 heads, 96 to 102 feet, and some 50 wings. How can we be arranged on 1 to 2 beds and lie still enough to sleep every night? We would shift shift shift, brushing against each other, breaking extra arms and legs, leaving bruises on anonymous skin.

While she was pregnant with me, my mother was a baby-changing table. Planted inside the womb, an embryo goes through different stages, evolving and eventually getting rid of gill slits— growing into and out of being a fish. I was an unexpected baby. When she first conceived she didn't know it and went to ride a horse in Inner Mongolia, drinking rice wine with shepherds. She only became aware of me after she came back and started to bleed. I could still have been a fish. Had this embryo failed to make it through, it would have flowed out of her body and she would know what it feels like to eject a fish egg. But it stayed and shifted and shifted on its changing table. If I ever have kids, it would be hard to resist the temptation to scare them in the following way: Place them on my stomach and tell them it is a baby-changing table capable of changing them back into fishes if I please because we have all been fishes and they are still inside us, we are neither here nor there, we are somewhere in the middle, swaying left to right, up and down, like riding your mother's belly, like riding a horse, a train, a table, a body, anything. Everything around you is a blur, everyone faceless, boundaries shaken loose and thrown into midair. You were a fish and when you were a fish you were also inside me sharing my boundaries so I had gill slits and I was a fish too. I hope you enjoyed it.

During the month when my mother almost lost her embryo, she was always lying in bed, her whole body still. Now that she was a table, she must do as a table would do: stay flat and open and wait for something else to occupy her. My father fed her soup. Strictly speaking they were not yet mother and father and they had considered getting rid of it, seeing that a baby would be a heavy burden they were not prepared to carry and already it had caused her to bleed, trapped at home, half paralyzed, forbidden to move. Eventually the embryo stabilized and my father got better at cooking. They both grew heavier, drinking the same soup.

I want to know the shape of my mother's desire, and maybe my father's as well. Only then would it be possible for me to offer them my own, in exchange, as a gift, a way to understand. My mother had been waiting for me to grow up, so that she could talk to me the way she'd talk to a fellow woman. Following this logic, my father never had his chance to begin with. He can't talk to me the way he'd talk to his brother. I can't tell them to see me as a little of both plus a little of neither. They don't seem very interested in my shape anyhow, so we silently avoid it. I am 5 feet 6 and weigh 105 pounds. To lay me down would only require 3 baby-changing tables, whereas my mother needs 4½ and my father needs 5, if we consider only weight. Imagine us on the train together, each lying on our changing-table beds. They would have to lie on their sides, and it is their choice whether I could see their faces or the backs of their heads. Even if I stay in the middle like I did 20 years ago, at any given moment there would be parts of them that I fail to see. Sometimes it's not enough to be in between.

One time ants crawled into our dorm and made a nest in the kitchen. They occupied every corner where they found food or water. Watching them struggle along the slippery bathroom sink, I realized they would never see me as a whole. If they climbed onto my arm and proceeded on this vast plateau of skin, they would not know that this was not the overall shape of my body. If I caught 1 of them and placed it on my nipple, suddenly there'd be a decrease in flat surface and the texture rougher, making it harder for the ant to move around. It would not know both areas belonged to me and I still had more. To those ants I existed neither as an idea nor as a body, even though I was huge. I could kill them if I wanted to, and their fellow ants would only recognize me as a location unsuitable for food hunting.

When my father called my mother an angel "sent by God to save him," what he meant was that she had her chance to make her fortune and eventually buy us a larger apartment. We moved to the center of the city. He felt lucky and he felt defeated. He said whoever had the chance should seize it and he asked her if she looked down on him because he had escaped Singapore and the humidity and drudgery that came with it. When my father was abroad, my mother sent him pictures of me. In one of the pictures I was sitting on the living-room table, gripping the telephone handset with both hands. I was playing my Friday-night game, Calling My Father. My father wrote back, the only time he ever sent my mother a letter. He wrote, "Will you blame me if I go home?"

A Chinese dragon is a symbol of potent and auspicious powers. My mother often says, "I have the help of the dragon." But it is also a creature that resembles a snake with 4 legs; a serpent. The serpent tempts and deceives through reason. It represents sexual desire. But does the symbol of desire itself also desire? What does it dream of?

Once my father dreamed he had 5 daughters, each the same as me. They stood in a line in our living room and he counted them, left to right, 1 through 5. He counted and recounted and recounted. He was happy. Then it suddenly occurred to him, how could there be so many? And he woke up and the other 4 were gone. He came to the breakfast table still fascinated by his dream. He said, "How nice would it be if we really had 5 daughters!" And I thought it all made sense given the extraordinary reproduction rates of rabbits. Rabbits are small mammals preyed on by carnivores and humans and they have no choice but to mate so as to preserve. Dragons, on the other hand, have a set number, since each has its own specialty and/or territory. They are not part of the food web or the carbon cycle.

From when I was born till the year I finished junior high, I shared a bedroom with my mother. After we moved, my father started to sleep alone. One day I walked into his room and saw the webpage he had left open. It was an article on the absence of sex in the daily life of middle-aged people.

To my mother I had made my adult confession, of being one human daughter who was in love with another. After calmly asking how C and I had sex, my mother asked what we would do once we were far apart. She said, "What would you do when you feel the need? Would you do it yourself?" I said, "Yes." She said, "Do you know how?" And I felt the urge to say, Do you?

After I learned how, the way I related to my body changed. I feel more continuous because now I understand how my skin caves in to form the inside. But it is also strange to feel the evidence of me as an open structure: open, not concealed, with multiple holes of various sizes and thus penetrable. It is hard not to think of my womb and bladder and large intestine. Sometimes I lie in bed and think, it is a special health checkup. And it has always been the pleasure of pretending: my hand is someone else's hand, my body someone else's body. I can shift into and out of another body, an imaginary identity, while remaining in my own. Such is the shape of my desire: it is ever-shifting and many-layered, each facet unfolding at the same moment. I don't know how to narrate this to my mother. It has moved beyond the scope of my confession, of whispering a name in the dark. I'm afraid she would want to take me to the baby-changing table and exchange me for another.

When I was a kid, our place was so small I could only play on the bed, and the TV set was facing it. Every day I stared at the dark screen and on it, my reflection. When I played pretending, I also played multiplying: the I on the screen was the villain dwelling in a dark cave, the I out in the open was the brave, innocent protagonist. I stabbed me with a dagger and fell down on my knees, and always either of us would die. It was a changing table of death too.

If a baby is brought to a changing table, it should realize right away that its parent is not satisfied with its current physical and/

or mental state. This is a place of renewal. When will we have an automatic baby-changing table where all we have to do is to place the baby in the middle, buckle the safety belt and press a button?

My mother has always wanted to transform me back to a baby so she could raise me all over again, this time with more precaution, spending more time with me and less on her work. She believes that, had it been this way, I would have grown up to be straight. When my mother or grandmother was around, I was easy to take care of. I would almost never cry. The only trouble was I refused all the baby food they tried to feed me. I puked everything out, demanding the same as what the adults had in their bowls. My grandmother once experimented on me. She didn't feed me the whole day and at the dinner table she gave me a spoonful of baby oatmeal and I didn't even open my mouth. Sometimes they still laugh at me. They'll say, "You wanted rice and meat and vegetables, like a tiny adult! You were determined to starve. How funny."

Before children's clothes came into being, there existed only clothes for adults and the same clothes for children in smaller sizes. So maybe before baby food there was only food and before baby talk only talk. Before any concreteness or division, there was only a fuzzy mess, a shadow shown on transvaginal ultrasound that would possibly grow to be a baby but could also end up being a fish, which is just as faceless as a newborn baby. My father says he recognized me as his child because I looked so much like him, but the only thing he recognized was my eyebrows. I had his eyebrows. When I was one, I got heat rash and scratched off part of my eyebrows and then they no longer looked like his.

Months ago I dreamed there was a wound on my mother's breast. It was fresh, still bleeding. On her way to the hospital she pressed a tissue against the wound, and it got stuck. After a minute she peeled it off, and I heard the sticky sound of tissue torn away from blood. My father stood by and watched.

The day before yesterday, I lost the notebook C had given me when I saw her last time. I was sitting in a coffee shop, my bag hung on the back of my chair, the notebook inside. A large man inserted himself between my chair and the one right behind. I turned to look. He smiled and said, "Too crowded here. I'd better go find another seat." Then he left to sit by the window. I stared at his back, at first thinking he might be a bus driver, then realizing the shirt only looked similar to a driver's uniform. He left after a while. I reached for my notebook and it was gone. Not sure if I'd left it at home, I took the bus back. It was not there. Later in the afternoon, I went to the coffee shop once more and gave the barista my phone number. As I turned around, I saw that man again. He was about to come in. We looked each other in the eye and he backed up, turned around, and walked down the street. I followed him. He kept turning his head to look at me, mumbling, lifting his left hand. In the end he darted into an alleyway. I dared not to follow him. I turned around and walked away and immediately regretted it. It was one moment when I wanted physical strength more than anything else. I wished I could turn into a giant.

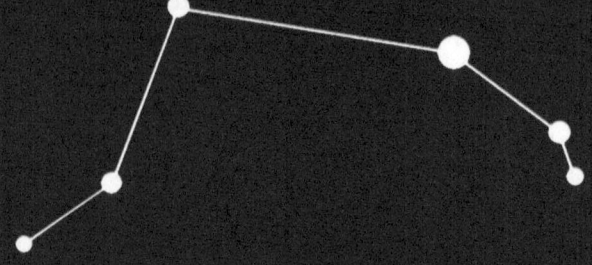

ARIES

3/3

1. the 2nd time i wake up this morning, i have sex with C. i have been worried about the lack of this kind of intimacy. even though i try and wake up at around 7 every morning, i am always sleepy and we barely have enough time to say good night. this morning eases my worries a little and i feel as if we are back at the starting point, from which the count will begin again until the next time we have sex. apart from imagination, virtual sex requires other efforts: me waking early, C staying up late. daylight saving time is going to start soon. this time change will allow us an extra hour. 1 piece of white bread with fried fish powder. 1 tea-leaf boiled egg.

2. run into A and he promises to do laundry tomorrow. he says, otherwise i'm going to die. spicy shrimp inari sushi (6 pieces) with green onions on top. medium boba milk tea (hot; half sugar). i've been watching free video recordings of a class on the history of ancient israel. last night the professor lectured on the story of adapa: fisherman, son/servant of patron god ea. he goes to apologize to anu, god of the world, for having broken the wing of the south wind. when i went to see C in the winter, her city was a flu-occupied city. though i managed to avoid getting sick, there had been several days when i felt a heavy fatigue while telling her i was fine. on the train back home i was sure i had caught a fever. i stared at the noisy group sitting everywhere around me, cheerfully eating their delivery food. i remember the nail polish of the woman on my left. it was a neon dark blue that reminded me of huge, poisonous tropical beetles. in the end i was fine, but i was half-hoping i would get sick so dad would show me more sympathy: forged or not, i didn't care. when i got home and found him nice to me nonetheless, it felt incorrect, irrational.

3. 1 espresso bread

3/5

1. had trouble sleeping—the same feeling of the ridiculousness of sleep. but it's not that i'm not sleeping at all, it just requires hours of effort. dream: someone has passed away and my mother thinks we should sell most of our belongings from my childhood. she finds a man to take away all my stuffed animals. i wake up and tell C i dreamed of my mother selling my stuffed lamb, though i've never had such a toy. she says she will buy me 1. then i dream of us in our bedroom, she lying on top of me, telling me we already have 4 lamps with paper lampshades. in my dream i remember the shape of each 1 clearly. i know we can start to arrange them in our living room. sandwich: dark rye, 1 fried egg, guacamole, spinach. medium watermelon lemonade. again, A says he'll do his laundry later tonight. he looks pained merely thinking of it.

2. my whole room smells like banana. 1 banana.

3. 1 beef burger with mushrooms and sour cream. when C wakes up it's already too late for class so she doesn't go. i tear open all the monopoly lottery games i've got from vons and find out i am the instant winner of a bottle of tomato sauce. C woke at 3 in the morning and i had a sudden desire to nibble her fingers.

3/6

1. went to sleep at 10 last night and slept surprisingly well. wake up at 6:40. dream: i am standing in my bathroom holding a rabbit. my parents want to get rid of it but i won't let them. i won't leave the bathroom. the rabbit bites my hand and it hurts pretty bad, though i find it bearable. then the rabbit turns into C, sitting on my right leg. when i wake up my right leg is bent and held up. a while ago C said she was sad and when i messaged her back, she didn't reply. yesterday i sent this journal to her again, and as i'm lying there waiting for her to message me back, i start to worry she might have grown angry. she wasn't yesterday, but maybe she has re-read it and found something she overlooked? then she shows up. she was on the phone with her friend. 1 buttermilk bread. C has bought a new pillow. she says it looks like a huge bun. she sends me a picture of her new pillow. it really looks like a huge bun.

2. 1 slice of pizza: bbq chicken, corns, black beans. still feel sleepy. because i get up too early? feeling very tired. my eyes are red.

3. at dusk the sky is very depressing: a cold, crispy blue grey, not entirely bright, not yet dark. the sun has gone, no clouds left. it is so entirely in between day and night and i hate it, maybe fear it, as i do the time between spring and summer. jasmine rice with spinach and beef, both korean style. can taste ginger in the spinach.

3/7

1. today also i wake up 3 times in total. C says i'm silly. before going to sleep she attempts to kiss me for longer than i've expected, and i try and fail to stop her. i consider sending her the safety sticker, the angry squirrel, but i end up not doing it because i'm not sure if she'll remember. i send another sticker instead, which i immediately regret. i'm afraid it might take away the seriousness in my statement of not wanting to be kissed. it results in her going to sleep later than she did yesterday. 1 small bowl of salad: noodles with onions, 3 tofu cubes, cucumbers with olives and goat cheese, green peas. eat lunch with W and 2 other friends and 1 of them tells a story of her friend eating raw yolks every year because it is a duty of the youngest person in the house. she says when you slaughter a chicken you can see yolks lined up in its body, ready for the days to come. it disgusts me. i almost want to throw up. then we start to talk about the diva cup and i tell them i've only just figured out how to use tampons last month. feel a little falling behind.

2. small chai (hot). sit in a history class to watch *simon of the desert* and *daisies*. i wonder how much discomfort we should allow ourselves. and of what kind? C once said she would be worried every time she felt the least bit of discomfort. she thought, will we be able to stay together till we're 80? but she also said she was fortunate she got to worry over such a question. yesterday in class people were talking about how they'd hurt themselves, which bones they'd accidentally broken: ribs, thumbs, wrists. what would simon do with a broken wrist? if he couldn't finish the gesture, would it still count as proper praying? halfway through

simon of the desert C gets afraid because i am not responding to her messages, even though she knows i'm watching a film. how much time does it take for "knowing" to turn into "not sure," then dash right into "not knowing" and "what if?" the more we're in love with each other, the shorter the effect of this "knowing" lasts. i have even grown worried for as short an absence as when C goes to the restroom.

3. 1 naan bread, hummus, 3 slices of cucumber, tomatoes, lettuce, chicken. i think watching *daisies* makes me feel hungry. then i watch the instructive video made by the diva cup company on how to use the diva cup. something about the flowy, fleshy pink background and the way the woman talks pushes it right onto the edge of appearing suspicious, superficial. maybe it is the fact that the whole video is green-screened and everything is floating in midair, looking like 3d models. but indeed it gives very clear instructions. watching it, feels unimaginable that such an object can be inserted into the vagina and also rotated 360 degrees. though i often find myself remembering the sentence in *valencia* by michelle tea: the vagina is stronger than you think. it is also fascinating to think that, during menstruation, so much pain can potentially be caused by very little blood.

3/8

1. wake up and find 2 male characters in *hunter x hunter* (a japanese manga/anime) are engaged, though this word may not mean what it often means because of how eccentric the manga is. C asks me when i want to make love with her the most. i can't really think of specific moments or things she has done. i tell her i thought she was very cute when we were eating tonkatsu in shanghai. she says she often thinks of the 1st time she came to visit me and slept in my bedroom. one night i told her i needed to go to the bathroom but she wouldn't let me. she tickled and kissed me and i was slightly annoyed but couldn't help giggling. she says it was cute. i tell her i like the moment when she was about to open the bedroom door and turned around to look at me. even now, sometimes i still don't dare to look her in the eye. i like it when she looks straight at me. scrambled eggs with hash browns. the cashier at the cafeteria says to me, happy

international women's day! today is your day.

2. 1 poppy seed bagel. 1 bite of the bagel tastes bitter. medium mocha (iced). today A finally does his laundry.

3/9

1. 1 small bowl of salad: macaroni salad, lettuce with goat cheese, 4 yellow curry tofu cubes. today C awakes at 4 in the morning. for a moment the heating is off and the ringing in her ears becomes so loud she feels afraid again.

2. 1 slice of roast beef, mashed potatoes, sweet corns with diced carrots. walking back to the dorm after dark, again i notice how many lights can be seen from the outside. there are those living room lights, bedroom lights, and emergency lights along the stairs. today i have learned that there is no security camera on campus. half a banana. in the past week the heat has been on so high that the peels of my 2 bananas get toasted. they are covered from head to toe with huge dark spots. when i go to throw them out, i see a strange animal strolling across the grass slope. in the dark i can't see it very clearly, it looks like a white lizard floating above ground. as it gets closer, i realize it's a skunk. i have mistaken the white stripe of fur for its whole. this is the 1st time i've ever seen a skunk. i tell it to C and recall her telling me about a bat that lived in the ventilation of her study. i was waiting for my flight to new york, wandering in the airport, taking pictures of timid lunch sandwiches with plastic wrappers. she told me her home was in the foothills of a mountain and sometimes there were wild boars. it was march. she was not yet my girlfriend. the flight got delayed and it started to snow. she said she wanted to get married because she would really like to propose. she said, 28 days in each month i think of how much i want to get married. i asked her if she was the moon. she said she had always had a proposal plan, but wouldn't tell me. she was also enthusiastic about designing her wedding, which in her imagination included flower crowns and a small log cabin. it was probably there and then, watching the spring snow, seeing her joking about me running into the love of my life among those delayed passengers, that i 1st admitted to myself that i was in love with her. this is something mom would

want to hear about. this past winter, after calling me abnormal and saying she couldn't understand my abnormality, mom asked me to give her some examples of my interaction with C that "are just like those in a normal relationship." when i refused, she criticized my overreaction and unnecessary sensitivity.

3/10

1. last night i got angry at C because she misread the words on my t-shirt and kept teasing me even after i told her what they were. she apologized. later when we were on the phone, she started to cry. she said i wasn't listening or responding to her. she said i didn't love her. i was confused and afraid and could feel my head spinning. she had to go to the lab at 2 in the afternoon and there wasn't enough time to talk. i sat in my room watching the online course, wondering if this was going to be the 1st time i failed to understand why she was upset. in the video the professor asked his female students if they believed they could get equal career opportunities after graduation, and then lectured on women and power in ancient israel. i felt sad throughout. eventually we talked before i went to bed. she said i had a habit of using single words when i was upset and when she was trying to get me to sleep. it made me sound cold and distant, even when i didn't mean to. i realized i had been criticized by dad on that too. i told her i wouldn't do it again. chicken quesadilla. small apple cider (hot). i scare a dog. i see it standing outside the window, so i press my face against the glass. it stares at me, startled, backs up, and quickly turns towards the 2 people holding its leash.

2. california rolls (6 pieces). today C says i don't praise her or post online about her enough. i tell her because of how stable the relationship is i find it hard to post about it. i've always thought it's enough if we can sense the love from each other. she says if i don't tell her, she won't know whether or not i think she is sweet. and i haven't written love letters to her in a long time. she asks if i don't love her anymore. in being pressed for a reason behind my behavior, there arises a strange, unexpected kind of sweetness and pleasure. for a while i feel as if i was lifted above myself and observing from outside my body. being pressed, questioned, called silly; imagining myself writing to her, posting about her:

there seems to be something enjoyable. i wonder if i am being masochistic. it has been raining on and off the whole day.

3/11

1. dream: trump buys a huge tv for his children and it is installed in the sea by helicopters. his children gather in front of their living room window, which looks out onto the sea, to watch. when the tv is turned on, it causes a tsunami that sends everyone floating down the street on top of a bus. 1 tea-leaf boiled egg. i've finished all the eggs and there has only been once when i got soy sauce on my pants. 66 blueberries.

2. 1 slice of pepperoni pizza. 91 blueberries. the last 1 is not the sweetest this time. today daylight saving time begins and now, instead of 7, i can get up at 8 in the morning.

3/12

1. dream: someone is killed in my home; another is being strangled and struggling with his feet in midair. i am the one who has told the killer how this person can be killed, and i escape out of fear. i take the elevator downstairs and sit on one of the chairs in a hidden corner of the lobby. i want to tell C what's happened and that i'm going to class with only my phone. as i sit down, however, a little boy starts to pull on the hood of my sweater shirt. his sister, a girl about 8, is holding him. i realize now we are on a bus driving across a bridge. i look out of the window and see the river. the little girl asks, are you worried that my brother is trying to steal? i say, no, i just don't want to get strangled by my hood. the boy lets go of my hood and inserts his fingers into my ears instead. i can feel him digging my earwax. then i wake up. another dream: i am back at home and plan to get bubble tea before class. i make a wrong turn and end up with too little time for anything. again i wake up. i remember hearing Z telling S yesterday that she had dreamed of her grandmother, who had passed away. sandwich: sourdough, tuna salad, lettuce, veggie spread, 1 slice of cheese.

2. 1 small bowl of salad: potato salad, pasta salad, sweet corns, 4 regular tofu cubes, 4 curry tofu cubes.

3/13

1. dream: i am deep down in the sea with several other people. we are standing in a line, collectively holding a long, sticky, grey fish. its huge body presses our backs tight against the wall. C comes. we start diving even deeper, swimming through clusters of manta rays. i feel afraid for a short while but soon not anymore. when i wake up i think of all the things i have done in a dream and feel no need to repeat in reality, like doing a handstand, eating the best cake i've ever had, and diving in the sea. they feel so authentic that i see them, quite literally, as both extensions of reality and an integrated part of it, not much less real than what has happened. 2 pieces of white bread with nutella.

2. 1 drumstick with bbq sauce, coleslaw, corn on cob. W told me the forecast said it would rain till sunday, and i didn't believe it. now i think that might actually be accurate.

3. mom asks if i have the time to make a video call. i tell her i'm about to go to dinner. she says, what about after dinner? but quickly retrieves the message and instead says, ok, maybe next time. 2 slices of spinach stuffed turkey loaf, green and yellow squashes, mushrooms, tomatoes, 1 piece of bread. baguette, maybe? the fire alarm in the dorm is making a strange sound, like the echo of water drops. maybe it's inside the ventilation? it has been repeated 24 times so far. a man from campus safety comes to check it. he knocks on S's door because she has called them; she doesn't answer. i get worried. what if this man is not really from campus safety? but he fixes the alarm and is gone.

3/14

1. dream: i want to go visit a former schoolmate down the street. she wants to change her job because the pay is too low and her plan is to learn data analysis via correspondence. i try and fail to recall her name, so i start to walk around a playground. a guy from my college approaches me and asks what i'm up to. once i've told him, he says, if you don't know her name, how will you find her? i say i know she lives right down the street; i just need to walk. we walk around the playground many times, passing a bathhouse. suddenly he is carrying me on his back. we keep walking and find

ourselves inside what looks like an art museum. he leads me to a short staircase. i walk to the top and ask him why it is so hard to walk on. he says, i have transformed the staircase into a pillar like those in a european palace. i realize i'm back down in front of it. the staircase looks like the pattern on a poker card, the joker. he bends down, grabs me, and carries me up the staircase. he says, i've carried you up and now you're my queen. i am outraged. i point my finger at him and say, don't you call me that. queens are the product of feudal and patriarchal societies. he gets mad and we start fighting, each holding a silver high heel that shoots multiple silver high heels towards the other. he keeps backing up while i use my silver heel to block his silver heels. 2 women are sitting on a sofa behind us, watching. the chest of 1 of them is pierced by 2 rivets with blue flowers on 1 end. she says, will i be able to cook like this? the other woman looks about in search of a doctor. i see the man sneaking back, with both eyeballs clawed out, eye sockets bleeding. the woman wants to approach him and ask for help, since he is a doctor. i tell her no, but she goes anyway. i walk towards the exit, thinking, this dream is getting so long; i'll call it *the man who keeps coming back*. i think, recently i've been having a lot of looping dreams. when i wake up i realize i have not. i tell C about my dream and she says, it's so long and complicated. she says she wants to punch the man in the face because he carries me twice. i notice that in my dream i'm talking to him in english. sandwich: wheat bread, tuna salad, sriracha mayo, cilantro, spinach. the new sandwich maker at the cafeteria is much nicer. though the cafeteria staff i was the most afraid of smiled at me, and i thought maybe i could be less afraid of him. W and i talk for a while after lunch and end up telling each other the times when we talked to strangers and something bad happened. she tells me about being followed by a man. i tell her 2 of my airbnb hosts attempted to harass me but what hurt me more than their attempts was D's response, if you don't want it, don't lead him on. reading her message was simultaneously surreal and funny: i couldn't believe i was actually reading this, but there was also part of me saying, almost triumphantly, *this really happens! people really say these kinds of things to their friends!*

2. chicken breast with jalapeño chili sauce, ziti, spinach. today my right arm is very sore. i tell C it's an occupational injury.

3/15

1. yesterday i told C i thought my pubic hair had grown less, and my eyebrows more sparse. she said my eyebrows looked fine when we made our latest video call. i said i wasn't sure about them, but i was sure i now had less pubic hair and it made me feel older, as if i were about to have my menopause. she said that was not the case. i believed i lacked iodine, and she said maybe it was iron. i thought of the time when she told me a few months ago she had wanted to live in a loft, and i had wanted that too. now neither of us wants a loft anymore. this morning i wake up twice so we say good night twice. sandwich: wheat bread, chicken salad, sriracha mayo, cilantro, 1 slice of swiss cheese. i still find it quite fascinating that people know the names of different kinds of cheese just by looking at them.

2. 1 small bowl of salad: 15 sections of asparagus, 11 spinach leaves, 8 bowtie pasta, 6 slices of cucumber, 2 slices of radish, 6 pieces of cauliflower (spicy). today in the training people are tossing clementines across the room and all of them are successfully caught. when someone talks she rubs 2 wedges of her clementine against each other. i want a tattoo like that, with the movement direction of each wedge marked out beside it.

3/16

1. dream: i go to work. when i walk into the writing center it looks like an indoor stadium. no one else is there and the lights are dim. i sit on the top of a high fence with my feet dangling. i sense someone coming and get scared. when i wake up i am chewing on the inside of my lower lip and a tiny tab of skin is hanging loose. i woke up 3 times throughout the night and every time i said good night to C because i didn't think i'd wake up early enough in the morning, but it is actually earlier than usual. 1 piece of white bread.

2. sandwich: sourdough, tuna salad, sriracha mayo, cilantro, 1 slice of cheddar cheese.

3. G asks me if it's ok for her to have video sex with her boyfriend. i say it depends on if she thinks it's ok. she says she doesn't. several days ago she told me her boyfriend yelled at

her because of something she'd said. she wouldn't tell me their whole conversation, only that she said jokingly, are you tired already after jerking off once? he got angry and said she didn't understand him. i wonder if there's some form of intimacy between them that she has not felt comfortable telling me. she says she may not go to singapore because her parents think it's an improper, almost scandalous act that will devalue her as a woman. she thinks it's too much trouble to fight against them. run into H and A after my shift and go out for thai food with them. stir-fried glass noodles with pork. A orders pineapple fried rice and it comes in a whole pineapple with its flesh carved out. A says, it wasn't like this last time. H says, maybe they do this for 1 out of 10 people who order pineapple fried rice. C tells me her dream: someone gives her a little panda and she is scared at first, so she ties its 4 paws together. but it has 6 paws. it grows angry and shows its sharp nails. she has to kiss it on the cheek. she wakes up and realizes the panda is actually the stuffed dog she has given me the past winter. we are on the phone for a short while but then her roommate comes back. C asks her roommate to buy her lunch so she can be alone and talk with me. we have sex. i think of the time when i had lunch with W and another friend and they mentioned a question they'd encountered: why do women moan?

3/17

1. dream: i am walking home from school carrying a huge notebook. it is so heavy that i can barely move my legs. i feel the heaviness in my knees. when i'm trying to cross a street, i get down on all 4s, thinking it might be easier to push the notebook forward. but it won't move and the signal turns red. finally i place the notebook on the top of my head which makes it feel lighter. when i wake up both my knees are bent and i think that might be why i had that dream. 1 plain bagel with cream cheese. medium iced raspberry black tea.

2. leftover glass noodles with rice from yesterday. spend a long time at the cafe chatting with people. when i come back, S is standing between Z's door and mine offering Z the chocolate pancakes she made. they both ignore me and i ignore them,

which is how our roommate relationship usually is. before the one and only time S and i talked and she asked if all my friends were immigrants, once i told B and her it would be hard for C to come to my graduation, since my parents wanted to come too. S said, they don't have to come to your graduation, but i understand graduation is a big thing for immigrant families. i don't know why she assumes that i come from an immigrant family. if she believes that's the case, why did she ask me if i wrote what i wrote in chinese 1st and then translated it into english? and what about, to throw in everything i don't understand about her, the time when she told me, as if it was the most natural thing in the world, why do your parents need to know you are queer? i am queer and i simply hide it from them; i never bring my partner home. now i am sitting here thinking of all these because of the pancake incident. not that i want chocolate pancakes (i'm trying to eat less sugar); it just makes me feel invisible and it calls to mind all the times when i felt invisible in her presence.

3/18

1. meet with a producer friend and a director to discuss the script of a musical they're making. in the car the director and i explain to each other what our names mean. they say the musical is a bit like *the shape of water* except the romance is substituted by friendship and the female protagonist is a 6-year-old girl. 6 pieces of chicken karaage. 1 bowl of tonkotsu ramen. forget to tell the waitress no kimchi. there are 2 shrimps in it. it is sunday and the director drives us to petco, where kittens waiting to be adopted are displayed in their cages near the entrance.

2. medium rose latte (iced). the producer orders a large latte and gets a 32-ounce glass mug. she says she has no idea how much 32 ounces really is. the director gets teased for placing condoms in a tin box in his backpack (*you have to always bring that backpack, and it takes so long to retrieve a condom from that tiny box*). casually mention C at sephora (me to the producer: *my girlfriend told me which facial cream to get*). it makes me happy.

3/19

1. dream: dad is piercing his right ear in the living room because he and my cousin are going to buy ear studs together. his right ear has been pierced 3 times. i try to tell him he can't just wear any ear stud he wants right after it's pierced, but he won't listen. and they don't bring me along, leaving me at home. i get up at 8 to work on the script and don't talk to C much. she doesn't go to sleep till 2 in the morning. though she says she really wants to kiss me, there isn't enough time. salad: rice noodles, chicken breast, shredded carrots, radish, cucumber, cilantro, red cabbage, thai dressing. medium decaf caramel macchiato (iced). A shows me 1 of his favorite music videos and points out how a band member's hair is always only covering his right eye. he says, how much hair wax do you think he has put on?

2. work from 1 to 7. 1 small bowl of salad: vegetable fried rice, rice noodles, green peas, 4 curry cauliflowers. when i get back to my dorm, C asks me if i'll forget what she looks like. she asks, will you forget how it feels to kiss me? i tell her i won't. another surge of her insecurity: we haven't talked much since yesterday morning. she says she wants to have a home and see me every day. i say we will. we will get married and live together. she says, you have to stay with me. you can't go far. i say i'm already far from her and we'll only get closer in the future. she says she will be strong and wait for me. then she goes back to sleep. at that moment, i wonder how difficult the relationship is for her, how painful and hard, how much effort it requires just so that it can go on. i wonder if 1 day she'll find it too much to carry around; i almost feel guilty for not suffering as much. G calls me and tells me she feels a little lost. after 3 months of talking to her boyfriend, who always has the same face and sits in the same office and leans against the same blank wall, she has grown tired of it. i say, but of course it's always the same face. she says, i know. it's just that, when i think of our relationship, it seems endlessly long and so futile. he has to stay in singapore for another 5 years because he's already signed the contract with a company. how can i go through it without seeing him? she still wants to go visit her boyfriend in may but her parents won't let her, since he's coming back only 2 weeks later than her. i want to ask her, if you already think it's

going to be futile, why do you care so much about how many times you can meet? but i'm afraid to put it into words and create a bad omen. then i remember C's accusation. she once said i wrote about us getting married as if it was something told to a kid so it could stop crying and go to sleep, as if what was being said would not actually happen. it made her feel silly.

3/20

1. C is still studying for a group meeting when i wake up. sometime past 4 in the morning over there, she wakes up because her roommate has turned the heating off, and the ringing in her ears gets louder because of the lack of ambient sound. we talk for a short while about whether we will be able to afford our own place and when we can start living together. she tells me about her dream: her mother urges her to find a boyfriend and she says, maybe i'll find a girlfriend. her mother doesn't respond, so she thinks it's time to come out and starts to consider how. she says it's a tiring dream. i tell her in my dream last night i saw a puppy lying on the floor and held it in my arms. i said to someone next to me, if a puppy is held like this it will rest its head against your shoulder. and the puppy rested its head against my shoulder. i realized it was C. 1 slice of roast beef, mashed potatoes, 6 steamed broccoli.

2. chicken flavored instant noodles. mom wants to see me and we video talk for 10 minutes. recently i've been feeling rejective towards talking to her. she keeps asking if i'm ok and i tell her i'm fine. she says our city has been cold like winter. she has washed and put away all her winter clothes, so she starts to wear dad's knit hat. she shows me her newly cut short hair and asks me how she looks. i say, but you always have your hair cut like this. she says, i haven't had such short hair for quite a while.

3/21

1. sandwich: wheat bread, tuna salad, cilantro, sriracha mayo, lettuce, 1 slice of swiss cheese.

2. waiting to meet with my mentor while listening to a podcast on people's secrets. in the 1st episode a woman describes her

father's death when she was 13. she says she was the one who found the body. she says, it is blue. it is a color that you're not when you're alive. my mentor says i'm lucky to not have trump as my president, although xi has modified the constitution so he can be the permanent president. i say sometimes i think i have neither of them, but other times i think i have both. small matcha (hot).

3. meet with the director, the producer, and the composer. we drive to a cantonese place to have dinner, roast pork, roast duck, roast chicken, rice, fried wide rice noodles, tofu pot, spicy pork rib, and then go to the chinese supermarket next door. i get very excited when i see that pointless japanese bottled iced tea, the one that is made to look exactly like water but tastes like regular iced tea. today C and many of her schoolmates are called to grade college entrance exams. she has to turn off her phone and give it to the teachers. today also, we don't talk much. not sure if i should be worried.

3/22

1. last night i tried to wait for C, but she didn't finish until 5:30 (2:30 in the morning here). i went to sleep at around 2. awoke at 4 and saw that C had sent me a post of a woman saying, all women should fix their boyfriends when they behave bad, since their ex-girlfriends have not taught them enough. she wrote, the goal is to make sure this product is satisfactory when it gets into the hands of the next woman. and it ended with her jokingly calling women to help their sisters. i was sleepy and the post made me sad. i asked C if she thought i had so many flaws that she felt she must spend a lot of time fixing me. she panicked and told me i was already very nice and she wasn't trying to say that she had taught me how to be in a relationship. i wondered if i was about to get my period. when i wake up this morning i feel dizzy. i can hardly keep my eyes open when i type so i only manage to say good night to C before falling back asleep. wake up multiple times throughout. today it is raining heavily; the forecasted storm finally happened, with possible mudflows. 2 dried figs.

2. leftover wide rice noodles. 1 small box of guava juice. thinking of the sugar going into me. yesterday during the meeting,

because of the way my mentor pronounced the word *xi*, at first i thought he was saying *she* and tried to remember where this female chinese political leader came from. then i realized it was *xi* and laughed.

3. C still has to get up at 6:30 and grade exams today! i sit in my room listening to the story of a woman who went through female genital mutilation at the age of 11, not wanting to move. 2 dried figs. leftover wide rice noodles.

3/23

1. today i am woken by a call at 6 am. it's from an old friend of mine who i haven't talked to for more than ½ a year. i have ignored her calls and messages. she calls me again at 6:30 and i am again startled awake. then she messages me and says she wants to explain why, exactly a year ago, 3am in the morning, she told me she liked me. despite feeling surprised, i considered it. i considered being together with her and came to the conclusion that it was worth trying. i stayed up till 5 thinking about this. the next day she acted as if it had all been a joke. that is why i have been ignoring her. the incident reminded me of D and when this friend wanted us to be friends like nothing had happened, i found it too demanding: i had no idea how i could talk with her normally; it would make me feel silly, easily deceived. several months ago i told our mutual friend everything and asked him to keep it a secret, but apparently he failed to do so. this, together with the fact that i found out weeks ago that his mother knew i had been in love with D during high school, throws me straight back into the past. lying in bed, unable to fall asleep, i start to consider if i have done something wrong and i want to cry but can't, since i can't settle on 1 reason to cry for. i am forced to recall the times when i realized that D's mother, her best friend in college, and her then boyfriend all knew i loved her and they all acted so friendly towards me; they said hi to me all the time and i could feel nothing but disgust, towards myself, for not trusting what they were saying to me, for wondering if there was something else hidden beneath every smile every hello if deep down they all found me disgusting and her then boyfriend triumphant on top of that. when my unrequited love was told

without permission i experienced what felt like the undoing of my boundaries. my boundaries were dissolved and i was liquified, destabilized, turned into open water for others to drink from. this friend of mine, as well as D, can't see what is wrong with that. they don't understand why even recalling it can make me feel so terrible. i keep saying i'm going to sleep. i keep saying, stop calling, stop talking to me, i'm going to sleep now. eventually i succeed. salad: mixed greens, sweet corns, black beans, tortilla chips, chicken breast, sliced tomatoes, southwestern dressing. 1 small box of guava juice.

2. beef bibimbap, bbq beef, bbq beef tongue, bbq broccoli. historical moment: today i learned how to play mahjong (taiwanese style) and have won 3 games in a row, starting from the very 1st 1. we play mahjong at the producer's place. she has 3 cats. she and the director hold the 4 legs of 1 of them so i can rub its stomach. it seems so unwilling to be touched that i feel guilty and only pet it twice. none of her cats like me. generally dogs seem to like me more.

3/24

1. went to sleep at 3:30 and get up at 10:30. awake multiple times. C asks if i prefer dating someone older than me or younger. i say i have no preference; it depends on the personality. 1 potato cheese bread. today C doesn't tell me she is going to sleep before going to sleep, so when i get up i'm not sure if she is sleeping. i message her and she doesn't respond. i know she must have gone to sleep but there is also the fear that she might have not, that she might be avoiding me, not wanting to talk to me, though we are not in a fight or anything.

2. 1 bacon and cheese bread. C is still grading exams. she says we can go see cherry blossoms the year after next because next year i still won't be there. she says the weather has been nice these days but they are only sitting there staring at the screen wasting their life. in the living room S is playing a song with a strange sound effect like someone is being whipped. with that whip, she is taking up even more space than she normally does.

3. 1 chocolate bread

3/25

1. C says she is anxious that something might happen, that the whole political situation in china and/or worldwide will change overnight. what are we going to do then? she says she has been especially worried this year. she doesn't dare to say too much to her schoolmates. she doesn't think it is ok right now for her to tell others she has a girlfriend. yesterday she was grading the exams and heard others talking about a girl, saying that she was the Party branch secretary and really had her way of talking to people. C says, hearing that, my very 1st thought was, she will be able to thrive even if something bad happens. then she says we haven't been talking much these days and only got to see each other for a very short time over winter break. she says she is afraid. it is painstaking. again i find myself in the fear of her finding it too hard, but i dare not ask. 1 cup of instant noodles (spicy lime chicken flavor). fall back asleep. wake up and hear S telling Z about the residency she has applied for. the residency, she says, is open exclusively to artists who identify as queer. she says, it will be fun to be by the water and making art. Z says, it sounds like a party.

2. 1 ham and cheese bread. again hear S and Z. S is going on a date and asks Z, should he pay for the movie tickets? Z says, sometimes i like to pay for myself. they discuss which outfit is better. S says she is on a diet because she realizes 1 pair of her pants is too tight. Z says, but you're already vegan, how much more on a diet can you be? just smaller portions, S says. C says last night she dreamed that there were many puppies at her grandfather's place, as well as a horse that had only 2 legs. her grandfather kept them and several other strange animals in the backyard. then she saw her ex-girlfriend accusing her with multiple social media accounts on 4 ipads. she wakes up and thinks she has a fever, but her body temperature is actually lower than usual.

3/26

1. couldn't sleep last night. worried that C would leave me. i had wanted to talk to her when she got out of a lecture, but then she said she was going to a mall with her friend. i reasoned i'd better not talk to her then, especially since i didn't know what to say.

dream: i have discarded my current phone and bought the 1st one i ever had, a sony ericsson. C calls me and when i look down, i see that my phone has turned into a pile of stapled paper. i frantically leaf through the pile, not sure on which page i can answer the call. i tear the pile apart. i see dad sitting at the table drinking beer with 3 friends, and 3 cats are idling around but start to attack me when i walk by. dad's 3 friends try to convince me the cats are not dangerous, but they are chasing me around, waving their claws at me, baring their teeth. i have to climb onto a high shelf. one of the cats has eaten a bird. i look down from the shelf and see a small pond of blood with messy, crimson flesh. 1 taro bread. it is a huge bread. i spend a lot of time eating it, and then i feel uncomfortable in my stomach.

2. 1 chicken sandwich. 1 small frosted lemonade. C says she dreamed that i went back home with her and accidentally mentioned something about us being in a relationship, and her aunt heard me. later when she was walking me home, i suddenly became very cold to her and refused to say anything. then i told her she was not good enough for me, neither was her family. she cried and begged me not to leave, but i left anyway. she found out that i had posted something terrible about her and all my friends thought it was a good choice to dump her, and we laughed together. she cried and cried and woke up crying. i have just finished eating when i get her messages, and i talk to her while we get into the car, arrive at the parking lot, walk to the theater, get the tickets, and walk into the bathroom. then i realize there is no signal in the bathroom and quickly walk back out with my bag still hung in the stall. she calms down more or less and gets up to go to class. i watch *pacific rim 2* with 3 other people. it is such a bad movie that after watching it i don't know why i agreed to come in the first place. later that night i hear Z crying while telling S her relationship problems. she says, i think men and women love differently; men love with their heads, and women love with their hearts.

3/27

1. again couldn't sleep last night. i didn't know what i was afraid of. 1 bag of almond cranberry oatmeal. it's from the grocery bag

distributed by the resident life office. finally watch *black panther* with P and we talk about whether the villain should have died. i say they could have just let him live. P says in terms of the story his character no longer has any purpose, since they don't need 2 black panthers.

2. 1 bag of instant mashed potatoes. the words on the package make me believe for a moment that there are whole potatoes inside.

3. 1 seafood louie salad. C sends me a picture of someone's nail polish collection. there are so many bottles, and several of the colors look very similar. i remember sometime last year, when i'd just got back to the states, she said she was going to get her nails done, since she wouldn't need to use her fingers to have sex with me for quite a while. in the end she never did. looking at the picture, i realize it is possible that neither of us will ever use nail polish again.

3/28

1. dream: my 3 front teeth fall off. i hold them in my hand, thinking, now this is real; it is actually happening. and then i think, maybe i should wake up 1st. then i wake up and realize that everything is fine. fallen teeth is a common theme of my dreams. i search for its meaning online and find out that they symbolize transition or loss. what kind of transition am i in? time after time i have drawn out tarot cards standing for transition. today C and i talk on the phone before she goes to sleep and to me everything feels normal again. 1 peach yogurt. 1 banana. G calls and tells me the story of a female friend of hers. this friend has a boyfriend 10 years older than her. they were having sex the other day and he wanted to go directly to the penetration part without any foreplay. she said it was uncomfortable, but he waved it off, saying it would be fine and they had to finish it. G asks me why her friend doesn't think much of this incident. i can only say she should have thought more of it because it is practically rape. before they painted over the bathroom stalls on the 1st floor, there was graffiti all over the walls and among those drawings and scribbles, someone had written, i was harassed, but no one believed me. then multiple

persons wrote *i believe you* beside it. now the walls are blank again and the words are gone. an information card is taped to the inside of each door, listing several contacts you can talk to in case of sexual harassments.

2. meet again with the director, the producer, and the composer to go over the script. the director drives me and the producer there. today the music is playing strangely loud. sitting in the back, i can't hear any of what they're saying in the front. it feels as if i've become a child again. far away among the mountains, the moon is faint like the moon's shed skin. 2 pieces of sashimi (white fish and salmon). 2 pieces of california roll. 1 bowl of lobster ramen.

3/29

1. talk to C on the phone. she says she sees 2 boys walking naked onto the balcony and from where she stands, since the boys' dorm is so close, she can see everything. she wonders if they're doing it on purpose. when her roommate joins her on the balcony to hang laundry, C says loudly, look, that boy's butt is so flat! he quickly walks inside. 1 piece of white bread with 1 banana.

2. there is almost no one on campus and the air conditioning feels extra cold. indian buffet: 3 different kinds of curry with vegetable fried rice, 1 drumstick. A sends me a picture of some chinese pastry. i ask him, what do you expect me to say? and i tell him the text literally means *chocolate large coconut mountain*. he says he just wanted to tell me he's at san francisco chinatown. C is supposed to get up at 9 in the morning to go to the lab, but she oversleeps. at first i am sure she is still asleep. gradually i start to wonder if she has gone to the lab without telling me. then i wonder if something bad could have happened to her. it is right at this moment that she messages me.

3/30

1. C says she wants to make love to me. in my dream we are looking for a room in a hotel and also trying not to pay for it. but as soon as we get the key to our room, i wake up. 1 piece of white bread with 1 banana and nutella.

2. 1 large lavender latte (iced). 2 pieces of crispy rice with spicy tuna. 4 pieces of valencia rolls. today we have another script meeting. C says she even kissed me in her dream. there was 1 day when i woke up really wanting her but too sleepy to tell her. i wonder if i should have. when i see the moon tonight, it is veiled by a light fog.

3/31

1. today is the international transgender day of visibility. when i was back home for winter, my parents asked me if H was a boy or a girl. i told them H was a trans man. at that time mom and dad both seemed quite interested, but then the next day, dad texted mom that he was worried about me. look who she is playing with, he said, homosexuals and trans people. mom showed it to me and asked me what i wanted to say. i told her i didn't want to say anything. so she went ahead and texted him, she is an adult, she won't be affected. i felt especially betrayed because he remembered the term. he had learned it from me and immediately used it to describe the group of people he found disgusting, a task that would have taken him many more words had he not heard and memorized this term. and then there came the feeling that i had done something wrong. maybe i should not have told them about H without knowing how they would react. today too i wake up 3 times and say good night to C 4 times, once over the phone, the other 3 via messages. again i find myself in that anxiety caused by our lack of intimacy. 112 blueberries. many of them are quite small.

2. 1 cup of instant noodles (beef flavor). 1 banana.

3. half a spicy salmon burrito. C gets up and goes to the lab. she has a full day today. mom says last night she dreamed that we were going out for barbecue, her, dad and me, each dragging a suitcase. but she is awoken by dad before reaching the barbecue place. knowing she'll be content with the response, i say, so you are craving barbecue. she says, haha.

4/1

1. dream: i am in a large classroom with some classmates,

reading the 6th chapter of a horror novel. it is after dusk. as soon as i finish, the electricity is cut and the room sinks into darkness. i try to turn my phone flashlight on, but it is very faint. gradually we all become scared and leave the room without our backpacks. i text C to tell her i am scared by a book about ghosts and am on my way home, but she seems unable to understand and keeps asking, what are you afraid of? what book? where are you? i run into a man carrying a cardboard box loaded with rolls of toilet paper, and he tells me he is responsible for distributing them to the whole neighborhood. he says, every time P has a tough tutoring session, she will come to greet me and just steal several rolls on her way out. i am still texting C when i step into my home and, for a moment, i grow worried that dad will ask who i am talking to. then i wake up. i tell C about my dream and get annoyed when she jumps right in and tries to comfort me. it is a feeling too hard for me to explain. i say, you always use the same words. but this is not exactly the reason. maybe i don't want her to say something generic every time i have a nightmare because i am usually not afraid anymore after waking up, and it is what has happened in the dream that's worth responding to, not my fear. sensing i am unhappy, she apologizes and says she is not being a good listener. i realize it is impossible for us to get into a real fight because at least 1 of us will always be quick to apologize. then we make love. i am surprised by how quick my body responds to words. before it would have struck me as a strange form of adaptation. G calls me right after C has gone to sleep. she is angry at her boyfriend because he says she asks him too many times if he finds her annoying. G has to affirm over and over that her boyfriend is not yet tired of her. then she mentions her friend who was once denied foreplay and tells me the same situation happened again twice last week. this friend blames it on herself, saying that she wasn't especially turned on. i wonder how that could be her fault. G says her parents still won't let her go to singapore. that is another reason why she's angry. she says, it's the same as when your parents didn't let you go to C's city, right? if you were me, what would your parents say? i tell her if i had a boyfriend instead they would have let me go wherever i felt like going with him. they would only have been too happy that i'd turned normal. G pauses and says she's never thought of that.

she says she's never thought i'm abnormal and i tell her i don't really care because what she thinks doesn't matter, at least not directly, not that much. the other half of the spicy salmon burrito. 1 yogurt: white chocolate lime crumbles.

2. in the shower i see a single hair on the wall. it is my hair, it is black. it has been there for 2 weeks, and i wonder why it has not been washed away. it is the only hair on the wall. 117 blueberries. many are even smaller than those i ate yesterday but sweeter. generally less juicy. i watch an ant struggle to crawl out of a drop of water near the bathroom sink. it looks pained, constantly lifting its front body as if to stand, as if having a seizure. could it be intoxicated by water? C once told me when she was a kid she'd tear off the wings of flying bugs for fun. i told her i once buried a dead goldfish behind the building where mom used to work. even to this day, i can't say for sure if it's a dream. did i kill a goldfish, whether intentionally or accidentally? if i did, how? why do i have no memory of the killing but only the burying?

4/2

1. dream: L is trying to invent a portable solar generator. today i say good night to C twice. later i go to the cafe and see L waiting for his coffee, dressed in a polo shirt. he waves at me. i've always wondered if it's acceptable to wave at someone when i walk past them within a fairly short distance. most people only nod or say hi verbally. 1 slice of turkey meatloaf (unexpectedly spicy), butternut squash, baked potatoes. medium mocha (iced). A tells me about his road trip to the desert. he says he threw a rock against the part of a hill that had been exposed to the sun. when he touched the spot, it felt warm. then he climbed up and threw another rock against the part in the shadow. it turned warm too. he lay his hand on it and felt a heartbeat. he thought, i have hurt it.

2. cilantro chicken salad. C says she really misses me. G asks me why her boyfriend doesn't respond to her messages right away. i wonder what could be taken as a proper distance and how we each define it. maybe i am a more secure person deep down. today C and i talk about observing one's own excrement. i once

read that almost all people observe before flushing; i am 1 of the few exceptions. i have a phobia about seeing feces, which is not coprophobia in the strict sense but maybe part of it. yet the kind of intimacy C wants includes us watching each other defecate and then looking at what's in the toilet. it is probably a goal i will never achieve.

3. 1 coffee flavored yogurt.

4/3

1. after saying good night and falling asleep again, i am woken up by a phone call from C. she says she can't sleep, i haven't been nice to her in the past week and she can't tell if i still love her. she says last night i went to do my things without telling her and it was like i just disappeared. after talking her to sleep, i start to panic. i feel uncertain of what will trigger her into saying i don't love her anymore, and this uncertainty frightens me. i sit in my room considering getting drunk, but i don't like alcohol. i am hungry but can't force myself to eat. my throat feels tight and i don't think i'll be able to swallow anything. eventually i decide to have coffee instead and admit this is the most harm i'd allow myself and it is not even real harm. leftover cilantro chicken salad from yesterday. medium vanilla latte (iced). and it is not even pure coffee. i am amazed by how much this fight, which is not even a real fight, affects my mood and body functions.

2. C wakes up and tries to tell me everything is fine. i am again hungry but too exhausted to leave my room and eat. when i finally go to the cafeteria and decide on what to eat, i find out that i've left all my cards in my room. i have to go back. walking up and down the stairs, i am worried that the cashier will forget that plate of food belongs to me and throw it away. it doesn't happen. chicken fried noodles with sweet corns.

4/4

1. dream: it is my birthday. i am sitting in the classroom between C and my chinese teacher. C stands up to tell my classmates it is my birthday. 1 sandwich: wheat bread, tuna salad, cilantro, 1 slice of cheese, mixed greens. 1 small cup of sprite.

2. 1 avocado and cheese crepe. C says she dreamed her father got depression. she tried to cheer him up by taking him to a discount shoe store. i tell her i've decided to get up at 5 in the morning on friday to watch the final episode of *idol producer*. she says it's not good for me. she downloads an app which can be used to find others with similar characteristics and talk with them. she says it looks ugly and all the people have bad usernames. then she gets upset because when she tells me she has bought 20 hair bands, i don't say 20 is a lot. i only say, so what? because i don't think 20 is a lot. i tell her i have been keeping all my hair bands in the same makeup bag and now it's almost full. she says, but some of them must have been worn out. i say, yes, but i still save them. i don't throw them away. she says i don't love her. she says, you're not being nice to me. are you being nice to someone else? i say, there's no one else. she keeps saying i don't love her and eventually i start to cry because i can't see a way out of it.

4/5

1. dream: the cultural revolution is happening again, and we are all called to a class on proper thinking. the textbooks we receive are dated from the older cultural revolution in the '70s, and when i open mine i see traces of photos that have been glued on top of the text and then torn away. there are also comments written in the margins by the previous owner, about how boring the book is. i'm sitting in the back row with my parents. the teacher walks up to us and asks me, so do you like it better now? i say, not yet. my parents are laughing. the teacher walks away. a friend of mine gets into a fight with 1 of the guards. she grabs the knife from the guard's hand. she can stab him or cut him open. she can do whatever she wants. but she only rolls up his shirt and slices gently along his rib cage once, and there is no blood. then she throws the knife aside. he quickly snatches it and cuts a deep open wound on her left hand. the blood gushes out and i can see her bones and flesh. i wake up. it's only 6:30. i keep touching my left hand, feeling it warm and intact under my fingers. i tell C i had a nightmare. she tells me to go back to sleep and tell her about it later. when i wake up for the 2nd time, she is ready to go to sleep. 1 drumstick, baked potatoes, rainbow vegetables.

2. before class i get a birthday card from someone in my cohort, but my birthday is not even close. there are still more than 2 months. the card reads, dear Y, i bet that you thought i forgot this ... only i didn't & thrilled you [smiling face with the tongue poking out] hope you like your present! your friend, [name of the sender]. the card is made by a company called american greetings. medium cold brew with half and half. bibimbap with beef (½). 1 box of guava juice. C says she hasn't seen me for a long time. we video chat for ½ an hour. she has a habit of staying in bed while doing this, which makes it almost impossible for me to see her face because her bed is shielded from the light with bed curtains. i can discern her eyes and occasionally her bangs. sometimes it leads to the strange feeling of me being exposed while she is in hiding, but the feeling is more or less neutralized by how frequently she tells me i'm cute.

4/6

1. get up at 5 in the morning and watch the final episode of *idol producer* with C. it's a chinese boy group survival show we've been following since january. in it, 100 trainees from multiple entertainment companies and agencies compete to be the final top 9, and these 9 will then form the official group. i remember feeling uncomfortable watching it. seeing 100 boys—many in their early 20s, some not even 20—bow down 90 degrees, so unified in their timing, their outfits resembling school uniforms, i feel as if i'm watching *the wave*. but we keep up with the show anyway because we think 2 of the boys are cute together. i've been writing fanfictions about them. we hope they can win 1st and 2nd place, which they eventually do. C is excited. she says, let's go watch their concert this summer. she goes to sleep at almost 4am. salad: lettuce, burrata cheese, chicken, avocado, heirloom tomato, orange, dijon dressing. i see the person who gave me the birthday card yesterday. he says, it's sunny, why is no one sitting outside? and goes outside. C says she can't sleep because she's too anxious about not being able to fall asleep. she says she doesn't want to sleep alone. medium latte (iced).

2. G says her boyfriend jerked off yesterday while they were in a video chat. i ask her why they have suddenly advanced to this

step and she says it's been happening since last month, when she 1st asked me what i thought about phone sex. unconsciously she was thinking that to ask such a question was to reveal they were doing it. i say, why are you telling me about this now? she says, no reason, it just comes to my mind. i ask her how she feels. she says she's ok. her boyfriend is the one with a stronger desire to do it. he says she is so sexy he can't help himself. i imagine G sitting on one side of the screen, saying, help yourself. leftover beef bibimbap from yesterday. C dreamed i had an extra breast on the side of my leg. in her dream she reflected on her not seeing it for so long. she thought it was strange but pretended to accept it, since she didn't want to make me unhappy. the longer she looked at it, the more she was actually able to convince herself it was indeed cute. but again, it seems unacceptable once she wakes up.

4/7

last night C said we hadn't been talking much and i didn't understand right away what she wanted to talk about, so i told her about school and a friend i had decided to stop talking to, at least temporarily. i told her i felt very lucky, that grad school and being in a relationship had changed my personality in a good way. at first she seemed happy but then started to tell me i was not treating her well enough. she told me i did not care about her and she could not feel my love and she started to cry. she said i was too silly and she had to teach me, and i did feel very stupid. i stayed awake till past 3 in the morning. it is the only thing i can think about the whole day. it is so tormenting that i can't write about it, so in fact it is now already

4/8

and still i can't bear to go too much into detail. today we have rehearsal. i am hungry. yesterday we went to the producer's place and played mahjong. i helped her make dinner. the kitchen window was open. every time a car drove by the garage light across the pathway would turn on for a minute. it was a cold green that reminded me of the lights hidden under potted plants on sidewalks. the breeze smelt like summer. today i go to denny's for the very 1st time. i've always wanted to go to a 24-hour diner late at night. the director says i should go to this diner up north in the middle of the mountains. his friend, a construction worker in his 50s, told him about it. "this friend," the director says, "he is a trump supporter. if you make a list of the common features of a trump supporter, he will match every single 1 of them: racist, sexist, anti-muslim, pro-guns, etc. he always introduces me to others as *my chinese friend*. but the last time i went on a road trip, he called and asked if anyone had looked at me weirdly, if anyone had made any strange remarks about me. it was a racist worrying about the possible racism his friend might encounter." double berry pancakes with 2 eggs scrambled and 2 sausage links.

4/9

1. leftover pancakes

2. medium caramel latte (iced)

3. 3 pieces of chicken tenders. C says she dreamed i was filling out a form for her and when she talked to me i told her i didn't have the time to respond. she got angry. then we went to the bathroom and i refused to close the door, even though she kept telling me to. she says, the reason why i got angry in my dream was not that you wouldn't close the door, it's that you didn't listen to me. you didn't do what i told you to do. today is hot like summer. i sit outside with H and A and many others come and talk to us for a while and leave. later, the sun sets. light slowly withdraws from the trees around us. we laugh so much that my cheeks are sore. i sit in the cafe wanting to buy chocolate and give it to everyone. then C asks me to translate 10 sentences from mandarin to english for her. they are pretty short sentences like *they teach us to cherish every opportunity* and *he detests his boss more and more*. i tell her i'll do it, though not today. but why don't i just translate all of them right here?

1. They teach us to cherish every opportunity.

2. As time goes by, he detests his boss more and more.

3. It is hard to categorize this book into a specific genre.

4. For a fairly long period of time, he has been used to making decisions in the last minute.

5. In addition to the computer, he is rather interested in tennis too.

6. The CEO of that company always likes to contemplate on a lot of issues.

7. We believe that every single person is decent, inviolable even.

8. She is so silly as to answer such a question.

9. It's safe to say that now they are at the peak of happiness.

10. She is truly the gentlest, the most considerate, and the most kindhearted!

4/10

1. had a dream i was in a stadium full of people, waiting for an event to start. all of a sudden we realized someone was carrying a bomb. everyone panicked and rushed towards the exit. i was nudged by all the bodies around me, pushed in every direction. i knew i was about to get stepped upon and crushed. as i came half-awake, stuck between my dream and reality, i thought, i don't mind dying, i want to see what it's like. so i closed my eyes and sank back into the dream and was stomped to death. the heaviness overwhelmed me. when i woke up i felt my heartbeat in the back of my mouth, and i was too afraid to sleep. i guess that's what it feels like to die in a dream. i couldn't bear it and told C about it, then we began to talk about the fight that had been going on before i went to sleep. i thought that if i didn't say something i was going to die in reality, but i was really bad at articulating it and she didn't understand what i was saying and thought i didn't want her to tell me what she was unhappy about. i tried to tell her it was just the way she said those things. if that's the case, she said, then teach me. but i couldn't. it was almost morning when i went to sleep again, and i had been crying so much my eyes were swollen and when i go to class this afternoon, they are still swollen. sandwich: ? bread, avocado sauce, roast vegetables. run into W in the cafeteria and almost cry when she asks me how i am. it is the worst sandwich i've ever had. get

asked how i am again before class and almost cry again. instead of telling them what happened, i tell them the dream i had in the morning: a friend and i decide to go for a walk at the seaside, but neither of us remembers if we should turn left or right. we pick a direction at random and as we walk we start to smell the sea and think we may have been right. but instead of the sea, we come across a graveyard with a forest of white crosses. in a distance are green mountains with a light fog lingering low upon the valley. i think to myself, we've taken the wrong way, but this is beautiful too.

2. 1 pork chop, 1 baked potato, roast vegetables. the price tag is wrong and i am charged 50 cents more than what i expected to pay. put it on the list of all the things that are giving me a bad day, as well as the irritation around my lips after eating the vegetables. am i allergic to something? what can possibly be causing it? i imagine myself suing the cafeteria for charging me an extra 50 cents and giving me an allergy, and immediately see myself defeated because all the ingredients are listed on that sheet of paper which also announces the price. but if the price can be wrong, the ingredients are questionable too. i sit outside eating my dinner, trying to make peace with C. she must have been really upset. i have never seen her talking in such a cold, detached tone. it scares me. she tells me not to put any more requests to her because she is tired and can't bear it. then she gets up and i go to a reading. afterwards we go to in-n-out, H driving me and another friend, V driving A because they are sharing a cigarette. chocolate milkshake. V gets scared by a man in a green shirt. she says he keeps stretching and wandering around. A tries to shield her. later when she stands up to leave, she pats A's head. we watch her walk out of the door and disappear into the night, and then talk about which super power we would like to have. i tell A i don't want any, all the while trying to figure out how C is feeling right now. i don't want to be able to read other people's minds or be strong enough to destroy a skyscraper. there's a moment after the reading when i look around the room and see people talking in small groups everywhere and wonder why they all seem so happy. it's probably only a social face but this face is also mature and flawless. when we dash into in-n-out at

10:30pm with a swirl of laughters we are actually a sad/angry
group consisting of a black man a black woman an asian american
trans man a half asian half canadian woman and an asian not very
woman woman. i can feel C's presence, as if she was right there
beside me.

4/11

1. sandwich: sourdough, tuna salad, sriracha mayo, apple slices,
1 slice of cheese, cilantro, mixed greens. talk with W and she says
she can practice breaking up with me if i want to, and i wonder
how that is going to work. we see a huge dog. it is gentle but W
is scared. its head is almost twice the size of W's head. medium
caramel latte with less caramel (iced). walking barefoot feels very
nice. if the lizards can do it i can too.

2. french fries. C gets seriously angry because i've been walking
around barefoot in the afternoon. she says, what if your feet get
hurt? what if someone drops food and you walk over it? what if
someone has fungus on their feet and it gets transmitted because
you touch their footprints? the only way for us to make peace is
to admit i've done something wrong and promise to buy a pair
of sandals. she softens a little afterwards. i tell her i'll go work on
the script. instead i go to a hookah bar with A and H so we can be
sad together. H orders onion rings. i get a cinnamon tea. but i am
having trouble inhaling the smoke and end up feeling nothing.
maybe i am not gifted in using any form of substance. A says
when he was younger he could breathe out full circles, but now
he can't do it anymore. the tv is on. lakers are playing clippers and
eventually win by 15 points. there comes a promotion video for
nascar. a man says, god created bumpers; bumpers were made
for bumping. so tonight i have learned 2 words, *hookah* and
bumper. pink flowers are pale under the cold white streetlights.

4/12

1. after the not-wearing-shoes incident yesterday, C got upset at
night because i couldn't remember which times she went to see
a movie by herself and which times she went with a friend. she
said i didn't care about her. she went to the hospital to get her

ears checked again but the doctor told her to go, saying there was nothing to worry about. then she left the hospital and called me and got upset. later, she said it is not really something i want you to remember, i was just unhappy so wanted to get it out on you. before i went to sleep she asked if i was unhappy. i said no. she said, i think you are unhappy, you don't want to tell me because you're afraid i'll get angry. i said, no. she said, ok, let's talk face to face when you come back so that we don't misunderstand each other. i said, ok. i went to sleep. when i wake up in the morning C says there's no water in her dorm and she can't wash her face. she goes downstairs with her roommates to get water so she can boil it in a pot. it is almost midnight. she says it's like going to a country fair. 1 orange.

2. 1 bagel with cream cheese, 4 curry tofu cubes, 2 slices of tomato, and honey. G has been trying to call me. i tell her to wait. wait till tomorrow, i say. she tells me about her stupid girl friend who always has unsafe sex with her boyfriend in order not to irritate him. G says, *je suis étonnée que mon amie ne sois intelligente pas*. today i finally see B after several weeks. she has not been living in the dorm. yesterday as we walked back, H said B is obviously not here. before her light was always on and i'd see the shadow of the wall, but now it's all dark.

3. medium mocha (iced). chips with guacamole, 2 mini brownies, cheese with crackers. C says she wants to buy me a dress for my birthday. she says, your birthday is in summer, so i can get you a dress every year. i say, then i'll have so many dresses. mom tells me diadia has been in the hospital for the past 3 days because he has erysipelas. i say i don't know what that is. she says she doesn't either. she says, it used to be a disease often found among the working class. it is almost 12:30 and Z is talking with S right outside my door. Z says her mother was telling her to keep her boundaries and to consider what she was willing to sacrifice (for love? from what i gather). i whisper, go away. yesterday as we drove back, A played *mama said* on his phone. H said, my mama never said that. now listening to Z and S, i think to myself, my mama never said that. what boundaries? that's not part of her language.

4/13

1. dream: the dinosaurs are back and start to chase humans, their helpless prey. some people gather inside an abandoned factory building. it has a ceiling that is almost 30 meters high. i stand on the windowsill outside, looking in through the window. the factory manager is standing close to me. i know the monster dinosaur is about to appear outside the window to my left, but when it comes i am still scared. it burns everyone in the building into 3 chunks of peanut brittle and hands them to me, forcing me to take a bite. i feel disgusted. i know if i want to survive under its reign, i will have to smoke 3 cigarettes every day. i don't want to smoke. i wake up and tell C i've had a nightmare but as i lie there typing, my fear goes away and i realize she won't be scared of peanut brittle and forced cigarette consumption. she says, let's go ride a dinosaur together. she has been having trouble sleeping because of her ears. today i am awoken by her call after falling back asleep, and she hangs up before i even speak. only afterwards do i see the messages she's sent me before calling. can i call you? she says, can i wake you up? i'm going to call you now. i'm going to wake you up. chicken breast with tomatoes, baked potatoes, green beans. G calls to ask about me and C. she says she still believes that if she tries harder, her mother will eventually turn around; she says, maybe my mother will understand me, listen to me, communicate with me, and treat me as an adult. most importantly: maybe G's mother will realize she is the reason why G was depressed last year and had sex with some random boy. right now her mother's understanding is that G is always overthinking. if only you don't think about everything so much, her mother says, it will all be fine. later i tell mom i'm going to chicago to attend O's wedding. she says, congratulations to her! hope you find your mr. right soon *smiling face*

2. 1 meatloaf, cauliflowers. E drives me and 2 other friends to a reading. in the car we talk about how the expectant lifespan of palm trees is around 70 years and since all the palm trees around here were planted at the same time, they will die at the same time too. E says, does it mean we will need to look out for falling palm trees? maybe it's wrong, maybe they'll live for 700 years. as i sit in the theater space, i am constantly worried that C might

wake up soon and get angry because i'm not there to talk to her. but she only wakes up when the reception is almost over. she asks me where i'm going now, and i tell her we're deciding on whether to go to a friend's house or go back. i'm surprised when she says, have fun. when i tell her we're going back, she says, this is good, going back is better. and for a moment i want to go to that friend's house just because she doesn't want me to. W is getting some more wine and, while opening the bottle, tells me she went to sweden with a friend when she was 16. they sat as models for the painting mentor of her friend's. 1 day, she said, we were dropped off at a friend's house and got really drunk after eating the fruits from jungle juice. i realize that earlier when we talk about palm trees, it doesn't cross my mind that none of us will live for 700 years.

4/14

1. this morning C doesn't want me to go back to sleep. she says i still haven't spent much time with her or posted about her. we talk about this for 3 hours. she brings up the time when we watched the *idol producer* finale. she mentions the 2 boys we paired together. she says, i told you the way they were hugging was exactly the same as how we hug, but you didn't say anything; you just ignored me. i say, maybe i wasn't paying attention. i keep apologizing. i think of how C wants the physical pleasure described in my fanfictions to be a reflection, a mirror image of our desire for each other, or to evoke desire between us. but i don't know how. when i wake up again it is almost 2 in the afternoon. i dream of the bombing of syria. missiles soar across the sky like moons. a man is taking a shower out in the open, and he farts water and vomits water while water runs down his body. not wanting to think about packing, i stay in bed and play candy crush soda saga. yesterday i told E and another friend that i stayed with X at venice beach for a week this past winter and he got mad at me for not cooking. in the morning i would always wait for him to get up, not doing anything, not making breakfast. one day he asked why i didn't cook the corns. i said, but you're eating too, right? he must have taken it as *if you're eating corns too, why don't i just wait for you to do it?* when actually i meant to say it would be better

to boil the water only once, since the stove is not functioning normally and takes 40 minutes for the water to boil, if i do it 1st, by the time you get up, the corns might not be warm anymore. this explanation requires too many words, so i chose to give him the shorter answer that immediately led to misunderstanding. i wonder if that's the nature of my problem with C too. 1 ahi salad. small jasmine green milk tea with crystal bubbles.

2. 1 bagel with cream cheese. the sesame seeds and poppy seeds keep falling down. i say to A, what's wrong with them? why won't they stay?

4/15

1. this morning when i wake up C is still making her slide show. i go back to sleep and wake up again right on time to say good night. for some reason she has a strong interest in calling me her daughter. she says she loves me like a mother, feeling protective towards me. that may be why she feels the need to teach me how to be in a relationship and is only content when i follow her words. 1 beef burger with mushrooms, sour cream, lettuce, 2 slices of tomato. H drives me to u-haul and we get cardboard boxes for packing. he mentions a road trip he has planned with A and i want to join them, which means i may end up not going home.

2. medium vanilla latte (iced). california rolls (8 pieces). i'm not wearing my shoes again and H jokes about it. you're not wearing your shoes again, H says. what if you get injured? what if you step on food? you know, H says, i love how the 2nd priority after getting injured is food. later i tell C about the road trip plan and she says, oh, i see, you could win an oscar with that cast.

3. sea salt edamame. A keeps calling it grasshoppers. i accidentally spill water all over our table. he says, i know. your grasshoppers are wet as hell. they're your wet insects.

4/16

1. last night i dreamed there was a lock on my vagina. today C calls me before sleep and tells me she has received her 2 boxes

of snacks. she lists the items: chestnuts, purple sweet potatoes, etc., all packaged up and ready to eat. she says she needs to start thinking about her research paper. in the next few weeks, come up with the topic, before june finish the whole paper. maybe, her mentor says, if you can submit it and get a result by september you can apply for the national scholarship. she says that's too rushed. i don't know anything about how such things work. i tell her i have the same kind of chestnuts too. salad: chicken, lettuce, cucumber, shredded carrot, grape tomato, red beans, garbanzo beans, feta cheese, pita, lemon pepper yogurt dressing. medium cold brew with half and half and honey.

2. finished packing everything that needs to be stored before summer break. i realize i may not be able to bring along the human size easter bunny i've mailed here from chicago. beef stir fry with rice and sauteed bok choy. someone emails me and says i'm qualified to be a part-time teacher for a company specialized in teaching chinese kids english. the email reads, are you looking for more ways to earn money in teaching? i saw you just updated your resume on [name of the job searching website], have teaching experience, and have a bachelor's degree. that makes you a great candidate to teach online for [name of the company]! on [name of the job searching website], you'll see our average online teacher makes $19/hour. you'll be teaching chinese kids, but the only language you need is english (we prepare everything for you and will give you everything you need). and the description says the company targets chinese kids aged 5 to 12. it looks very much like a scam, but after looking up the name online, i come to the conclusion it is probably a legit company. the problem is that parents who are willing to pay for such all-english courses are likely to prefer real americans. but at the same time, i'm curious to see what they provide for their teachers.

3. large winter melon green tea.

4/17

1. C says she has never been in love with a straight woman and does not know how that feels. sometimes she likes to imagine me being together with another person, one that she thinks

would have been a nice match for me. sometimes she imagines terrible things. this is what she likes to imagine: after being in love with multiple straight women and feeling miserable and finally meeting her, who has put my misery to an end, i wake up one day and discover she has become straight, which throws me back into the same old misery. there is a certain kind of pleasure, she says, in imagining such scenarios. i have yet to figure out the reasoning behind this and therefore find it a bit terrifying. it is purely imaginative and that is why there is pleasure: if it was not, she would have lost me. but does the pleasure come from the process of returning to reality? from imagining a situation where she has total control over my happiness and misery? 2 pieces of white bread.

2. sandwich: sourdough, tuna salad, cilantro, mixed greens, 1 slice of provolone cheese. is that provolone? i'm not sure. medium cold brew with 2% milk.

3. 1 slice of pesto and shrimp pizza. flying to chicago tonight.

THE HIDDEN TABLE

THE HIDDEN TABLE

One afternoon in high school, a boy locked me out of the classroom. When I knocked, he pressed his face against the door and stared at me, laughing. Upon entering, I brushed past him and said, "Fuck you." He said, "You don't have the organ for that." Another afternoon, a different boy asked how many times I masturbated every week. Before I said anything he added, "It's a natural thing to do, but many people don't talk about it. I know you're different. You're not too shy." A 3rd boy sitting to his right laughed. I said, "Sure. The same number of times as you." He said, "I do it every day." Now sometimes I regret it. I should have combined the 2 of them together and said, if a human is a human and I know how to satisfy myself who is a human, I can also fuck a boy.

In 5th grade I came across a love story/fanfiction between 2 male characters from an anime I was watching and thought, So this could happen too. That was my initiation into queerness and desire. When my mother said, "Do you know how?" I did not tell her I learned how to come in unto myself through reading how men come in unto men. This is the only confession I am still hiding away from her. Slowly my focus shifts from anime characters to pop idols, which are often likened to angels and praised to be "as beautiful as the sons of God." Now, lying in the dark, at the same moment I am penetrated and penetrating and it is all the better if it's a man, my idol, that is penetrated by me or his fellow idol who's faceless in the height of desire and is also me because then I know, So this could happen too.

My father has the habit of looking at my phone without asking. He always says, "I just wanted to see the time." Then he always comments on my wallpaper. Sceneries are generally acceptable, anime characters are less welcomed because they are childish though essentially OK, yet most times he encounters a portrait of strangers, 2 young men he doesn't know. Then he'll say, "Who are these 2? Your idols? Only stupid youngsters have idols. Your family does not support that. Why don't you use a picture of me and your mother?" But there are things I can do to these strangers that would never happen between me and my parents. My father might have been a human son who married a daughter of God, I would rather be a human daughter who sleeps with sons of God and has them bear children instead.

Idols are heterosexual by default. The 2 men on my wallpaper are always asked to describe their ideal girlfriend, not ideal partner. They are young, almost still boys—one is 19, the other 17. We love them for their faces but they are faceless in the same way that my mother on a bicycle and the serpent in Eden were faceless. They are labeled as idols, and they are expected to do all the conventional idol things: dance, sing, look good on stage, like women (because most of their fans are women), tell these women screaming their names from under the stage, some within arm's length, some 300 feet away, that they love them too and love every one of them equally as much. They form a familiar imagery: man standing in the center of a crowd, arms stretched open, lit by bright white lights pouring down from high above—even the word "idol" can go both ways. Watching from far back in the dark stadium, these idols become the only source of illumination. All this is fine but also expected and sometimes veering towards the edge of boredom. Idols only reveal what they see fit and during every concert, every fan meeting, occasions we believe to be a vis-à-vis, the face is, at its best, a carefully constructed mask. An idol is nothing but an image painted by themselves and their followers collectively. We settle on a specific set of characteristics, as well as what the idol should look like, how the idol should act and react, what the idol likes and dislikes—everything is considered and gathered together and portrayed in this image, and we recognize the idol as who they are only when they meet the image requirements that have been agreed upon. But occasionally the image does not suffice. If the idols follow their routines too perfectly, we start to demand their "real characteristics," their vulnerabilities. For me, the one vulnerability I want to see in my male idols is specific and simple: there is no fun in leaving them be, seeing them as angels that could come in unto the daughters of men. They might as well step down and become something on the boundaries and hard to define. They might as well take turns doing what is usually done by human daughters, to fall in love in a way that is not their default. Instead of God saying, "Let us make man in our image," I would love to create a case in which I say, "Let me (re)make gods in my image; let me queer gods."

It can't be mere coincidence that, sometimes while they are dancing, the facial expressions of the idols bring to mind those during an orgasm. It is intentional yet also feels like a crack, a moment when someone far away and high above becomes flesh and the flesh becomes sensual. With it comes the urge to penetrate that crack, to reach my hand in, tear it open, to account for it and thereby ensure its reappearance, through the process of imagining an alternative reality: where the symbols of desire themselves also desire and desire in such a way that I can relate, or even participate, where I can say, "Fuck you," and not be questioned, and really fuck. The easiest and most common approach to achieving this is to read and/or write fanfiction.

Reflecting on my history of reading/writing such work, I've realized this alternative portrayal makes me feel less threatened: both by masculinity and heterosexuality. It is my way of both avoiding the potential threats to my female body and reaching into the crack on these men's surfaces, their perfection, their normativity. When the other followers call them husband and boyfriend I feel vulnerable and alienated, erased, because I don't want to be the wife or girlfriend of my male idols. My type of follower lies outside the expected zone of how one should desire these idols and will likely not be recognized by them. Fanfiction reading and writing is almost the only way to create interactions, sexual or nonsexual, as how I would want such encounters with these idols to be. Now there comes the sense of freedom and agency, of "I will make you not interested in demonstrating your masculinity by showing off muscles or calling every follower your girlfriend," of "I will decide who and who make the hottest couple in this boy group." Most times frustration is not part of the picture because idols are usually distant from our daily routines and a majority of followers won't interact directly with them anyway. I am satisfied with projecting my desire for one idol onto another and realizing it through the latter's body. Together they form an open surface, the changing table of desire, where I have the choice of shifting into another person or observing from a distance. It plays with impersonation and voyeurism at the same time.

About my lack of a penis and the necessity to "borrow" one from another man in my fantasy:

To me it is more a matter of convenience. Since this man is an idol from the same group and thus closer to the other idol, it is easier to imagine what could happen between them. When it comes to sexual fantasy, the penis is abstract: it is their facial expressions and emotional responses, rather than actual body parts, that I want to see. It could be something else, but I've chosen this penis because its owner is close by and meets my requirements for logical and attractive coupling. Instead of the actual organ I don't have, it is my desire that is inside my idol's body, it is my anger that punched in the face of the boy who locked me out for no reason.

Sometimes when C said I had not written a love letter to her for a while, I would write her a piece of fanfiction instead. It would be about a pair of idols we both liked at that time. Later I would find out that she liked to recite the dialogue I wrote and it embarrassed me to no end. She would say to me what 1 character had said in my fanfiction, and it automatically put me in the position of the other character. Such a situation was embarrassing because, even though I'd written the piece for her, I never imagined her in it. She had also asked me if I was thinking of us while writing and I told her it was totally separate. To a slight extent it felt like being caught in bed with someone else, with my fantasy, which was sometimes too personal to share even with C. And the shadowing annoyance, "Why would you assume I projected our experiences onto the idols? Why would you assume you are my only subject of desire and fantasy?"

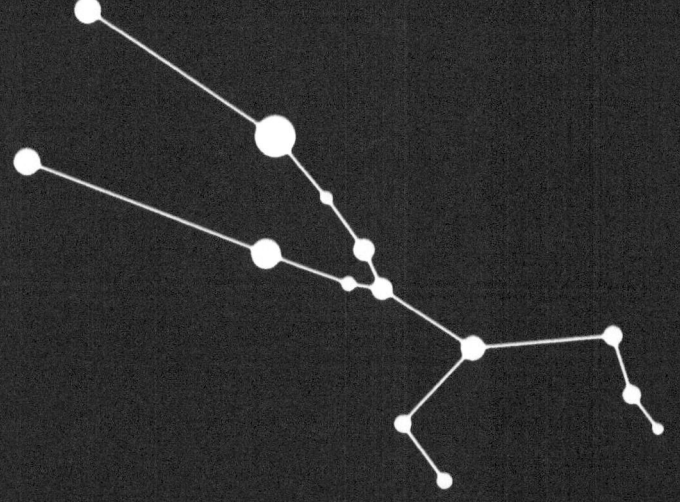

TAURUS

4/26

1. i broke up with C 3 days ago. she is still talking to me as if we were together. this morning i wake up to 150 messages of her writing out my future: i fall in love with an american woman with brown hair but we break up because my opt visa expires and i don't want to get married; then i go to africa to work for an ngo and marry a woman from australia. 1 of us gives birth to a daughter and then we separate because the kid drains our affection for each other; my daughter goes to work for a newspaper and has a crush on the chief editor, who turns out to be my american ex-girlfriend with brown hair. also according to her, later this year i will go back to china and happen to see her sitting in a coffee shop. standing outside looking at her, i give her a regretful facial expression. she writes on the window, reversed, *never mind*. the reason why i write in english, she says, is that it is too hard to write reversed chinese words. sandwich: wheat bread, chicken salad, cilantro, mixed greens, 1 slice of cheddar cheese. medium strawberry black tea (iced).

2. 1 bowl of chicken noodle soup. soft serve ice cream (vanilla and chocolate).

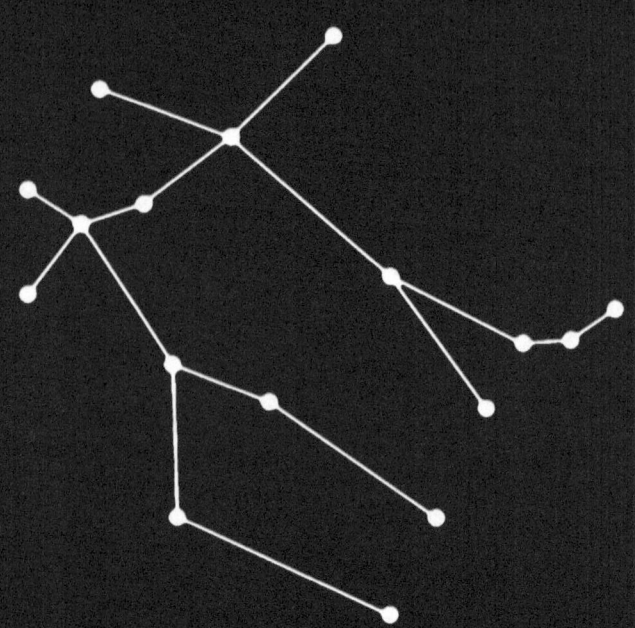

GEMINI

5/18

it's been 25 days since we broke up, and it feels as if we have broken up multiple times and still counting. the 1st few things we did after it happened were: changed profile pictures, bios, and background pictures on every personal page; changed relationship status on social media; made all posts about the relationship private; deleted stickers, memes, and photos that would remind us of the past. for a time we kept going back and forth, and i thought we might be able to stay friends. today she tells me about a story she tried to write in college. it was a love story between the female version of the mathematician brook taylor (brooke) and the female version of joseph-louis lagrange (jossie). she says there is a moment when wind blows over jossie's body like a current flows past a lump. then she tells me she's been depressed ever since we got together. she was afraid of the uncertainty, of the distance between us, and she was constantly sad that she could only be with me for this short period of time which is the rest of our life. now hopefully she won't feel that way anymore. she says, i think 23 is still very young. we are arguing over whether i ought to go back this summer. without me telling her face to face that i don't love her anymore, she says she can't move on. during the past 25 days, we still occur in each other's dreams. she would tell me every time she dreamed about me until i asked her, why am i always being bad to you in your dreams? she said she didn't realize. i felt she was blaming me subconsciously. sometimes she would call me the worst person in the world and being with me the most terrible decision she'd made since she turned 18, sometimes she would take it back and say she didn't mean it. i thought she was tormenting me and she thought i was exaggerating things, then she said she wanted to make me feel miserable because she didn't know if i felt miserable and wanted to make sure. also today, she asks me to tell her i don't love her and don't want to be with her. why do you want me to say it again? i say. i already said it once 2 days ago. that night i couldn't say it but she insisted and we both started crying. she said, it's simple, just follow me. so i followed her. i said, i don't love you. we won't get back together in the future. you'll meet someone else and you'll be better together. but in the end i still couldn't say, don't talk to me anymore. because of this failure, now she wants me to repeat everything and say it will be the last phone call between us. when i say i'm ready, she makes a video call instead. i say i won't accept video calls. the phone call lasts for a long time. when she calls back again after hanging up, i hear birds on that side. i say, you can go sleep now. she says, you don't love me anymore, why do you care if i sleep? i do what she tells me to do and make a post telling everyone we have broken up. she immediately reposts it, saying it was me who initiated it.

many times i cried for hours, considered getting back together with her. eventually i didn't. now i don't think she still wants it. the way i relate to other parts of the world has changed. i can sense that something is missing, but it feels more like a calm opening than a wound. 1 night C said, your mother must be extremely happy to hear this news. when i told mom, she asked if i was ok. i said i was fine because i initiated it. i had wanted to keep it a secret but ended up even talking about this with our program director, after running into her in the hallway. she recommended the spa and going to the beach with any friend who had a car. she said, i once had a relationship with someone in london. it's hard; you have to switch modes. when you're up and ready to go out to the world, the other person is about to go to bed. you have to switch to the night mode so you can talk to them in the right way. sitting across from her, i began to calculate the time difference between london and china and that between china and los angeles. today C says, you never considered how hard such a relationship would be. if you like someone you just tell them without thinking and once you lose interest, you disappear. i think she has a point. several hours before we broke up, i had made up my mind not to say it, seeing she still had that ringing sound in her ears and couldn't sleep very well. but when she asked me, all of a sudden, why i never had time for her, i failed to hold it back. days after she said that would be the last time she brought up that question, she said her plan was to sort everything out once and for all and never bother me with the same question ever again. and i just let go.

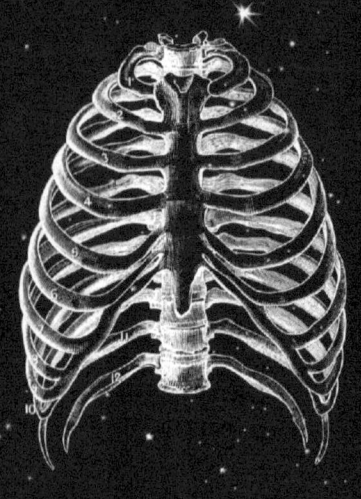

CHEST IS THE BEST STORAGE SPACE

G: Yesterday I went to the choir concert you
were singing in. You told me not to go because
you were bad, but I thought it was in fact a
fine concert. There was a girl who had her
hair braided and piled on the top of her head
and I kept looking at her because she was in
the front row. She seemed very into singing
the lyrics. She held her folder with one hand
and it lay completely flat on her palm. But
she kept yawning. At first I thought maybe
she was adjusting her jaws, because how could
she be yawning while being so serious about
singing the mass? I watched her and I started
to yawn myself, so I knew she must have been
yawning. She was wearing crimson lipstick and
pushed her glasses up again and again. After
the concert she came down from the stage and
I saw she had not worn braces, or maybe she
had and they failed. She let someone hold her
waist and rest their head against her stomach.
I wondered if she was pregnant. I could imagine
her being pregnant, but not raising children.
Sitting in the concert hall, I had a sudden
realization. I realized none of us was going
to grow any taller, and that made me sad. That
was yesterday. Today I observed some fallen red
leaves and have come to a conclusion on how
they are going to die after their departure
from the branch. They are going to die from the
tip down. The tip always goes black first. The
leaves, though partially dead, have a beautiful
red color. I wish I could be this transparent

in the sun. What else do you know about that
girl in your choir? What's her name? Is she good
at singing? How old is she? I mean, she looked
relatively childlike, like a high-schooler,
despite that lipstick. Maybe that was why I
couldn't imagine her raising children. Anyway,
call me back when you get off work.

G: If I have a crush on someone but don't
particularly like his nose, how should I tell
him? *C'est trop grand!*

Y: Why do you have to tell him?

G: I think he needs to know there is something I
don't like about him. There may be more, but I
am still in the process of finding them.

Y: I don't think it's necessary. If he's a
delicate person, you might destroy him.

G: *D'accord.*

Y: Stop saying that to me. What does that mean?
I know you told me. I forgot.

G: I went back home last month for Grandma's
funeral. Grandpa's almost entirely deaf now.
After the funeral we went out together for
dinner and there were so many of us, more than
20 I think, that we had to have an extra table
set up and the small room was warm enough
without heating. Elbows kept hitting me in my
back. Grandpa sat in the middle of the middle
table and when someone wanted to make a toast
to him they would scream. He couldn't really
hear screams either. It seems that once you lose
your hearing, you also lose the ability to eat,
especially when you're surrounded by so many
people and every one of them is making so much
noise, which to you probably sounds close to
silence. At a certain point my father started
to tell others about my color-vision deficiency
and how it had been discovered. "I went to the
hospital with my daughter last weekend," he

said, "and the doctor showed her a color test
plate. The doctor asked her, 'What animal are
you seeing?' She said, 'A cow.' The doctor said,
'Very good. Now where is the head of the cow?'
And my daughter pointed at its tail. Before
that I had no idea what color blindness was. It
was so funny, I couldn't stop laughing!" And he
laughed and laughed. I don't know why he found
it so laughable.

Y: How was your grandpa doing?

G: Other than his poor hearing, he was fine.

Y: When did your grandma pass away?

G: A little over 2 months ago. I still think of
her every day, though I don't know what exactly
about her I should be thinking of. We weren't
very close, not blood relatives. You must have
been sadder when your grandpa passed away.

Y: I doubt it. On the contrary, I think. What
exactly does *d'accod* mean?

G: It means OK.

Y: It seems to mean a lot more than OK.

G: Towards the end of the funeral dinner my
father got really drunk. He made 3 toasts in
a row to me. He said to me, "Your grandpa is
90 years old. Your grandpa sits here but hears
nothing, he doesn't know what everyone else is
talking about. Now you can go up to him and read
French to his ear and make him happy! He is 90
years old and has no idea what French sounds
like." I refused. I said no. That's too strange!
He won't understand what I am saying even if
he hears it. My father insisted. You know him,
that's how he is. He said, "If you don't want
to, just read something in English and tell
him it's French. He won't know the difference
anyway." Eventually I got away with singing.
When Grandpa grasped that I was going to sing a
song, he said, "No, forget it. It's too tiring."
Yet still, I stood up and sang.

Y: I remember the other time when your father
insisted you read something. Eventually you read
a short story of a prisoner breaking out of jail
after seeing a snail on his windowsill.

G: That's right! Do you really think I shouldn't
tell my crush about his nose?

Y: You really shouldn't. What don't you like
about his nose?

G: It's not very pointy. Somehow I feel that
there must be a way to improve it, like if
your front teeth are protruding, you can lick
them inward every night before sleep and after
a certain period of time, they will not be
protruding anymore. Do you think the choir girl
knows this? Should I tell her?

Y: I don't even know who you're talking about.

Y: I went back home last month. My grandmother
scared me. I wasn't sure why until it finally
hit me: my grandmother's face looks different
than it did before. It used to be firmer,
smaller even, the contours more explicit. Now it
has loosened a bit, the lines turning fuzzy like
the whole face might someday liquify. I followed
her around everywhere until I came to accept her
current face as the new normal face. I convinced
myself she had not aged since I was 10 and she
would now begin aging again. I could observe her
like a leaf fallen into my hand. But this is
not the point. The point is, I was on the plane
back here and during takeoff the man sitting to
my right stretched his left foot out, so for
a while we were all watching that foot: me,
another man sitting to his right, and a flight
attendant sitting on her special chair facing
him directly. His foot was surrounded by our
seated bodies. We stared at it because it was in
a bright white sneaker. I keep thinking of that
foot like how you keep thinking of the choir
girl, that beautiful anonymity. On the plane

back, I invented a sex game: stand naked in the
middle of a circle made by flight attendants and
passengers and let them throw snack sandwiches
at you. Snack sandwiches are made of sourdough,
cheddar cheese, and chicken breast. Anyway, call
me back.

G: I told him. I told him *Je n'aime pas ton nez*
and he said, "What don't you like about it? Is
it a major issue? Maybe I can change it." Do you
think he is in love with me? Maybe he'll get
plastic surgery.

Y: It's hard to say. He could have been joking.

G: I thought he looked very serious. But now I'm
unsure.

Y: Have you heard it?

G: Heard what?

Y: Chest is the best storage space for men.

G: What does that mean?

Y: It means you should store men in a chest.

G: What? No, it means if there's a man in your
family you should have some chests installed at
home.

Y: It works either way.

G: I don't think so.

Y: If you chest your crush, you will figure
out what he is thinking. That choir girl, she
stomached someone instead of chesting them.
That's not the best option.

G: I really don't think so.

Y: But if his nose is too pointy, you may get
hurt when you chest him. A pointy surface
creates too much pressure.

Y: I invented a sex game on the plane.

G: You told me already.

Y: I revised it for you: chest your crush and let him throw his nose at you. It would feel like standing face-to-face in the lavatory with 1 flight attendant and letting them throw 1 snack sandwich at you repeatedly.

G: My father used to say: "When we look for ruins from ancient times, we always dig into the surface of Earth and find them deep underneath. The more ancient the time, the deeper the pit gets. Does it mean the earth naturally grows thicker and thicker over time? If that is so, the surface area will gradually increase too, and everyone will move farther and farther apart from everyone else."

Y: But that's only the case if we all remain still for millions of years.

G: Today I observed what's left of those leaves. They totally turned into a powder before they blackened all over. I had wrong expectations of how they would die. I heard that before Grandma died, she sent her 4 sons to look for all the unorthodox ways of treatment available out there. Later they said, "That was how much she didn't want to die." Grandpa used to go out in the afternoons and play poker with neighbors. Sometimes they would play mahjong too. After they carried Grandma to that facility on the mountain, he only played mahjong. He always lost. Once a week my father gave him some money so he could keep playing, and once a week he went to that mountain to see Grandma. Then she was gone. They say a deaf man can live past 100 years because he hears no bad words about himself ... I wonder if constantly losing mahjong games has the same effect. Over the winter at home, I would usually message my crush in the morning, while eating breakfast. I told him, "Did you know that on a Boeing 787, when you reach a certain altitude or when it's time to sleep, all the windows automatically dim into

a cold purple? Before this they had to go down
the aisles and ask every passenger to shut their
curtain, but now the windows just turn purple on
their own. If you fall asleep before your window
changes color, you wake up and the sea and
mountains underneath look like ruins after an
explosion. It makes you feel far away. Maybe in
your doze there has been a 4-dimensional leap.
How could you tell?" He responded, "I didn't
know." In fact, the idea of someone throwing
snack sandwiches at me can be comforting. I like
snack sandwiches, no matter how many times I
have eaten them, I am always surprised by how
soft they are. Anyway, call me back.

G: Do you remember that tiny fruit store 2
blocks away?

Y: The 1 run by a middle-aged man, where
sometimes we saw his wife and daughter too?

G: Right.

Y: I remember buying watermelon from him in the
summer, when I went to play with you at your
place. Must have been more than 10 years ago.

G: It's no longer a fruit store. He started
to make a living by giving newly dead people
formalin shots, so said a cardboard sign near
the entrance. I wondered how one could do that,
how much formalin a dead body would need and
what would happen if it received too much or
too little. For a time, I thought there was
a connection between injecting formalin and
choosing a watermelon, that requirement for the
perfect amount of suppleness under your hands.
But when the watermelon is over-matured or
unripe, we eat it anyway. Most of the time you
make do with the amount of formalin you receive
too. If you're not very experienced, you won't
be able to tell the difference.

Y: After my grandfather died and my grandmother
started to scare me, I had trouble not seeing

everything in their apartment as objects of the
deceased. There were newspapers on the living-
room desk. One of them was all about telling
elders what they should know about their health.
On the front page it said, "Flu Season!" Lying
close by was a nail clipper. Mounted towards the
end of the handle was a fake emerald-green gem,
probably made from plastic. Why would a nail
clipper need a fake emerald? My grandmother was
sitting next to me. We watched TV, the sports
channel, a tennis match. It was the 3rd day of
the Australian Open. I thought, in Australia it
is summer, my grandmother doesn't know how to
use the heater, but she can turn the TV on and
off by herself. She can switch channels.

G: I came back and you were singing in that
choir concert and it was a mass, a funeral mass
in Latin. I couldn't understand a word. I sat
through the flight home, then I sat through the
concert. We were all facing forward. Some people
fell asleep. Some snuck peeks at their phones.
The lights were dim and I felt as if I was back
on the plane.

Y: You were watching that choir girl. Because of
the horrible lighting her whole face was gold
and she looked like the Sun King. Sometimes she
was blue, then her lips stood out.

G: Do you know who she is?

Y: You were just looking for a distraction.

G: Was my crush there? If I can chest him, maybe
I would see him every day. *Peut-être, peut-être.*
But do I really want to see his nose every day?

Y: To chest a man is simple, simply store them
in a chest, and it doesn't have to be your
chest. If you play the airplane sex game in
a lavatory with your crush, the lavatory is
your chest. You are practicing, practicing,
practicing. It's good for him to get used to
being in a chest anyway.

G: Sometimes I hear the vibration of a phone. I heard the same sound halfway through that funeral. There are moments when I want to be stored, buried, put away. There are moments when I believe I am put away and frozen. Do you ever feel like this?

Y: Imagine millions of years later there will be a special population whose only task is to increase the pressure against the surface of Earth.

G: It doesn't work that way.

Y: In my grandmother's chest there is everything that's no longer necessary to the family, which now consists only of herself. I remember seeing a fine set of glassware when I was little, something I had always been afraid of breaking, and later it was removed from the display and safely stored in that chest. I was told about how my uncle skipped lunch every day for a week and bought a piece of coral, which had been deep pink but gradually faded to pearl white. My grandmother said it was dyed, a fake. It went into the chest too. We observe the chest the way we watch TV, opening and closing every drawer, like switching channels. While we were watching the tennis match, my grandmother said, "Summer dress." Then she said, "They should be more careful and protect their knees." Then I flew back in a metal chest whose windows changed color in my sleep. The choir girl stood in the front row and twice a week we rehearsed and the last time everyone was dressed in black. The choir girl said, "Yesterday my dog died. Why did we open death's box? He had a dysfunctional liver that evolved into a dysfunctional body. I went to the hospital to watch and I didn't stay after he was euthanized. I watched and, I held, his paws, which were barely 9 years old, and it was like, living, the climax, of a documentary,

on a healthy, owner, pet, relationship, which
is now complete, in a benign way. What was I
doing? Why did I watch? I, skipped, ahead, and,
there in my mind, he was already buried. Do
you know the kind of drawer in a morgue that
opens to reveal a body inside? Why did we open
death's box?" When I first received my binder,
of all the words in it, I understood only 3.
Now I'm no better. See this as a do-as-told,
mouth-as-eye contest. Call me back.

G: I asked my crush if I could chest him. He
asked what I meant by "chest." I sent him a
picture of a home-decoration magazine, and on
the 1st page was the sentence you told me about.
He said, "How did your grandmother die?" and
I didn't think it was relevant. I told him to
be chested by someone was to squeeze 2 bodies
into a small space by resting your head against
their chest. Or you could open a chest and hide
inside it. Or you could take a plane or go to a
concert or watch TV, all of which would confine
you within a small space and force you to stare
forward. Just in case. Let's get prepared. Let's
help each other get better at this.

Y: Then I found myself touching my grandmother
a lot. This happened after she started to go
to bed at 7 p.m. I'd wonder, Is she practicing
being chested? How many hours does she spend
sleeping every day?

G: When my father insisted I read something to
Grandpa, I thought of how I cried every time I
was sent to their place. My parents didn't have
enough time to look after me. Maybe I sensed she
was not my real grandmother. I would always say
the lunch she made was too salty.

Y: If it's too salty, it's bad for your heart.

G: I tried to talk my crush into boarding a
plane with me. I asked him where he would like
to go. He said it was a hard question. *Très*

difficile. I said, "*Pouvons-nous parler de ton nez?*" He said, "What?" I said, "Nothing."

Y: So I went back. I went back and I took the bus and after I got off the bus I walked through my grandmother's neighborhood. It was a neighborhood for all the retired faculty from a certain university. Children grew up there and usually after high school, they left. I saw my kindergarten, where I first discovered my fear of swings. Who would be living here after all the children are gone and their grandparents gone too? I saw my grandmother and she said, "In a few years this place will be vacant."

G: I say, "We could start by taking a train together." He says, "OK." We board the train. I tell him once in grade school some students from another country came to visit, and upon the request of our teacher they taught us their national anthem. We all stood up, face-to-face with them, and they sang it twice. Most of the words we didn't understand, but it sounded nice. The 3rd time we sang each sentence after them and it felt like taking a vow. Then the teacher let us try and sing along with them. It didn't work out.

Y: What did you sing to your grandfather?

G: I don't think he heard it. Sometimes even when your ears have deteriorated, you can be much better at hearing people sing than speak. But that wasn't the case.

Y: Then, right outside the apartment building where my grandmother lived, I saw an older man. I knew he had just been to 1 of the apartments. The 2 men in suits and ties next to him were telling him how nice the neighborhood was. They said, "Here you have all kinds of facilities. Whatever you need. A supermarket, a kindergarten, a gym ... the subway right across the street." But the subway wasn't finished yet. Did the man know? I wanted to tell him. The

subway is not ready! It is a terrible pit, all
dirt and mud. Wait till it rains! Do you know
how much water runs under our feet?

G: We board the train. We sit down next to each
other. If we are fortunate enough, after 1.5
hours, we start to lean in. We shift our torsos.
It is not a natural way to lean against each
other on a train. We shift and shift and shift
shift shift. Here is what I sang to my grandpa
and everyone else at the funeral dinner.

[G hums a voice message]

Y: What's that?

G: A song the sport channel used to play every
day at 7:30 p.m., when I was 5 years old.

G: Someone drove us all to the funeral home. It
was early in the morning. I remember a coldness
that felt sticky and made me want to shower.
For most of the funeral, we merely stood in
silence. There wasn't a strong expectation of
crying, neither for me, as the youngest person
present, nor for anyone else. As a child I
was often required to react, to perform. Now
I was recognized as an adult. I stood in the
funeral home listening to the silent vibration
of someone's phone. We didn't have to walk up
to the coffin and take a last look at Grandma.
She was carried away. There was music. Later at
the dinner my father told me to read something
in another language or sing a song in whichever
language and I felt very confused. Am I a child
again? Later aboard the plane I became as dying
as all the other passengers. We ate and drank
and stuffed ourselves till we suffered from
constipation like some elderly patients making
the most out of their last breath, till it was
time for sleep and the lights were dimmed and we
were buried under our blankets and finally dead.
That choir girl was such a child that, sitting
there listening to her, everyone felt old. I

wondered how Grandpa felt when he listened to me
singing. Had he heard me or not, there wasn't
any difference. Anyway, call me back.

Y: We shift and shift and shift shift shift. On
the plane back here I invented another sex game:
remain in your seat with someone of your choice
sitting next to you. Shift your torso until you
face each other directly. Let them bury their
face in your chest, with their nose as the point
of contact.

G: *Je n'aime pas son nez!* It is not pointy
enough. But if it were, it would hurt too much.

Y: Since it's not pointy, it won't create enough
pressure and will be harder for you to really
chest him.

G: I felt very dead. Had there been a point of
contact, even the point of a nose I didn't like,
I would have felt much better.

Y: Now I think it doesn't even have to be that
way. This sex game, I mean. If the 2 of you walk
straight towards each other, his nose will be
the 1st part of his body that comes into contact
with you. The slight touch of his nose indicates
the existence of his whole person and the
possibility of you being hugged and more, which
is a solid proof of your non-death. When you are
sitting rigid on a plane, the slight touch of
his nose can give you much comfort. Other than
that, the softest thing you'll lay your hands on
is your snack sandwich.

G: I think I should take back what I've said to
him.

Y: That you don't like his nose?

G: It doesn't really matter. What we should do
now is compare the shape of my fingertip to that
of his nose. If they bear enough resemblance, I
can simply poke my own chest and pretend to be
chesting him. That would be so much easier.

Y: It is something worth introducing to almost
everyone.

G: When we were on the train, there was a haze
hovering over the field and a grey residue of
snow from last month, some frozen into ice, some
melting away. The whole train was fixated into
that long strip of space. If one knows the area
of that train's cross section and the length of
its trip, they can multiply the 2 and come to a
result of the exact volume it will ever occupy
in the duration of its life. So its metal skin
will brush against and only against the haze
forming next to its set volume.

Y: If you're going to get married, you should
only marry someone whose nose tip resembles
your fingertip in terms of shape, softness, and
texture, so that you can keep yourself company
in every death moment like sitting on a plane,
on a train trapped in a sour haze, at a choir
concert, or sitting at the dinner table with
your family again after 3 years, at the table
with your family after your spouse's funeral
and hearing or not hearing your granddaughter
sing, sitting on the bed pulling out each drawer
of your chest, on the bed preparing for sleep at
7 p.m.

G: I suppose Grandpa didn't really care to know
what I was singing, or reading, we hadn't cared
to know the lyrics of that national anthem
either.

Y: I suppose I can move into my grandparents'
apartment sometime in the future.

G: How tall is the whole building?

Y: It has a total of 22 stories and a basement,
the height of which doesn't really count.

G: But why not? I won't stop you. We can just
say this building starts from a layer that
used to be the surface of Earth but is now
underground.

Y: Sure. So it is an apartment building with
23 stories, therefore the height will come to
around 72 meters, or 236 feet. My grandparents
used to live together on the 12th floor. Now
it's only my grandmother.

G: What does the building look like?

Y: Like a huge chest. The facade is painted
brown with no ornaments. The longer you stare at
it, the more you feel the urge to walk up to it
and pull out every window like you would those
small drawers of a chest.

G: Do they like living there?

Y: It is a perfect location to practice being
chested.

G: I suppose we can all move back into our
grandparents' place, when it's the time for us
to do so.

Y: My grandparents argued a lot. After they
retired, there wasn't much for them to do. Get
up early in the morning, eat breakfast, eat
lunch, watch TV, eat dinner, go to bed early
in the evening, and the same the next day. It
was as if they'd boarded a plane that wouldn't
allow them to get off. So they argued for fun.
Sometimes I wonder, Why aren't people arguing
for fun on the plane?

G: So many other passengers are sleeping near
them.

Y: I will only go back if I have a mission.
If someone tells me, "Go back, otherwise the
building won't be heavy enough," I will settle
down at their place in a second, like a free
refill.

G: But how heavy is heavy enough?

Y: It depends on the weight of that
neighborhood. The apartment buildings, the
kindergarten, the supermarket, the gym, the
subway station, everything. And the people

living both above and under the surface of
Earth.

G: It was there and then *sur le train* that I
told him *je n'ai pas aimé son nez* but to be fair
now I think it might be somewhat acceptable.

Y: That's good news.

G: Should I tell him? When should I tell him? I
don't want him to think I'm really attached to
him. If I can find something other than his nose
...

Y: Don't forget to practice. You still need to
practice.

Y: I will move into that apartment only if I
have a mission. If the neighborhood is not
heavy enough, all the children who have left it
at a certain point may be asked to come back,
so that a proper pressure will be maintained
and the surface area of Earth won't keep
expanding and everyone won't be moving farther
and farther away from everyone else once they
are chested and stored away. The mission might
even include walking barefoot because shoes
are only extra, an unnecessary area of contact
that will decrease pressure. High heels will
still be allowed though. Either barefoot or
high heels. Then my grandmother wouldn't want
to go outside because she doesn't like walking
barefoot, nor does she like heels. Maybe she'd
receive extra-thick wool socks, though I feel
unsure about whether she'd agree to wander
around like that. After my grandfather passed
away I found myself touching her arms now and
then, as if to hold her there, to brush down
tiny invisible bits of her and save them under
my fingernails. She would hide my hand under
her armpit, where layers of clothes gathered. I
have a pretty detailed idea about what she does
every day. I know on which part of the couch she
sits when she trims her fingernails with that

shiny nail clipper. Yet still, I hadn't observed
my grandfather's nose. The correlation between
that nose and my grandmother's fingertip was
never examined and what exactly she does while
lying in bed after her regular visit to the
bathroom I won't know. It was such a risk to
marry someone with an unmatched nose. And the
situation might become so much worse that we
can't walk with our feet anymore. We will create
just enough pressure for Earth to remain in its
equilibrium, not expanding, nor dwindling. And
worse and worse still, the day might come when
we can only walk on our fingertips. By then,
every time right after going out we will begin
to look forward to coming back home, or to any
random pause, any chested moment. But it is also
possible that we will have become so familiar
with walking on our fingertips that it doesn't
bother us at all. Why did we open death's box?
Of all the lyrics I understand only 3 words and
so do you, maybe it's not us, maybe we didn't
open anything. Chest is the best storage space
because it's the quickest and most convenient
enclosure you can form with someone else's
body and, sitting upright, facing forward, in
stiffness, in silence, you will like it very
much. Call me back.